Padgett, Abigail.

Strawgirl.

$18.95

DATE			

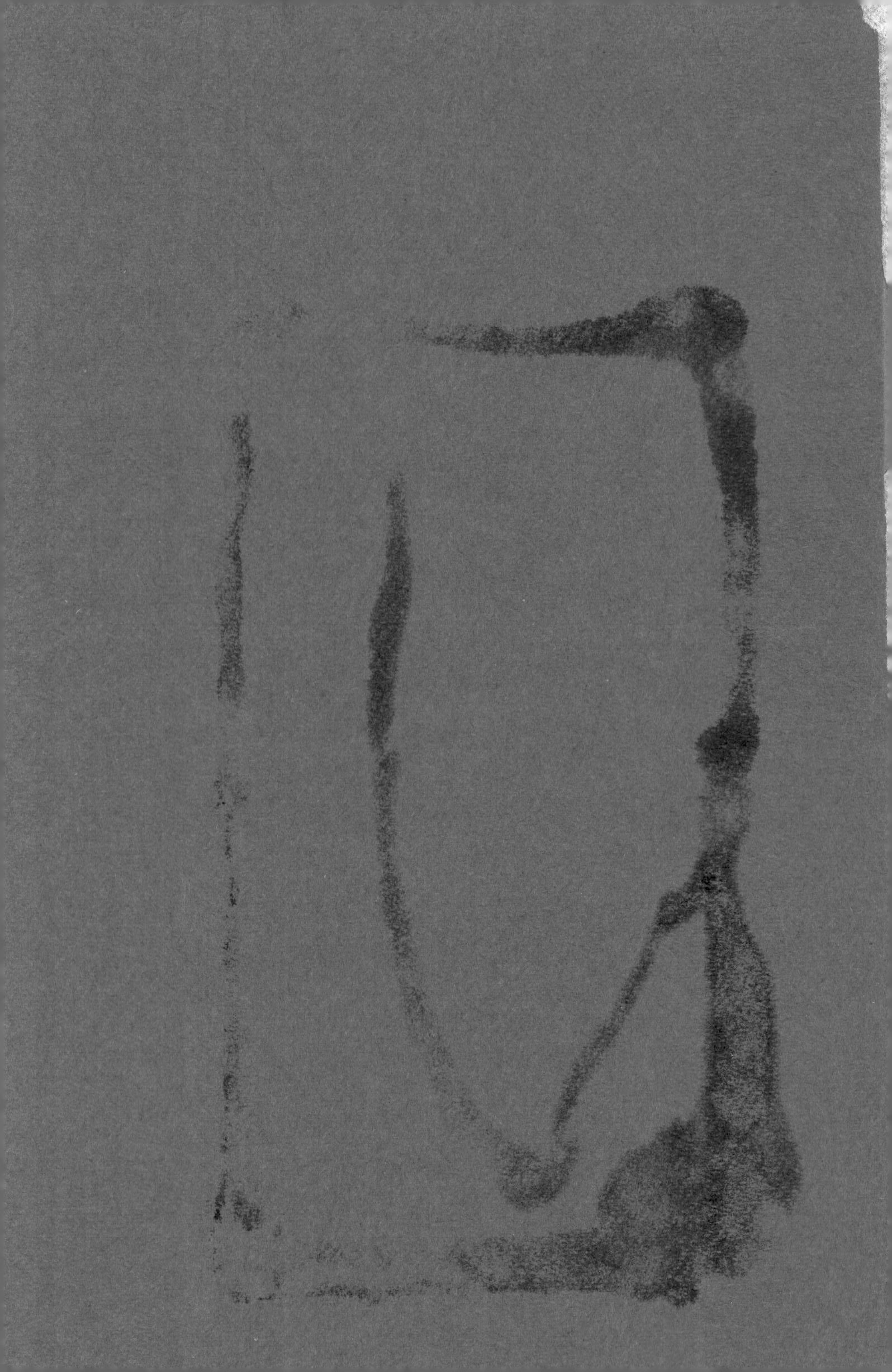

STRAWGIRL

Novels by Abigail Padgett

Child of Silence
Strawgirl

STRAWGIRL

ABIGAIL PADGETT

THE MYSTERIOUS PRESS

Published by Warner Books

A Time Warner Company

Grateful acknowledgment is given for permission to quote from "In Response to Those Who Say The Mad Are Like Prophets," by Pamela Spiro Wagner, © 1993, from *CAMI*, the Journal of the California Alliance for the Mentally Ill. Permission granted by Dan E. Weisburd, editor and publisher.

Mysterious Press books are published by Warner Books, Inc.,
1271 Avenue of the Americas, New York, NY 10020.

A Time Warner Company

Printed in the United States of America
First printing: February 1994

10 9 8 7 6 5 4 3 2 1

Library of Congress Cataloging-in-Publication Data

Padgett, Abigail.
Strawgirl / Abigail Padgett.
p. cm.
ISBN 0-89296-489-8
1. Government investigators—California—San Diego—Fiction. 2. Women detectives—California—San Diego—Fiction. 3. Child abuse—California—San Diego—Fiction. 4. Manic-depressive psychoses—Fiction. I. Title. II. Title: Strawgirl.
PS3566.A3197S77 1994
813′.54—dc20 93-24179
CIP

In Memory of a Friendship
Joan Garfinkel Glantz and Dassia Porper

Acknowledgments

To Adirondack poets Adelaide Crapsey and Jeanne Robert Foster, and Hudson River painter Charlotte Buell Coman, for the inspiration of their work.

To the Iroquois Indian Museum of Schoharie, New York, for research assistance.

To Mary Schifferli of the Albany Institute of History and Art, Albany, New York, for dis-covering women artists of the Hudson River School.

To Robert Pell Dechame and Fort Ticonderoga Director Nicholas Westbrook for their gracious permission to view privately held work of artist Ella Ferris Pell.

To Professor Marilyn J. Ireland of San Diego's California Western School of Law, for technical legal advice.

Note: Shadow Mountain and its Seekers exist only in my imagination. The lodge, however, is really there in the guise of Hemlock Hall, near the town of Blue Mountain Lake, New York.

". . . and in the bloodshed
of a yawning barn there is only
straw, all there is,
and she grasps for it."

Pamela Spiro Wagner

Chapter 1

Bo Bradley watched the day unfold with the wary eye of a Cornish hen touring a fox farm. Days were never this benign; something was peculiar. She had been leery of the day since it started. An ordinary Wednesday, stolidly constructing itself of midweek events so unremarkable they seemed fake. Early-morning San Diego traffic drifting inland too smoothly. Coffee in the chilly Department of Social Services cafeteria too aromatic. The outdated rotary phones too quiet, the footsteps of other investigators in the hall too unhurried.

It wasn't the lithium, couldn't be. The medication she took when necessary to control symptoms of a manic-depressive disorder could do that. It could blur the razor-sharp edges of reality, slow the frenzied input of detail to a manageable, waltzy tempo. It could make everything seem sluggishly *nice*. Except she'd stopped taking the lithium eighteen days ago. So far so good. But this dreamy, dull Wednesday was hiding something. Bo acknowledged the prescient feeling, blunted for the last six months by medication, as a familiar if unpredictable friend.

The feeling had brought a grin to her face when at 8:15 supervisor Madge Aldenhoven burst into the office Bo shared with one other child abuse investigator, flapping an interdepartmental memo in one hand.

"Bo, you're third on today's rotation for new cases. You won't get one until this afternoon, and I know your paperwork is caught up. Please don't waste my time and yours trying to weasel out of what I'm about to ask you."

Aldenhoven had tucked a stray wisp of floury hair into an otherwise impeccable chignon and smiled beatifically. Bo recognized the look as one turn-of-the-century artists would have lavished on the faces of dewy-eyed mothers surrounded by hordes of children in formal attire. The supervisor's gaze was directed at the neat row of orange-banded case files between plastic, county-issue bookends on Bo's desk. A painting of Madge Aldenhoven in biblical robes sweetly cradling a copy of the Department of Social Services procedures manual took shape in Bo's mind. The painting would be done in thick oils, with an ornate gold-leafed frame. Bo sighed and experienced the bone-deep antipathy that characterized her relationship with her supervisor. The daily jousting of bureaucrat and iconoclast without which the job might just be tolerable.

"You know the department is sponsoring a workshop today on Satanic cults and child abuse," Madge went on, waving the memo as if it were a command from the White House. "Estrella was going to represent our unit, but we got another toddler trapped on the freeway median last night . . ."

"And the mother?" Bo asked with genuine concern. Mexican families illegally crossing the border from Tijuana to San Diego's southernmost community often made a run for it across the eight lanes of Interstate 5 to the scrubby, unpopulated safety of the flatlands on the other side. Some didn't make it.

"Hit by a bakery truck in the northbound lane," the supervisor answered briskly. "Fortunately not fatal, just broken bones. The two-year-old was thrown clear, made it to the median. Estrella's over at St. Mary's with him now."

Bo's officemate, Estrella Benedict, was the Spanish-speaking investigator in Madge Aldenhoven's unit, and Bo's best friend.

"Sure," Bo said, brushing an imaginary bit of lint from the arm of her chair, "I'll go sit through your devil worship seminar for Es. Do I get extra points if I bring back a bloody ceremonial dagger or cloven hoof still reeking of sulfur?"

It had been impossible to keep the cynical edge from her answer, and Aldenhoven's renowned insubordination sensors hadn't failed to go off the scale in response.

"Don't take that attitude, Bo," Madge warned from the door. "The department's brought an expert on the subject down from Los Angeles at great expense. Representatives of the police department will be there as well. It's a serious topic. Bound, printed guidelines for recognizing Satanic abuse will be distributed. I want to be sure our unit has its own copy." Bo could see one of Madge's contact lenses drifting precariously off center against the hyacinth-colored iris. Tracking the lens's progress precluded proper attention to the woman's words, which continued. "You've been doing so well these last six months. I'd like to keep it that way."

Bo folded the workshop memo into an origami swan and left it dead center on the gray Formica surface of her desk.

The workshop itself had been ludicrous. A rented hotel conference room with Berber carpet on the walls and what appeared to be woven steel wool on the floor. Lukewarm coffee, several dozen cops and social workers with preformed personal ideas about the devil, and a presentation that in Bo's opinion had not changed since the thirteenth century.

"Some of you will find this hard to believe," a very blonde psychologist named Dr. Cynthia Ganage told the group, "but right now, today, right here in the United States . . . there is a growing and powerful Satanic conspiracy." The psychologist was so fashionably dressed and made up, her expression so glowing, it occurred to Bo that she might be picking up a little money on the side doing bathroom cleanser commercials.

"I don't find this hard to believe," Bo whispered to a social worker from the probation department seated beside her, "I find it impossible to believe!"

"Shh," the woman replied, writing "Satanic conspiracy" in purple ink on a lavender legal pad. "That's how they operate. They *know* people won't believe it."

". . . even at the highest levels of society," Ganage continued, "and the principal Satanic ritual invariably involves sexual defilement, torture, and sometimes murder . . . of innocent children."

"Oh, God," Bo sighed.

"Praise God," said the social worker from probation.

"You're not going to believe this!" Bo told Estrella when she returned at noon. "I've seen a lot of nuts in my day. I've *been* a nut in my day. But nothing can touch this overdressed psychologist the department imported from la-la land. The woman's either delusional or she's found the best money-maker since junk bonds. According to her, every school, church, day-care center, even 'the United States government,' is crawling with secret Satanists panting to torture children. Not to mention rock stars, pop bands, and everybody connected to the entertainment industry!"

"Does that include TV evangelists?" Estrella grinned over a steaming cup of instant noodle soup on her desk. The sun streaming through miniblinds over their single window sliced Estrella's braceleted arm with wavy black and white lines.

"I think it includes the Pope," Bo sighed. "But what really bugs me is that this woman is billing enormous consulting fees to stand around in a five-hundred-dollar suit showing pictures of rock bands whose lyrics, if played backward on the wrong speed underwater, may or may not contain messages urging people to sacrifice babies."

"Wanna know what bugs *me*?" Estrella queried vaguely, examining in a thin band of sunlight the chipped polish on a manicured nail.

"What?" Bo answered, distracted by her own reflection in the mirrored office door. Her appearance had not altered appreciably since she'd checked it that morning. Silver-red shoulder-length curls in typical disarray. Changeable green eyes that today had adopted a shade Bo ruefully identified as 'cucumber.' Less-than-flat midriff and thighs that, if not stopped, would soon resemble Dickensian sausages. Even the loosely cut hip-length jacket she wore nearly every day could not re-create her prelithium lankiness.

"What bugs me," Estrella told the cup of Ramen noodles, "is when manic-depressive friends of mine stop taking their medication and don't tell me."

Bo turned slowly from the mirror and tossed a xeroxed pamphlet entitled *Casework Intervention in Ritual Abuse* onto her desk. The pamphlet's jacket, of folded legal-size yellow card stock, was decorated with a clip-art head of a little boy in a sailor cap, circa 1939, facing the head of a horned devil with an obscenely protuberant tongue. "How did you know I stopped the lithium?" she whispered.

"When I'm not dancing in cantinas, feeding my faithful burro, or strewing rose petals in dusty religious processions," Estrella sang in an accent as broad as it was phony, "I have been known to see what is in front of my face!" The dark eyes looked straight at Bo. "So why didn't you tell me?"

Bo studied the back of one freckled hand as if the answer were written there. "I knew you'd worry?" What was it about psychiatric problems, she pondered, that caused people with no medical training whatever to dispense pharmacological opinions so freely?

"You knew I'd worry," Estrella repeated as if translating a difficult phrase from High German. "Why should I worry? You almost got yourself killed in a mine shaft last year, crazy as a tumbleweed on that case with the deaf boy. You almost blew it permanently, but why should I worry?"

Bo sat in her desk chair and spun to face an exquisitely dressed woman of Hispanic parentage who was about to assault her with a Styrofoam cup of lukewarm Ramen noodles. "I'm sorry, Es," Bo said through the tumble of hair shielding her penitently bowed head. "I should have told you."

The act, which wasn't entirely an act, worked. Head-ducking, a simple primate conciliatory gesture learned from watching *Gorillas in the Mist*, had proven useful to Bo more than once in defusing aggressive humans.

"So how come you stopped the lithium?" Estrella inquired with slightly less feeling. "You've been doing okay."

"Some people with mood disorders have to take medications all the time," Bo explained. "I just have to take it some of the time, and the side effects aren't exactly fun."

Estrella adjusted a mother-of-pearl comb in her sleek coif and narrowed her eyes. "What side effects?"

Bo saw no civilized way to avoid answering the question.

"Weight gain, for one. On lithium I tend to feel like a jumbo marshmallow with the personality of a road kill. I long to pick up small objects in less than two minutes and react to cataclysmic world events in under a week. It's sort of like snorkeling in potato soup."

"And it doesn't help your love life either, right?"

"Es . . . !"

"Well, I knew it was something."

"Es, I keep telling you I don't want a love life, as you so quaintly put it. Too many complications. I want to paint, that's all. Did I tell you two of the Indian primitives sold last week? I'm thinking of spending the money on a weekend at an elegant spa like the movie stars go to. You know, where they feed you grapes and pack you in warm mud?"

"You can do that in my backyard for free," Estrella suggested. "So tell me why you're so antsy about that cult workshop this morning."

The ordinariness of the day was wearing on Bo. The endless, nonsensical details juggled in elaborate patterns behind which, she sensed, other things hid.

"It was just so stupid . . ." she began as Madge Aldenhoven knocked, opened the door and swept into the small office in one efficient gesture.

"I think you're going to be glad you attended the workshop on Satanism, Bo," the supervisor announced in tones resonant with vindication.

"Why is that, Madge?" Bo queried, scanning the ceiling for cobwebs.

"Your new case is a molest. The little girl was just brought to St. Mary's in an ambulance, badly injured. We have reason to believe this case may involve ritual abuse because some sort of bizarre symbol was painted on the child's abdomen. There's an older sister. What little information we have suggests that the most likely perpetrator is the mother's live-in boyfriend, known to be a member of a cult. I want you to go to St. Mary's immediately and assess the situation. It will probably be necessary to pick up the sister from school while the family is still at the hospital. Do your best. This is going to be a messy one."

Bo admired a pearl and lapis ring on Aldenhoven's hand as it slid a new case file onto the desktop. The ring went well with a Chinese-blue linen mantua the supervisor wore over a simple knit sheath dress the color of alabaster. Madge, who never went out of the building, never confronted the reality documented in reports she merely read, could cultivate the illusion that this was a desirable line of work. Madge could dress as though she were the ladies' wear buyer for a conservative department store. It was, Bo acknowledged, a healthy self-deception. Across the manila folder's orange band the words

"FRANER, SAMANTHA, 3 YEARS 6 MONTHS/HANNAH, 8 YEARS 1 MONTH" had been penned in heavy black marker. A chemical scent drifted from the fresh ink, dissolving the day's facade like rain on a dusty window. It wasn't an ordinary Wednesday after all. Bo had known it all along.

"I don't want this case," she told Estrella when Madge had closed the door behind her. An odd feeling, similar to panic but full of sadness, rose in her throat. Another unthinkable set of horrors to sort through. Against the deceptive vapidity of the day the new case loomed like a signpost to hell, offering no hope in any direction. "I don't even want to *work* here," she groused with a petulance that seemed to have come from nowhere. "I can't face another molest case, with or without Satanic conspiracies. I just want to stay home and paint pictures."

Bo listened to herself and heard the whiny voice of a spoiled brat. Still, the words were true. The case file on her desk shimmered poisonously.

"I knew it!" Estrella pounced on the moment. "You're off your medication and you're getting weird. You never let work get to you before. You need the lithium, Bo. You can't handle this job without it."

"Maybe," Bo pondered, stuffing the unread case file into a battered briefcase and grabbing her keys, "and then maybe there's just something peculiar about today . . ."

"May first," Estrella pointed sharply to a wall calendar. "We don't celebrate the Russian Revolution here, and Cinco de Mayo is still four days off. Nothing noteworthy about today."

Bo's lips curled upward in a knowing grin. May first? Beltane! The day Caillech Bera ceased her wintry wailing and turned to stone until the following All Hallow's. Bo could almost hear her Irish grandmother telling the tale.

"Aye, an' old Cally's a-turned to stone some lonely place tonight, her staff a-lost i' the gorse. We'll not see 'er for all the bright summer, we won't, not hear 'er, neither!"

A comforting revelation, Bo smiled broadly. With the ancient symbol of madness put out of commission by a warming sun, people might safely walk the land without lithium. People might just quit whining and hang on to whatever jobs were paying their rent.

"Thanks, Es," Bo waved at the door. "You're more help than you know."

Chapter 2

During a recently completed renovation St. Mary's Hospital for Children had retained the services of an image consultant. Bo, swiftly assessing that the hospital's parking lot was full, eased her dowdy blue BMW into the only remaining parking spot—one marked RESERVED FOR CLERGY. Then she stuck out her tongue at the smiling magenta wooly mammoth whose painted fiberboard figure adorned every light pole. "Mabel," as the logo had been named by the image consultants, held strings to multicolored balloons in its long-extinct trunk, and wore a stethoscope around its neck. Bo found the creature aesthetically atrocious.

"Why," she'd asked Dr. Andrew LaMarche, director of the hospital's child abuse unit, "would a children's hospital in southern California use a logo depicting an extinct elephant that never set foot south of Schenectady, New York?"

LaMarche had, uncharacteristically, laughed aloud over his roasted Anaheim chili at a five-star steak house on the one occasion in six months on which Bo had agreed to dinner with him.

"The idea," he explained, "was that children would see a prehistoric, long-haired elephant as strange, like being in the hospital is strange. And that the smile and bright colors would make the strangeness friendly. Of course the thing is hideous, but the concept's sound. Young children, basically, are able to identify familiar/unfamiliar and friendly/unfriendly constructs. It's helpful to adorn the hospital with repetitions of a figure that's at once unfamiliar and friendly. Hence, Mabel!"

Bo sneered dramatically at the Mabel smiling into her windshield and pulled the Franer case file from her briefcase. Samantha Alice Franer, it told her, was a three-and-a-half-year-old Caucasian female who had been brought to St. Mary's Hospital after her mother, Bonnie Corman Franer, had taken her to a local pediatrician. The pediatrician, Susan Ling, M.D., had phoned the police after arranging for an ambulance to transport Samantha from her office to St. Mary's. According to Susan Ling's report, Samantha Franer had suffered internal injuries consistent with a sexual assault perpetrated sometime the previous day. According to Susan Ling, those injuries were serious.

Stuffing the case file back into a saddle-stitched cowhide briefcase whose brass clasp was the Mayan snake-head glyph for rain, Bo tugged down the cuffs of her black knit slacks and headed toward the hospital's lobby. A sound truck from local TV station KTUV was parked in front of the hospital's sliding glass doors.

"Uh-oh . . ." Bo breathed uneasily, and grabbed for the case file again. No TV news team worth its journalism credentials would sink to invading a hospital where children lay sick and in pain. Not unless the story were irresistible. And TV station "K-TOUGH," as it chose to be known, had built a reputation on scooping San Diego's most bizarre, or bloodthirsty, events.

"A symbol of some sort has been painted on the child's lower abdomen in what appears to be yellow Magic Marker," Dr. Ling's report went on. "It is a strange face surrounded by spikes. This may or may not have any bearing on the child's injuries, which I do not hesitate to define as having resulted from rape."

"Shit," Bo said flatly as the automatic doors opened with a whoosh. Dr. Ling, obviously new to San Diego County and its procedures for reporting child abuse, had phoned her report directly to the police instead of to the Child Abuse Hotline. In the systemic relay of the report to an assignment desk and then back out to detectives in the field, the information might have been carried on one of the standard police radio bands. Accessible to anyone with a short-wave radio who happened to be listening. And somebody *had* been listening. The sound truck made that evident.

"It's somebody from Child Protective Services!" a voice noted from a cluster of people surrounding the lobby information desk. Bo watched a woman approaching her from the group. She was followed by an unshaven boy with stringy blond hair wearing a Grateful Dead T-shirt and carrying a Minicam. The woman was still wearing the oversized ecru silk jacket she'd chosen for the morning workshop. Bo had hoped never to see the matching bleached lizard three-inch heels again. It was Dr. Devil, the sensationalist psychologist from L.A. who could find Satan-worshippers at any convenience store but clearly couldn't grasp the concept of cruelty-free footwear. A sound bite of the woman being gummed to death by geckos flashed across Bo's brain.

"I'm afraid I've forgotten your name," Bo said, cheerfully jerking her elbow out of the woman's well-manicured grasp. "What on earth are you doing here at St. Mary's?"

Besides skating on a child's pain right into your own personal spotlight?

"Cynthia Ganage. *Doctor* Cynthia Ganage," the woman announced urgently. At close range Bo could see lipstick in two shades, skillfully applied with a brush, a dusting of blush over flawlessly creamy cheekbones, smallish hazel eyes set too close together but widened by artful application of gray eyeliner. The hammered hoop earrings were not brass, but gold. "As you know from my workshop this morning," Ganage went on,

"I'm a psychologist specializing in the cult-related ritual abuse of children."

Ganage's voice, Bo realized with renewed contempt, was just loud enough to be heard by two newspaper reporters hurrying through a side door from the ambulance bay. The lobby of St. Mary's was gradually assuming the frenzied atmosphere of a shark tank at feeding time.

"I'd love to chat, but duty calls," Bo smiled with patent insincerity, handing her identification badge to a security guard at the elevators.

Cynthia Ganage raised her voice another two notches. "Are you here to investigate the Franer case? From available information I'm certain that Satanism is involved. I'm here to volunteer my professional services, free of charge—"

As the elevator doors smothered the blonde woman's words, Bo took deliberately deep breaths and reminded herself that sensationalism was not really a criminal offense, even though it should be. In publicly revealing the child's name and details of the case, Cynthia Ganage had just violated every protocol observed by police and Child Protective Services personnel alike. Staring at the Mayan snake-face clasp on her briefcase, Bo decided that compared to Ganage the snake was actually cute.

"I'm here on the Franer case," she said at the fifth-floor nurses' station. "Is the child still being examined? I need to speak with the mother, too. I assume she's with Samantha?"

"The child's still in surgery," a heavyset black nurse with whom Bo had worked on previous cases answered quietly. A look in the hooded eyes issued a warning. Bo had seen the look before. The silent language of medical personnel.

"Put the walls up," it said. "Get ready to face the intolerable."

"You can go on down to the observation deck," the nurse suggested. "See how much longer it'll be. The mother's in the surgical waiting room."

Every nuance of the softly spoken words told Bo things were not going well. Nodding, she forced herself to walk through the unmarked door at the back of an office behind the nurses' station. The door opened into a short corridor that led to a small observation cage through which activities in the operating room could be observed. The observation chamber, always dark, held a row of chairs bolted to the floor for silence, and a speaker projecting voices from the brightly lit operating arena below. It was, Bo thought, like entering the interior of a Christmas tree ornament.

". . . unable to effect substantive prophylactic measures already described . . ." the familiar voice of Dr. Andrew LaMarche pronounced slowly as Bo made herself focus on the scene seven feet beneath her. Something wasn't right. The green-clad surgical team was too quiet, moving too slowly. The surgical nurse empty-handed. The anesthesiologist failing to monitor his bank of screens, which appeared to be blank. One surgeon walking away, another closing a wide incision across the child's abdomen with unusually large stitches. The little girl's skin was as pale as the cap of short blonde curls above her closed eyes. She seemed more representational than real, a chunky Raphaelesque cherub on an unfinished canvas. In the intense operating room lights the tousled blonde curls seemed crystalline. Like spun glass. Bo fought a realization that blurred her vision. The realization that the child's body was merely an empty and fading husk from which the personality of someone named Samantha Alice Franer had already fled.

"The cause of death . . ." Andrew LaMarche pronounced into a microphone suspended above the operating table, "is internal hemorrhage secondary to . . ."

Bo turned back into the small corridor and pressed her forehead against its cool tile wall. What was it like to be three years old? She searched her memory and found very little. A favorite green plaid sunsuit with white eyelet ruffles on the straps. Her grandmother had embroidered the first three bars of "Kitty of Coleraine" on the sunsuit's bib and taught Bo to pick out the melody with one finger on the piano. And a Cairn terrier named McDermott who howled when her mother practiced the violin and slept every night with his head on Bo's pillow. Vague, innocent memories devoid of the complexity only possible after the brain has completed its circuitry between five and six years of age. "The age of reason" defined by the ancients. The age when it is possible to learn to read, to manipulate symbols, to frame ideas of right and wrong. Samantha Franer would never be six years old now. She would remain forever three, just a memory of a flaxen-curled toddler frozen in the minds of those who loved her. Like Bo's sister, Laurie, who twelve years after her death was still twenty. Who would always be twenty.

Bo squeezed her eyes shut and felt tears spill and run down her flushed cheeks. But was she crying for the dead child on the operating table or for her own sister whose suicide twelve years ago had triggered in Bo a depression so profound she'd been hospitalized for three months? It was hard to tell. But she was going to have to get control of herself.

"So what will it take?" the imagined voice of her best-loved psychiatrist, the sprightly Dr. Lois Bittner, echoed from the past. "A piano has to drop on your head out of the sky before you see you're in trouble?"

"I'm not in trouble," Bo told the gray ceramic wall. "I'm okay without the lithium. I've just never seen a child dead on an operating table before. I mean anybody might *decompensate* a little . . ." she exaggerated the psychiatric term, ". . . seeing that."

"You're not anybody," the memory pointed out with dogged good cheer. "You have manic depression. You have to protect yourself."

Bo considered the savage arrogance necessary for the act of rape, and realized that she would never comprehend it, only hate it. An act somehow generated in the chemistry of the male, where apelike charades of dominance could go wrong and become brutal defilement. But to defile a thing with no defenses, no hope of resistance or self-protection? Even though her job required near-daily brushes with its not uncommon reality, the rape of children continued to shock Bo. A sickening horror endured by millions of children every day. And this one was magnified by its deadly outcome—the pale, still body below.

Bo wished Lois Bittner were still alive. Wished she could talk about what she'd just seen. Wished she could climb the wooden stairs to the shrink's comfortable loft office in a seasoned downtown St. Louis building that had been new when Teddy Roosevelt took office, kick off her shoes, and talk. Bittner had been a complete fluke, a coincidence, a mistake. And the best thing that had happened in Bo's train wreck of a life.

Turning to hunker on her heels with her back to the wall, Bo massaged her skull to erase the scene in the operating room and let herself remember Lois Bittner. A reassuring memory in spite of its beginning. A mental earthwork buffering the shadowless image of the dead child below.

A depression, the worst ever, had crept like an iron fog into Bo's brain after Laurie's funeral. In the beginning she'd thought she could handle it. Driving the new BMW Mark had bequeathed her as compensation for annulling their marriage of three years, she'd left Boston a week after the funeral and begun the cross-country trek. The long drive back to Los Alamos where she'd continued to work on the Navajo reservation after her husband left to find a wife who would bear his children. A wife with no history of psychiatric problems. The BMW had held up well, but by St. Louis the same could not be said of Bo. Everything had turned dark, colorless, without hope.

Waking in a Holiday Inn overlooking the Mississippi River, Bo had looked out the window and understood that to go outside was to succumb. To go outside was to walk over the roughly cobbled bank and into mud-brown water that would swiftly cover her, swiftly drag her downward to an utter, final silence. There was no question about it; something in her brain had signaled that it was time to die. The neurochemical pathway for dissolution, hardwired into every brain for an inevitable future when it would be needed, could be activated prematurely. It could happen in an acute depression. It had happened.

But something else said "No!" Something in the very cells of her body screamed that death made no sense. It was an intelligence even more primitive than the most ancient segment of her brain, the pons, nestled at the base of her skull. An intelligence of a billion mere cells that pulled her from the window and locked her body in a fetal curl on the floor of a hotel room closet. It would not let her go outside to the cold, swift water. It would hide her in the preconscious darkness of the unborn until something came to derail the brain's grim command.

Twelve hours later the hotel manager, alerted by complaints of a guttural moaning heard in the next room, had unlocked the door with a passkey, and phoned the police. In the emergency room of a state mental hospital Bo was asked to select a psychiatrist from a typed list. Unable to talk, she had barely succeeded in organizing her thoughts sufficiently to identify the first letter of each name. Somehow the letter B seemed familiar, and Bo pointed to one of the B names.

"Lois Bittner?" The emergency room physician chuckled. "She's a little unorthodox. You sure you want Bittner?"

Bo was sure of nothing but the battle raging between her own life and the urge to drown in a strange midcontinental river whose name she couldn't at the moment pronounce, much less spell. "Uh," she'd answered, nodding. A pain like dull acid filled her, outlining her body darkly against the white room. She felt like a demon, a cartoon figure filled with black ink. When the admitting psychiatrist muttered, "This is thorazine; it'll pinch a little," and eased a sparkling hypodermic needle into her left hip, she couldn't feel it.

They'd taken her to a musty, high-ceilinged room and fastened leather cuffs to her wrists. At some point the door opened and a pastrami-scented woman who looked like a miniature schnauzer in a batik dashiki, long skirt, and Frye boots, burst in. "I'm Lois Bittner," the woman said as if her name were the answer to some amusing conundrum. "So why are you here?" The accent was clearly German, the aging dark eyes full of mirth. Bo felt a smile struggle through the darkness inside her and twitch at the corners of her mouth. The smile had felt like a lifeline, a hint of a way out.

That night Lois Bittner sat by Bo's bedside and regaled her with tales of St. Louis eateries—the fried ravioli at Garivelli's, floating in butter, the Steak'n'Shake French fry, perfect in its crispness, the Caesar salad at Al Baker's, mouth-watering. "Good food here," the diminutive doctor had grinned, "not a place for death."

Not a place for death.

Bo shook her head and forced herself back to the present. San Diego was not a place for death, either. Just a sun-washed desert city with a beach. A pastel city of nursery colors where three-year-olds in ruffled sunsuits would build things in sand, not be buried in it. "I've got to find another way to make a living," she told the empty corridor as she struggled to her feet. "My psychiatrist recommends something involving fried foods."

In the office behind the nurses' station Bo recognized the oxlike frame of Dar Reinert, the San Diego Police Department's most experienced child abuse detective. A former tackle at Notre Dame, the hulking cop had yet to find a suit that didn't make him look like one of Rembrandt's syndics.

"She didn't make it," Bo answered the question in Reinert's gentle, delft blue eyes. "She's dead."

"Sonofabitch," Reinert huffed softly. "You'd better grab the sister now! We figure the perp's this wacko boyfriend of mom's—guy named Paul Massieu—lives with 'em. Better get the eight-year-old outta the loop. I'll send a coupla uniforms out to the kid's school, back you up. You meet 'em there. What's the older one's name?"

"Hannah," Bo remembered from the case file. "Hannah Franer. Why do you think the boyfriend's the perp?"

The small room was airless, dim.

"Nine times outta ten it is, isn't it?" Reinert sighed, jabbing numbers into the phone. "You look like spoiled milk, Bradley. Go out in the hall. Get a drink of water or something. Besides," he said into a blue and gold striped tie askew over a blue oxford cloth shirt unbuttoned at its size eighteen collar, "this Massieu's known to be involved with a cult."

Bo noted the small stainless-steel Ruger revolver tucked in the waistband of Dar Reinert's wash-and-wear dress pants, and grimaced. This was the job. It often felt like an old episode of *Dragnet*.

Over a water fountain in the hall she breathed the flat chemical scent of San Diego's multiply recycled water, and assessed her future. How many more months, years of this could she take? How many more tortured children? And how many more officious remarks from Madge Aldenhoven, who would undoubtedly die on the job at ninety-three? In the living room of Bo's beach apartment a newly stretched canvas waited on its easel. Two coats of gesso applied over the weekend would be thoroughly dry. Time to paint, but paint what? No inspiration twitched before her eyes. Only the lifeless image of a chubby blonde girl.

Get a grip, Bradley. Let it go. Just go pick up the sister and then do something fun tonight, something distracting.

Bo tried to imagine what fun, distracting thing she could do that wouldn't involve sugar or saturated fats, and drew a blank.

At the end of the hall she could see Andrew LaMarche, elegant even in green surgical scrubs, somberly closing the door of the waiting room. His head was bowed. In seconds Samantha Franer's mother would be told as compassionately as possible that her younger daughter had ceased to exist. Bo considered the reality behind the closed door and shuddered.

"Bradley!" Dar Reinert's scratchy tenor voice bawled from the nurses' station, "you're going with me. Come on!"

"Going where?" Bo asked, joining the burly detective at a near-run toward the elevators.

"Franer place," came the reply. "Seems this Paul Massieu character showed up at the sister's school forty-five minutes ago, told the staff Samantha was in the hospital, and took Hannah. There's an outside chance they're still at home."

In the elevator Reinert shrugged on a navy blazer that effectively hid the gun in his belt. Bo could taste his fear like a metallic film in her own mouth. They both knew that if the older child had been victimized as well, the perpetrator might kill her to ensure her silence.

"Any news?" Cynthia Ganage asked in the lobby.

"Rats live on no evil star," Bo said, her eyes wide with apparent meaning.

"What was *that* all about?" Reinert scowled.

"The woman's a snake," Bo answered as Ganage made a note of the remark. "Do you really think we'll find Hannah with this Paul Massieu at home?" she asked once they were out of earshot.

Dar Reinert glared at the horizon beyond the hospital parking lot as if it had just maligned his mother's virtue. "Ganage may be a snake, but she may also be right," he said. "And no, I don't think we're going to find Hannah Franer at all."

Chapter 3

By 4:30 in the afternoon the windows of the five-sided tower atop the Victorian lodge gleamed amber in the setting sun. The tower had been added to the sprawling camp when the original owner's young wife contracted tuberculosis. Local Adirondack legend maintained that the desperate man confined his beloved in the tower, imploring her to breathe the famous, healing air. But before the renowned mountain cure could return the blush to her cheeks, the frail consumptive had tumbled mysteriously from one of the tower's windows. In the three-story fall her neck snapped cleanly as a twig, killing her in a second that, had her death not filled it, would surely have escaped the notice of history. A cascade of flowers, century-wild descendants of those the young wife had planted, still spilled beside the lawn. Her ghost was said to roam among them, weeping.

Eva Broussard sat motionless in one of the hickory rockers on the broad porch below the tower. The story of the consumptive bride was to her a soothing mantra, a mental chant possessing infinite avenues for inquiry. Had the Victorian lady jumped, or fallen? Was she pushed? And why a tower of five sides, crafted with such obvious architectural difficulty, buttressed between second-story casement windows? Had the tower been, really, a prison? Had death been the only possible escape?

Eva pondered a similar, if evolutionarily recent, human hunger for a way out of biological bondage. The hunger for something beyond the demands, and then decay, of flesh. That hunger had produced religions. And it had undoubtedly produced the experience that brought her here to document its influence on a hundred people. A hundred people who had in the Adirondack night seen beings who seemed not of this planet. A hundred people frightened and exalted, forever altered, longing for a return of the strange visitors who might, just might, know a way out other than death.

A tall, ropelike woman of mixed French-Canadian and Iroquois blood, Eva exhibited the tensionless grace of a high-wire artist even when still. But her otter-brown eyes were pure French, a Gallic amalgam of passion and rationality. Tugging a creamy knit turban from her head, she ran bronzed fingers through two inches of stubby, chalk-white hair. The chemotherapy that had caused her ebony mane to fall out in clumps was a necessary hedge against a cancer that might or might not abridge a life already sixty years in the making. But it had drained the color from her hair forever. Not that it mattered.

A uniquely beautiful woman by any standard, Eva had cherished only that part of her body which lay behind her eyes. Her mind—superbly trained, boundlessly curious, always rational. She had observed no evidence that her mind would survive her bodily death, however desirable that hope might seem. And after the sharp warning implicit in cancer, the realization had brought her to this odd locale in the mountains of New York State, where she watched and documented a particular groping of the human soul toward understanding. The endeavor would be the last work of her life; its significance was paramount to her. She wanted to leave behind a record, something useful to future generations. The study would be her legacy.

Eva Broussard did not believe that actual spacecraft had

brought extraterrestrial beings to earth. The near-impossibility of transporting anything with physical mass across cosmic distances precluded that occurrence, and probably always would. Neither did she dismiss all claims of sightings as error or delusion. Hadn't the pioneering psychologist Carl Jung suggested that the first sightings in the 1940s might herald a change in the human brain? Perhaps that change, occurring for unknown reasons in some people but not in others, enabled certain individuals under certain circumstances to perceive weightless images beamed from elsewhere in the universe. And perhaps these images, routinely described as "silvery" and only visible at night, had been here all along, their creators waiting millennia in the past for the brain of a race of apes to mature. To "see." Eva's curiosity about those who "saw" and about how that experience would reorder their behavior was the thrumming pulse of her life. The only thing she cared about. Until now. Before today's phone call from California. Before the incomprehensible death of Samantha Franer.

Eva searched her mind for a link to the child, some particular memory that would define the personality now vanished. But there was nothing. A healthy, attractive little girl, toddling energetically behind the other children last summer when members of the group with school-age children were present. Eva remembered chubby exuberance, platinum curls, an obvious contrast with the older sister, Hannah, who was shy and reclusive. But nothing more. Samantha had still been a baby, and Eva did not share the traditional womanly fascination with barely verbal people. The sadness, she realized as conflicting winds raised angled ripples on the lake below, lay in the fact that whatever Samantha Franer might have become was now an impossibility. In the face of that, Eva wondered if her own intellectual pursuits might not seem ludicrous.

She had purchased the lodge for its proximity to areas of the Adirondacks in which sightings were reported. Paul Massieu and others who'd seen lights, saucer-shaped vehicles, and frail, shimmering humanoid figures while alone on some mountain escarpment spent as much time as possible at the compound, assessing their similar experiences. The expenses of utilities, food, and a kitchen staff from nearby Night Heron Village were shared on a monthly basis by everyone present. And in exchange for accommodations the Seekers willingly signed releases and underwent exhaustive interviews with Dr. Eva Blindhawk Broussard, who had never seen one of the silver people, but who took their stories seriously. Each Seeker provided a social and family history as well as medical and psychiatric records, and agreed to update all information twice yearly for the next decade. A comprehensive database. An intriguing longitudinal study that promised to provide clues to the psychosocial bedrock of an important shift in human awareness. A paradigm shift that as yet made no sense, although one day it would. The same could not be said of Samantha Franer, whose future had been canceled. Eva pondered a suprahuman ethic that permitted immortality for computerized data, but allowed an innocent life to be snuffed by another's depravity. The model brought her to her feet in rage at its cruelty.

Skating barefoot across a lawn only faintly green with spring grass, Eva Broussard stopped beside the woody spill of Madagascar periwinkle, legacy of a woman whose death, like Samantha's, remained a mystery. Amid the million pale green leaves not a single bud had emerged. It was too early.

It was, she admitted, gazing over the lake her own Iroquois ancestors had named, probably too early for many things. Too early to comprehend a human behavior that could result in the death of a child. Certainly too early to comprehend the human endeavor to find a link with the universe. The purpose for which she'd bought Night Heron Lodge, nestled beneath Shadow Mountain. The purpose for which a hundred people came there to stare into the sky and wait for visitors who might come again. Who might have answers to questions about life and death. Who might show the way out.

That it was too early had been made clear by the unconscionable death of a little girl. That death would destroy the group. It would curtail the intent of Eva Broussard's carefully framed research. It would confuse the mystery that had by whatever means created an experience that several rational people interpreted as visitation by nonearthly beings.

Now outsiders would come, asking questions for which there would be no solid answers. The Seekers on Shadow Mountain would be dragged into a very earthly, and very ugly, reality. They would be ridiculed, labeled. The bond of their common experience would be eroded. Worse, they would be accused of complicity in one of the most loathsome crimes possible—the sexual violation and murder of an innocent child. Beside that reality the hope of an end to cosmic loneliness seemed pitifully premature.

Eva Broussard pulled a blade of grass and held it to the waxy, dimming sun. What possible set of facts, she thought, could explain the senseless horror of Samantha Franer's death?

From the darkening lake a chill breeze wrapped her skirts about her legs. There was no answer.

Chapter 4

According to a check run by police on the address given St. Mary's Hospital, Bonnie Franer had signed a six-month lease on the three-bedroom house in a quiet central San Diego neighborhood shortly after Christmas. Dar Reinert shared the information with Bo as he drove and wolfed a Mounds bar. The candy's sweetish coconut smell gave the interior of the car a sickly tropical flavor.

"Why would Franer have signed the lease rather than Massieu?" Bo said from the passenger's seat, trying to ignore the odor. She felt oddly uninvolved with the case, and yet pulled toward some dimension of it that seemed peripheral. Something distant, almost cerebral. If she really decided to quit her job, she realized, this would be her last case. Maybe the nagging tug toward irrelevant facts was just a way of making the break. At least it wasn't manicky. She felt none of the dramatic emotional response that would signal a need for lithium.

"We ran a check. Massieu's Canadian, not a U.S. citizen," Reinert replied, easing his eight-cylinder Olds diagonally across the driveway of the house. "Some people will only rent to legal citizens. Cuts down on the problem of a bunch of illegal Mexicans renting a place and tearing it apart."

Bo considered launching an argument that "illegal Mexicans" were no more likely to tear a house apart than, say, "legal Norwegians," but abandoned the idea. What Reinert suggested was often true. A cultural dilemma created when agrarian people from villages as yet unblessed by electricity or modern plumbing walked hundreds of miles to work north of an invisible line called "U.S.–Mexico Border." Unsophisticated people, who might keep chickens in the laundry room of a rental house or cook them over Sterno in the living room. Reinert's expansive maroon car, she noticed, effectively blocked any possible exit from the closed, two-car garage.

"Nobody's here," she said. The beige stucco ranch with its fading brown shutters and bare, weedy lawn provided a wealth of information. Keenly aware of nuance, Bo missed none of it. "They haven't lived here long, and they don't intend to stay." A network of cracks in the unwatered lawn created a miniature badland. "There aren't any bikes or toys in the yard, which means they haven't bought any. And no personal touches. The house looks exactly as it did when they rented it."

"Whaddaya mean?" Reinert sniffed, watching the living room picture window for movement. "Place looks okay to me."

"That's the point," Bo went on. "People invariably mark their living spaces, personalize them. A butterfly decal on the mailbox, plaster St. Francis in the yard. Maybe a plant or a lamp visible in a window. Something that changes the physical structure into a habitation. This place is just a structure. The people haven't created any identity here. Their hearts are someplace else."

"So?" Reinert opened his door.

"So they're not going to stay. It's temporary, like a motel room. Nobody feels compelled to personalize a motel room; there's no point."

"Women pick up stuff like that." The detective nodded fondly as Bo followed him toward the slightly warped front door. She kept to herself the fact that any man with a diagnosis of manic depression would probably exhibit the same sensibilities. It came with the territory.

The house seeped a sort of breathy grayness, the hallmark of places where no one is. There would, Bo sensed as Reinert removed the Ruger from beneath his blazer, also be no dog or cat. The grayness lacked even an animal presence.

Dar Reinert's fist thumped on the hollow-core door as he bellowed, "Massieu? Open up. Police."

Beside the drab rental the adjoining property seemed to have been groomed as a set for a country-and-western video. A picket fence banked with waist-high scarlet geraniums bordered a verdant lawn punctuated by an artistically placed birdbath, a small gazebo of white lath, and an unidentifiable piece of antique farm equipment. From a bed of Charlotte Armstrong roses between the geraniums a salty male voice roared, "There's nobody home over there! They've been gone since 7:00. You won't need that gun!" The man, about seventy and dressed in painter's pants and a pajama shirt, grinned sheepishly from his position flat on the ground amid the roses. "Been skittish around guns since the war," he explained. "Lost an eye at Pearl."

Bo wondered for the millionth time in her life just how she was able to know, without even *caring*, that the old codger was lying. He had a glass eye, all right. But he hadn't lost the real one defending Pearl Harbor.

"It's an acute sensitivity to tone and presentation," Lois Bittner had tried to explain years ago. "You're a walking litmus test for imperceptible clues that anyone else would miss. Have you given any thought," the wiry psychiatrist lapsed into her characteristic accent, "to a chob as a chypsy?"

Bo smiled to herself as Reinert made easy work of unlocking the flimsy door with the edge of his tie clasp.

"Isn't this illegal?" she said.

"Door was unlocked," the detective recited. "I feared that the older child might be alone in the house, injured and unable to call out. On that cause I entered the premises accompanied by a representative of Child Protective Services, Ms. Bradley."

Reinert's written report of the entry would say precisely that. But they couldn't stay beyond a few minutes or remove any evidence.

The living room, carpeted in a threadbare chartreuse shag, was completely empty. A dining ell to the left contained a Formica table and four mismatched chairs that could have been purchased in any thrift store in North America. Four plastic placemats in a sunny yellow showed evidence of regular cleaning, and matched a basket of silk daisies in the table's center. The kitchen was equally tidy, if devoid of personality. There was nothing about the place to suggest that anybody really lived there. There was also nothing to suggest diabolical secrets.

"I don't get a sense of anything unwholesome going on here," Bo said tentatively. Houses sometimes seemed to whisper of events they had sheltered. This one merely yawned. "What makes you think this Massieu's involved in a cult?"

Reinert was checking the contents of the refrigerator. "The mother told the admitting clerk at St. Mary's that they were in San Diego so Massieu could buy some land out in the desert for this New York group she called the Seekers."

"So? California's full of people *seeking* something different. It's the primary pastime. Crystals, channeling, past lives, Eastern mysticism, Zen dentistry—it's just openness, curiosity. What's wrong with that?"

"People get a little *too* curious, you ask me," Reinert answered enigmatically from a cabinet beneath the sink. "Makes 'em crazy."

Marveling at the non sequitur, Bo chose not to respond to it and congratulated herself. There would be no point in explaining to Dar Reinert what "crazy" really meant or that it could not be the result of curiosity, a quality already erroneously damned for its ability to kill cats. Moving into a hall accessible from both kitchen and living room, Bo inspected a bathroom situated between two bedrooms. On a shelf was a half-used pack of pink bathroom tissue and a large bottle of baby shampoo. Bo remembered pale curls and shivered. The baby shampoo would have been for Samantha. On the toilet seat and on the floor bright red stains were already drying.

"Dar," she whispered, "better see this."

"Mother said she was bleeding this morning," he said gruffly behind her. "Bastard must've torn her up last night. She goes to bed. The blood pools in her abdominal cavity while she's sleeping. Then when she gets up . . ."

Bo touched the door frame in an attempt to curb a wave of nausea. What had been done to Samantha Franer did not bear close scrutiny. Not without throwing up, at least.

You've seen this before, Bradley. Remember your job is to protect the sister. Let the police worry about the perp.

"Well, well, looka here . . ." Reinert singsonged from one of the bedrooms. The tone made it clear that he'd found something he was looking for.

Bo smoothed her forehead with the heels of both hands. "What is it?" she asked, entering the room Samantha and Hannah Franer had obviously shared. Red, white, and blue Raggedy Ann sheets adorned a double-bed mattress on the floor. Above a red-enameled bureau whose half-open drawers revealed children's socks, T-shirts, pajamas, hung a face. Or a head. A thing woven of straw with protuberant, empty eye sockets, a sharp nose, and an oval mouth that appeared to be blowing. Bo recognized the mouth as similar to one in an Irish children's book her sister, Laurie, had loved. The north wind's mouth in a cloud, gusting winter over Lough Derg. The memory of Laurie was, as usual, unsettling.

"I dunno what the hell it is," the detective snarled at the hollow eyes, "but didn't the pediatrician's report say somebody painted a spiked face on the poor kid's belly before he raped her? This looks like a spiked face to me, made of straw or something. So what does that say?"

"I don't know what it says," Bo answered. The straw face seemed to tell some story far removed from the terrible stains in the bathroom. A story Bo sensed in the same way she could tell, even in windowless rooms, when clouds covered the sun. But a closer story was that Hannah Franer, if she were still alive, had just entered a world Bo knew very well. A world in which there only used to be a little sister.

"It says these people are into some weird stuff that may involve sex with children. Ritual abuse stuff. That psychologist, Ganage, says they do it because destroying innocence pleases Satan, or something like that. And with this devil mask right here in the kids' room, it's safe to guess Mom might just have gone along with it. Time for a warrant—at least accessory to felony child sexual assault. I'm gonna call it in . . ."

Bo watched the straw mask. It stared wildly at nothing, howling soundlessly. Things were moving too fast, assumptions being made with senseless velocity. Accustomed to occasional manic episodes in which her own perceptions accelerated beyond the boundaries of reality, Bo now felt like an inert stump rooted in a hurricane. Something was off, wrong, skewed. Why was everybody in such a hurry to jump on the devil worship thing? The situation, Bo gauged uneasily, was assuming the framework of mania. Too fast. Out of control. But recognizing it didn't mean there was anything she could do about it.

"I want you to interview the mother as soon as we get back to the hospital," Reinert said from the kitchen where he was on the phone arranging a warrant for the arrest of Bonnie Franer. "I hear you're magic getting the truth outta people. I want you to break her. Now. Before she gets a lawyer."

It was perfectly legal. The cops and CPS workers did it

whenever necessary. A suspect could not be interrogated by police without counsel. But a social worker could interview the suspect in order to secure information that might affect the welfare of that suspect's children. Whatever was said in that interview would be submitted to juvenile court in a confidential report prepared to document recommendations for the child's placement and protection. In theory, that report could be seen by no one outside juvenile court. In practice, the report or even the social worker could be subpoenaed to other courts, and the CPS worker could simply tell the cops anything she or he thought they needed to know. In actuality, if Bonnie Franer chose to tell Bo Bradley that her live-in boyfriend, Paul Massieu, raped her three-year-old daughter, Samantha, in a Satanic ritual involving bug-eyed masks, she might as well have told KTUV's evening news.

Bo experienced the weight of her own role in the mercurial sequence of events, and sighed. A hundred-pound raven perched on her head would have been more comfortable.

"Mind if I smoke in your car?" she asked Reinert, lighting a Gauloise and exhaling thoughtfully.

"Hang it out the window," Reinert replied.

Bo bit her lip and did not produce any of the twenty-seven possible comebacks crossing her mind.

Chapter 5

Andrew LaMarche clasped long, bony fingers atop a desk calendar advertising soy-based infant formula. On a bookcase to his right a Seth Thomas clock informed Bo in gilded Roman numerals that it was 2:15 and that time, in fact, possessed wings.

"Why do you have to interview the poor woman right now, Bo?" he asked quietly. The edge of a French accent never lost from his New Orleans upbringing betrayed emotion otherwise scrupulously contained. The death of Samantha Franer seemed to have upset him inordinately. Bo wondered why. As director of the hospital's child abuse unit, the world-famous expert on brutalized children had undoubtedly seen more than one small cadaver.

"The suspected perp has taken off with the older sister," Bo explained. "The mother may know where he's taken her." On the physician's desk was a rough potter's clay sculpture of a human baby in the arms of a Barbary ape. "Where did you find that piece?" she asked, intrigued. The ape's eyes were wide with fear.

"I made it," he replied without interest. "Bo, Bonnie Franer had nothing to do with the death of her daughter. Neither did Paul Massieu. They're both innocent. I'm sure of it."

Bo raised her eyes from the sculpture to gaze levelly at Andrew LaMarche. "The police think differently."

"The police think *obviously*," he said from beneath a graying mustache. "I had expected better from you. I simply can't allow you to interrogate Bonnie Franer right now, Bo." His voice dropped to a husky whisper. "She's just lost a child."

Bo examined her patience and found it worn to translucent thinness. Every minute ticking by might increase the danger to Hannah. "I know she's just lost a child! And I'm not here to discuss it with you. I'm here to get information that might just save the sister from a similar fate. Now where's Bonnie Franer?"

The baritone voice rasped with anger. "Do you think I don't know what you and Reinert are up to? The woman's in shock. She could say anything. You'll concoct enough evidence to hang her by tomorrow. I won't permit it!"

His hands, Bo noticed as he stood and wrenched a mole-gray pinstriped jacket from the back of his desk chair, seemed wooden. Beneath close-cropped hair the color of loam his eyes swept the room as if searching for hidden assassins. Bo would not have been surprised if he'd grabbed the odd little sculpture and smashed it against the wall of diplomas at her back. The framed documents proclaimed Andrew Jacques LaMarche a doctor of pediatrics, a fellow at three universities, and a legal expert on criminal pediatric trauma. None of them mentioned that the dashing baby doctor had the temperament of a coloratura soprano opening *La Traviata* at the Met. But the peculiar thing was the direction of his anger. Long a defender of the rights of children, Andrew LaMarche had never before evinced any interest in the feelings of parents.

Puzzled, Bo showed her ace. "I think Bonnie Franer has told you what happened to Samantha, and I think she's told you where Paul Massieu has taken Hannah."

"She told me Samantha seemed strange last night, refusing to eat her dinner. She said that Paul Massieu returned from the property their group is purchasing out in the desert near Jamul at about 7:00, when he and the mother checked on Samantha, who was asleep, and decided not to call a doctor because she wasn't feverish. After that, she said she, Paul, and the older sister, Hannah, watched television until Hannah went to bed at 9:00. Apparently there was some muted talking and activity in the girls' room at that time, indicating that Samantha had awakened when her sister came to bed. But since neither girl came back out to say anything was wrong, Bonnie and Paul didn't check further. Bonnie said that Paul was not alone with Samantha at any time last night, and so couldn't have been the one who raped her, even if he'd been capable of such a thing. The couple went to bed at 10:00 and heard nothing from the girl's room during the night. Paul rose at 5:00 to breakfast with an earthmoving contractor they've apparently hired to clear a road into the desert property. He was gone when Bonnie heard Samantha's cries from the bathroom and then saw that the child was pale and bleeding from the pelvic region. She told me she phoned a local pediatrician's service then, at about 6:30, and made arrangements to meet in the doctor's office after dropping the older sister at her school." There was a pause. "And that's it, Bo. Anything else she may have said is privileged."

"Another child's life is at risk," Bo told him. "Against that fact your privilege means nothing. If Hannah is harmed because you kept me from interviewing the mother, you're accountable."

They'd both known it all along. Bo couldn't imagine what lay behind the verbal grandstanding. His eyes were the color of wet slate.

"She's in the surgical social worker's office with a priest," he muttered, tugging French cuffs to a point precisely a half inch below his jacket sleeves. "But you're wasting your time."

Bo had scraped knuckles on the renowned LaMarche pomposity before. "Oh, thank you, massa," she bowed, shuffling across what she realized was an Aubusson carpet. "I's jus' doin' my job."

"Don't push me, Bo." The deep voice held an unaccountable dagger edge.

Bo merely pulled the office door closed behind her and wondered why everyone seemed mad as hatters. The thought found form on an imaginary canvas in her head. LaMarche in a top hat and cutaway coat, pouring tea for a March Hare who was Madge Aldenhoven, while a burly dormouse with a Ruger revolver in its belt snored with its head in a plate of crumpets. The day was not going well, despite its bland beginning. Bo found a measure of comfort in the accuracy of her earlier foreboding. And in her decision to explore the possibility of quitting this torturous job. In the surgical social worker's office that comfort evaporated like water on a heated stone.

"Hannah is fine," Bonnie Franer pronounced with wrenching effort after Bo explained her own function in the nightmare. "Please, dear God please, just leave me alone!" The gaunt woman had doubled over in a series of shallow, racking gulps that would only later become sobs. The gulping and breathing created a rocking motion. Bo watched with growing alarm as Bonnie Franer's tattered fingers roamed aimlessly over the suede surface of a purse. Most of her fingernails were bitten to the quick. A glance at the woman's skeletal forearms revealed long, fine scratches threading the pallid skin. Similar marks raked the sides of her face and neck. Some were fresh, trickling spidery filaments of blood. More were dried and healing. Bo had seen it before. Even with her gnawed fingernails, Bonnie Franer made a habit of scratching herself. A bad sign.

The priest, who in Bo's estimation couldn't have been a day over fourteen, sat boyishly on the social worker's desk and reeked concern. "I'm Frank Goodman," he curbed a naturally wide smile tugging at the corners of his mouth, "from St. Theresa's."

"Hi, Father," Bo replied and ran a freckled hand through her hair, then tapped a Bic pen against her teeth. Bonnie Franer presented a textbook picture that screamed "victim." Had Paul Massieu done this as well? Stripped the mother of her very personality while using her daughters as sexual toys? Maybe this *was* one of those tabloid cases beloved of talk show hosts, cases in which secretly monstrous men held thrall over helpless women and their children. In three years with Child Protective Services, Bo had never seen such a case. They were never that simple. But this might be a first.

Bonnie Franer's agitated, crablike hands seemed to be searching for something. Bo recognized the behavior. A pair of scissors, a drapery cord, even a ballpoint pen might become a weapon in those hands. A weapon turned against the woman holding it. Bonnie Franer, Bo noted glumly, was a Class A candidate for suicide.

"Did Paul Massieu ever molest or sexually assault your daughter Samantha?" Bo forced herself to address the pathetic figure.

What do you do for an encore, Bradley? Bite the heads off kittens?

As the woman continued to rock from the waist, hanks of fine, dust-blonde hair pulled loose from a hastily brushed bun at the nape of her neck. In the artificial light of the social worker's office, the floating tendrils might have been the hair of a swimmer. Underwater. Riding currents no words could penetrate.

The tiny office seemed to be shrinking. There was no air. Bo wished the priest would go out into the hall rather than witness the spectacular barbarism indigenous to her job. But he merely sat gazing with kind, basset-brown eyes at the grieving mother.

"Paul loves the girls," Bonnie Franer whispered in a final attempt at coherence. Then her eyes rolled back and she began to rock harder. "It's my fault, my fault, always all my fault." The last words emerged as a moan, continued as a mindless chant. The rocking and moaning would go on, Bo realized, until the woman was medicated. There would be no more communication. Gently Bo placed a hand on the woman's frail wrist, but there was no response.

"Let me." Father Frank Goodman jumped off the desk and slid a muscular arm around the woman's shoulders. Inexplicably, he began to sing something that sounded remarkably like "Send in the Clowns" in a soft tenor. His singing actually seemed to relax the frenzied rocking.

Bo wondered what had happened to the Catholic church since she left it twenty years ago.

"Had enough?"

It was Andrew LaMarche, glacially present at the door.

"Reinert's issued a warrant," she said in tones designed to encourage a professional response. "But this woman won't survive a night in jail. She'll . . ." her voice began to crack, "she'll find a way to . . ." The words were cardboard stuck in her throat. The same words required in describing Laurie's death. "She's got to have a suicide watch."

"I've called for a psychiatric consult." LaMarche conceded the point while ignoring Bo's discomfiture. "Mrs. Franer will be taken to County Psychiatric. I hope this will end the involvement of Child Protective Services with this unfortunate woman."

Bo regarded the man who'd sent long-stemmed roses to her office and phoned every week since saving her life in an unusual case the previous fall. A tin statue would have produced more warmth.

"Nothing would please me more, Doctor," she emphasized the title, "but a child has been killed. The district attorney will order the immediate filing of a sibling petition. Fifteen minutes after I leave here, Hannah Franer will legally be in the custody of San Diego County's Juvenile Court for her own protection. It's my case until she's found and her safety is protected."

"You're destroying innocent people. Can't you see that?"

"At least one innocent person has already been destroyed," Bo said as she pushed past him. "Or had you forgotten?"

In the parking lot Bo found a small picture of St. Theresa under her driver's-side windshield wiper. On the back a large hand had penned, "This is *clergy* parking, bozo! Fr. F. Goodman"

Climbing on the hood of her car, Bo tucked the prayer card onto the left foot of Mabel Mammoth, clambered down and lit a cigarette.

"I have the most noxious job on the planet," she told the creature, "involving not only malignant acts and vile individuals, but pompous pediatricians and priests who should still be playing video games after school. Someone has slaughtered a child, and I have a sense that everyone connected to the case is locked into dead-end viewpoints that are obscuring the truth. I don't know why I feel that way, Mabel, but I do. Is it because I stopped the lithium? Am I getting too imaginative here? And is there any chance I can find a job somewhere that doesn't surpass Dante's Inferno in wretchedness?"

The magenta mammoth said nothing but continued to smile at an oleander blooming profusely at its feet. Bo sighed and scrounged through the jumble of tape cassettes in her glove compartment until she found the one she was looking for. *Carmina Burana*. Its "O Fortuna" had been the anthem of her adolescent rebellion, wholly approved by her violinist mother.

"If you've got to lurk about in excessive eye makeup," Margot O'Reilly had said one long-past Boston morning, "then I suppose it's best you lurk to some enduring music."

Bo drove the few blocks back to her office with a dog-Latin chorus to spring and fate blasting from her car. Its invocation of rebellion created a focus for her discomfort with everything so far connected to the Franer case. A child brutally dead, her mother plunging into a hellish depression, her sister vanished with the only suspect, and the odd coincidence of a Satanic workshop the same day a purportedly Satanic case turned up. None of the pieces really fit. But then they never did. Not at first. Bo decided to start eliminating pieces, narrow the field. And she knew just where to start.

Back in her office she nudged the door closed and picked up the phone. "Information for Quantico, Virginia, please. I'd like the number for the Federal Bureau of Investigation's task force on ritual crime."

It was after 5:00 in Virginia, but somebody answered his phone anyway. And in ten minutes provided Bo with enough information to tar and feather Cynthia Ganage. Not that anybody would listen.

Bo mentally filed what she'd heard and then stared into her own green eyes in the mirror on the office door. Those eyes didn't always see exactly what everybody else saw. The brain behind them was different, its neural pathways prone to the odd bypass, the occasional derailment. But that brain, her brain, her *self*, would never cling to an insubstantial fantasy to avoid facing a truth. The realization was centering, like opening the door to a personal integrity she'd known was there but couldn't name. She was pretty tough, she acknowledged, to be able to face a world in which human behavior could not be blamed on a Satan. One tough crazy lady. She wished everyone else involved in the Franer case could say the same.

Chapter 6

An early ground fog already drifted luminously in the stand of paper birch east of the lake path. Towering behind her, Eva Broussard felt more than saw the thick, crumbled silhouette of Shadow Mountain. Its vastness had taken form countless millions of years in some unknowable past. Webbed at its base by veins of glassy quartz and pink feldspar, its highest peak was of a rare stone found also in lunar rock samples—anorthosite. In a leap of near-mindless concatenation Eva had at one point allowed herself to wonder if the moon rock itself might somehow figure in the curious experience related by Paul Massieu and the others. The Adirondack peaks consisted of some fifteen hundred square miles of erosion-resistant, metamorphosed anorthosite. A huge expanse. Did it in its massiveness create a magnetic field capable of producing realistic hallucinations? The theory made as much sense as any. Which wasn't saying much. After three years Eva Broussard had yet to frame a coherent theory of why a number of demonstrably rational people insisted they'd had contact with extraterrestrials on or near Shadow Mountain.

Padding across the porch to the inlaid maple floor in fringed moccasins pulled on against the evening chill, the graceful woman knelt to lay a fire in the largest of three fireplaces.

There would be a community meeting after dinner to deal with the grim news of Samantha Franer's death. Later she would drive to Albany to pick up Paul Massieu and Hannah at the airport. After settling Hannah, Paul would flee to Canada. The decision had not been an easy one to make. Yet everyone was certain Paul was innocent, and that by the time he could be extradited from Canada, Samantha's real murderer would have been apprehended. The level of confidence exhibited by the group in California's law enforcement agencies reflected nothing so much as a familiarity with American television. Eva found herself staring into the stacked wood.

Could she be wrong about Paul? Could her fondness for the quiet, lonely man have obscured her judgment? *Could* Paul Massieu be a pederast, a child-molester, the rapist and murderer of a little girl?

As she lit a match to the kindling she stripped herself of the layered identities that might blind her to a distasteful truth. Like barely perceptible cloaks, she removed the personae of psychiatrist, Bolduc Chair in Social Psychology at the Séminaire de Sainte Jeanne d'Arc, and author of the popular self-help series, *The Meaning of Your Life*, as well as a highly praised biography of the Christian mystic Hildegard of Bingen. When the intellectual trappings of forty years had fallen away, Eva addressed her core being—a mature Iroquois woman. The fire caught and flared, its dancing light a filigree on her broad hands.

"What do I want?" she thought inwardly to a gallery of masks floating near her subconscious. "Do I need to believe in the normalcy of this man's personality so much for the sake of my own research that I've overlooked a terrible inadequacy? Have I wanted the project more than the truth?"

The Iroquois mask Eva named "Pride," an elongated visage woven of age-darkened willow with mere slits for eyes and a clown's wide smile, did not drift into view behind her closed eyes. She'd more than half expected it, the quality called pride having been a continual stumbling block in her adult life. But it wasn't there. Nothing was there. Just a reversed-out image of flames, black on a gray background. If Eva Broussard had failed to perceive a disturbing sickness in Paul Massieu, there was nothing in her mind to account for it. Still, she acknowledged, there was always the minuscule margin for error. The margin in which wholly inexplicable events could occur. This might be one of them, but Eva was prepared to contend that it wasn't. Eva was comfortable with a ninety-eight percent certainty that Paul Massieu was innocent.

Rising from the stone hearth, she stretched bronze, muscular arms toward Night Heron Lake, now gray marble beneath a patchy scarf of fog, and thought about the other victims of Samantha's killer. The child's death would destroy the mother. That realization scarcely required the plethora of professional sensitivities possessed by Dr. Eva Blindhawk Broussard.

Bonnie Franer had been beaten by a drunken sod of a father on a bleak farm outside Syracuse, New York, until marrying at nineteen an arcade games salesman she'd met at the truck stop where she worked as a cashier. Eight years later and three months into the pregnancy that would produce Samantha, Seth Franer had taken the remaining two hundred dollars in their bank account and vanished. A postcard from Niagara Falls informed Bonnie that he was sorry, but he guessed he was just a rolling stone. He wouldn't be back. The day the postcard came Bonnie Franer had taken her daughter Hannah to kindergarten, returned home, and swallowed a hundred and thirty-six over-the-counter sleeping pills. A neighbor found her vomiting on the rickety wooden porch of the Franers' rented duplex in Troy, New York. After her stomach was pumped, the defeated woman's only fear was that she had harmed the child growing within her. Now that child was dead.

Eva Broussard shivered slightly and hugged herself against the flimsy substance of Bonnie Franer's life. Nothing had been given the woman to uphold her during difficulty. No family or cultural ties, no education, no financial resources. No substance of any kind. The woman was prey to every vagary of emotion, every whim in the shifting winds of her time. When Paul Massieu met Bonnie Franer working the food concession at one of Eva's lucrative self-help lectures in Buffalo, he'd fallen in love with his own need to protect something. A cultural anthropologist specializing in the nineteenth-century United States, he'd seemed to grieve for everything lost in time. Suffrage banners, quart-sized beer bottles, the Elizabethan dialect still spoken on the Outer Banks of North Carolina before a causeway to the mainland was built. Everything lost filled him with a helpless urgency to protect it, save it from an annihilation already accomplished. Bonnie Franer and her daughters had represented a fragility he *could* protect. Until now.

Over the mantel a small oil painting reflected the flames below. A gloomy local New York State landscape painted on cardboard in 1874 by an artist named Ella Pell who would later achieve renown in the great salons of Europe. Eva had discovered the painting among rubbish stored in the tower when she bought the lodge. Probably, she thought, a gift of the artist to the lodge's first owners. Perhaps a gift to the woman who'd died falling from the tower itself. Paul Massieu had insisted that the painting be framed and hung.

In its lower left corner dim figures occupied a small boat, dwarfed by looming, mist-covered mountains and the lampblack surface of the lake. But the seated figure, a woman in a black hat, wore at her neck a scarlet kerchief. The minuscule banner, barely visible in its dark field, was to Eva a symbol for the very striving she'd come here to document. A frail emblem of hope in a tumult of darkness. But there would be no hope for Bonnie Franer now. Too much had hurt that defenseless soul for too long. And Paul Massieu could no longer protect her.

The little picture with its single thread of color was for the inquisitive Broussard an apt standard for their whole endeavor. An unusual, perhaps irrational endeavor. Now doomed. Idly she adjusted the painting on the stone wall and remembered her first meeting with the somber anthropologist.

He'd come unannounced to her office in Montreal three years ago.

"I want you to tell me if I'm insane," he'd explained in the familiar Canadian French. "I'll pay whatever the standard rate is for such things."

A soft-spoken man of about thirty-five, dressed in rumpled corduroys, a forest green turtleneck sweater, and the predictable professor's tweed jacket. Strong, clean-shaven jaw. Shaggy black hair showing inherited evidence of male pattern baldness. Raven-dark eyes with thick, curling lashes. Black French, Eva decided. Or part Indian, like herself. Whatever his genetic heritage, it, and a mutilated right hand injured, he said, on an archaeological dig, gave him a sinister quality that was misleading. Paul Massieu would prove himself to be one of the gentlest men Eva had ever met. He'd hunched his wide shoulders and clasped stocky hands, the right of which was missing the little finger, in his lap as she outlined the reasons his request couldn't be met.

There was in actuality no measurable quality named "sanity." The term could be defined only by its absence or impairment, and even that was subject to wide fluctuations based on social and cultural expectations. Certain patterns of behavior had been given certain names, and certain medications were known to control certain symptoms. But literally no one could define sanity, much less measure it.

"But you're a psychiatrist, aren't you?" he'd insisted.

"Among other things," Broussard answered. "Tell me why you've come to me."

Paul Massieu had leaned forward nervously, his elbows on his knees. "I remembered something that happened a year ago. Something that *couldn't* have happened, and yet the memory is there . . . details, feelings, everything. So either it *did* happen, or I'm somehow making up this whole memory, and I'm crazy."

"And you want me to . . . ?"

"I read one of your books. You sound, well, practical. I want somebody objective. Somebody who's not connected to any of this weird stuff . . ."

"Connected to what weird stuff?" Broussard had inquired, curious.

Massieu straightened his shoulders. "To any of these people running around saying they've seen flying saucers and creatures from other planets."

"I'm afraid you've come to the wrong place," Broussard began professionally. "I really can't—"

"Please," his appeal had been direct and unflinching. "You've got to help me."

She had agreed. And after polygraphs, hypnosis, batteries of tests, and analysis, Paul Massieu, an adjunct professor of anthropology at McGill University who loved camping in the Adirondacks, was revealed to be a marginally introverted personality with no evidence whatever of thought or affective disorder. Either he had been abducted by wraithlike humanoid figures in metallic clothing, and examined by them, or he had hallucinated the experience in whole or in part for reasons completely inconsistent with the entire history and practice of psychiatry. Eva Broussard didn't dismiss that possibility.

But then, when word of her work with Massieu got out in Montreal's psychiatric community, others began to show up at her office. Most were so impaired that their narratives of extraterrestrial contacts were specious, either attention-seeking or delusional. Still, for every ten of them, one believable witness would appear. A fifty-four-year-old grocer from Malone, New York. A young computer skills teacher from Quebec City who wanted to be a fashion designer. A Roman Catholic grandmother of ten from Mishawawka, Indiana, who'd been on a tour of religious shrines when she, too, saw the strange beings.

Eva Broussard had gone into seclusion for two months at a Carmelite convent on the St. Lawrence River near Cap-de-la-Madeleine. In silence and barefoot on the old limestone floors she'd considered the nature of cancer, which had claimed her left breast and might eventually claim her life. She had watched her dreams in the Iroquois way for the masked faces who would reveal her deepest need. "To know," the masks had murmured. "Your great need is simply to know." Then she'd pondered the motley collection of frightened people who told of a near-identical experience—contact with beings unlike any known human form.

An original text of F. H. Bradley's *Appearance and Reality* arrived from Oxford and was carefully read. Experience, the Victorian philosopher told Eva, is what matters. Thinking about experience is a maze of misleading relational complexity. The experience is what it is; interpretations of it are flawed by attempts to describe it as like something else. Paul Massieu and the others had known an experience. Describing it in relational terms was just the way of the human mind. It might be like science-fiction fantasies familiar to Massieu and the others from novels and movies, but it was not, in reality, any kind of fiction at all. Something had happened in the experience of these people. Eva Broussard decided to spend the remaining years of her life trying to identify what that something was. At sixty she felt that her very life, her experience and training, her travel and writing, had groomed her, prepared her, for precisely this. She regarded her decision to pursue the research as the most exciting moment of her life.

Within another month she had closed her office and liquidated enough assets to purchase the old Adirondack camp beneath a mountain where Paul Massieu was examined in a silver craft by papery beings with huge, glassy-black eyes. The creatures smelled, he said, like the aromatic spice called mace.

For Eva it had been a homecoming. Born on the Onondaga Reservation near Nedrow, New York, young Eva Blindhawk had only been taken in by relatives of her father in Montreal at seven, when her mother died of the same cancer Eva herself now fought. In the critical first five years of life she'd been an Iroquois Indian, an Onondaga from whose ranks the chief of the six Iroquois nations must, by ancient tradition, be chosen. She'd been the daughter of Naomi Blindhawk and granddaughter of a dream-woman who ordered the midwinter rituals. Tracing her lineage to one of the oldest longhouses, she knew herself a member of the Heron Clan. One of her great-great-grandmothers had named the very lake now hidden in mist below the lodge. Eva Broussard was home. But trouble was winging its desperate way from California. A fugitive man and frightened child, and all that would follow them.

As members of the community gathered from adjacent cottages and climbed the maple tower stairs for the evening chant, Eva sighed and relaxed. Some of the Seekers, as they called themselves, believed that a technically perfect plainsong in human voice, beamed regularly into space from a transmitter atop Shadow Mountain, would entice a return of the frail, terrifying visitors. The chants, performed at sunrise and at sunset from the five-sided tower, were the most lovely, plaintive sound Eva had ever heard.

Chapter 7

Bo had delivered the paperwork on Hannah Franer to the district attorney's office at 3:00 P.M. His signature scrawled across the petition at 3:10 ensured that the eight-year-old girl was legally under the jurisdiction of San Diego County's Juvenile Court. A formality under the circumstances, the legal documents would ensure that police could seize the child without hindrance in the event that she were found. A "sibling petition," no more than a handful of paper in which a county assumed the duties of a parent when the real parent had "failed to protect."

For the rest of the afternoon Bo worked another case, and brooded. The case involved an abandoned ten-year-old found by police in the closet of a fleabag hotel room where his mother lay dead on the floor, having freebased her way into the next world. The boy, now waiting at the county receiving home for whatever would happen next, said he had no relatives except a father named Lee John who'd "killed some dude" in Iowa, or maybe it was Idaho. When twenty-seven phone calls to corrections agencies in states beginning with I turned up no information whatever on a Lee John or John Lee Crowley, Bo wrote up a court report recommending that the boy be released for adoption. Then she stood outside the window of Madge Aldenhoven's office, smoking.

No one would adopt Jonas Lee Crowley. That was a joke. In fact, hell would freeze before the hypothetical nice couple would welcome into their hypothetical loving home a skinny, snarling boy with hate in his ice-blue eyes, lice in his hair, and a hobby of peeing on shoppers from the top of department store escalators. Jonas would spend the next eight years in foster homes and correctional schools. After that he would be released to the streets where he would unquestionably sire another generation of misery. If there were a way to stop the cycle of ruin she saw every day, Bo couldn't imagine what it might be.

Her own childhood home in Boston had seemed perfectly awful at the time. A little sister who was deaf, everybody having to use sign language. Her mother, a violinist with the Boston Symphony, constantly practicing in the dining room. The scent of imported tobacco drifting from her father's meerschaum in a living room converted to library for his endless and highly paid research into antiquated patents and copyrights. And a paternal grandmother whose annual summer visits from Ireland wreaked havoc. In retrospect Bo knew her childhood to have been a well-managed haven, despite the problems her family faced. This job had forced her to see what hell life could be for children, and the hell those children would later create for *their* children, ad infinitum. She wished her parents had lived long enough for her to thank them.

"You look like your best friend *es morte*." Estrella butchered the common remark while struggling through the parched bushes outside their supervisor's office. "You just smoke out here to irritate her, don't you?"

"No, I like the view," Bo answered, gazing through a chain-link fence at four lanes of traffic on Genesee Avenue. "It's the best part of this job."

Estrella grabbed a limb of a relatively healthy bottlebrush

tree for balance and stood squarely on two-inch heels. "I hate it when you get nasty," she said. "I think—"

"I know. You think I should go back on the lithium." Bo ground the cigarette under a shoe and retrieved the smashed filter. "But it's not that. I *know* when I need medication, and right now I don't. I'm just tired of pretending it's normal to spend my days chatting about things that would gag most convicted felons. I mean, how many people do you know in the real world who schmooze over lunch about how to get evidence of oral copulation on infants? Or show each other pictures of roach-infested diapers, not to mention tire marks on—"

Estrella grimaced and held up a hand. "Spare me. I work here, too. You just don't think about it, is all. You just do the job and then go home and *forget* it, which reminds me—"

"The kid on the case I got this morning," Bo interrupted, tossing the filter into a trash can by the door, "died on the operating table. She looked like a cherub, a Rubens maybe, and she's dead. The mother creates a whole new meaning for the term 'self-hatred,' the boyfriend's run off with the older sister, and that publicity shark of a psychologist is getting miles of exposure screaming 'The devil did it!' Reinert seems to believe there's ritual abuse involved simply because the boyfriend's in some cult, even though we don't know what kind of cult. LaMarche has gone off the deep end defending the suspected perp and the mother . . ." Bo paused for a breath, "and even though I've eaten nothing but one Granny Smith apple and a half pint of skim milk all day, I'm still fat. I think it's time to find another job."

"You're not fat, but hunger can make people mean," said Estrella, unaccountably beaming. "You don't need another job. I think we've found the answer."

"What was the question?" Bo asked suspiciously. Estrella looked like a cat with the keys to the parakeet sanctuary.

"Will you promise me something?"

"No promises on Wednesday. Old Irish superstition."

Back in the office Estrella fussed over a tube of lipstick found in the bottom of her purse. "Not even for an *amiga* who may or may not take care of your dog while you run off to a fat farm this weekend?"

"You win," Bo conceded. She wouldn't entrust Mildred, her crotchety old fox terrier, to anyone else. "What do I have to promise?"

Estrella appeared to inspect the glazing of their office window. "That you'll go out with LaMarche the next time he asks you. Just go out and relax and have a good time."

"Deal." After the day's encounter Bo was sure his interest had waned, perhaps perished entirely. Just as well.

Later at home in her Ocean Beach apartment, Bo retrieved Mildred from day care with an elderly neighbor, slipped on faded jeans that had, in another life, belonged to her ex-husband, and headed for Dog Beach. The expanse of sand designated for San Diego's canine population had cinched Bo's decision to relocate to the coastal city after federal money for social service programs on New Mexico's reservations dried up. Where else would they set aside a whole beach for dogs? And just up the street was a fashionable dogwash designed specifically for Dog Beach patrons. She'd bought Mildred a vinyl-coated foam life vest at the dogwash boutique, signed a contract with Child Protective Services, and found a nearby apartment with an ocean view the same day.

Mildred dug in the sand as if hundreds of prime filets lay just beneath the surface, and barked greetings at a neighboring basset. Bo sat and threw a ratty tennis ball for Mildred until it was appropriated by a show-off Doberman puppy whose owner also owned the local pizza parlor.

"You owe me one slab with garlic and anchovies," she yelled at the man. "That tennis ball's an antique!"

"So are my anchovies," he yelled back.

Offshore a fuzzy gray band hovered at the horizon, moving

toward land. The marine layer. Perennial bane of tourists who believed the myth of southern California's endless sun. In fact, until late June San Diego would be awash in weak, salty haze until 11:00 every morning when it burned off, only to return at dusk. It was coming in again. Bo relished the fog's predictability. Found its slow approach comforting as Mildred flung arcs of sand in all directions, including into Bo's hair. Without interest she noticed a pair of denimed legs bisecting the horizon. Ragged cowboy boots that might have been new at the siege of the Alamo. When they didn't move she glanced upward, straight into a shadowed face she associated mainly with windsor knots and antiseptic.

"I'm sorry I've been a beast today," said Andrew LaMarche. "If you'll permit . . ." The word came out "*pear*-mit." "I'd like to repair the damage."

How? By rounding up a few stray longhorns before the lariat tricks?

"Don't tell me. Let me guess." Bo sighed. "Estrella has asked you to rescue me from madness by doing John Wayne imitations, right?" Under a mound of sand between her hands Bo imagined she was burying Estrella Benedict slowly, alive.

"I'd like to take you to dinner," LaMarche suggested in businesslike tones, "and explain my behavior about the Franer case."

The pediatrician looked, Bo thought, like an ad for designer prisonwear. His blue workshirt lacked only a number stenciled over its pocket.

"I've been set up," she told Mildred.

"So it would seem," Andrew LaMarche agreed happily.

Chapter 8

"Where are we going?" Bo inquired through cool, road-scented air whipping her hair into tangles a forklift couldn't separate. LaMarche had removed the Jaguar's roof in what she assumed was an attempt at savoir faire.

"Santa Ysabel," he replied as the last, muted bars of Respighi's *Pines of Rome* faded from the car's speakers. Bo found the music an uncomfortable reminder. Her ex-husband, Mark, an aspiring choreographer of radio drama, had as a graduate student read the athletic final chapter of John Updike's *Rabbit Run* over the climactic music so many times Bo couldn't hear it without gasping. Later Mark Bradley had produced an award-winning series of Navajo children's stories, recorded over tracks of Indian flute, wind, and an occasional howling coyote. Bo knew the recordings were inspired by Nicholas and Jaana, his children of a second and happy marriage to a hearty nutritionist from Minnesota whom Bo never ceased envisioning in a Wagnerian chorus. Mark's wife's name had been Ingrid Soderblom. Impossible not to think of metal bras and the entire Wagnerian Ring Cycle. With a smile, Bo forced her attention to the present.

"Santa Ysabel? We're having dinner at a mission?"

Andrew LaMarche's gray eyes glowed with a pewterlike

patina, signaling his enjoyment of the moment as well as his knowledge of a pleasant answer to her question. The answer would, she knew, not be given without some tangential discourse. It was his style. Bo wondered if the discomfort with straightforward speech, the maddening verbal perambulations, had something to do with his French-speaking childhood. Or maybe he was nervous. Or maybe he just liked to talk.

"The church was built as an *asistencia*, or sub-mission in 1818," he said as if Bo had asked for a detailed history of California missions instead of the location of her next meal. The glow in his eyes became a twinkle. "Fascinating, really. They say pirated gold is buried among the old graves, although no one has ever—"

"Andy," Bo employed the familiar name out of desperation, "we've been driving for thirty-five minutes, I have enough dirt in my teeth to plant geraniums and my hair's something mice would kill to nest in. Why are we going to Santa Ysabel?"

"Duhon Robicheaux's in town with his Cajun band. There's a *fais-do-do*," the baritone voice explained with excitement. "I hope you like *andouille*!"

The setting sun created pastoral landscapes in shades of gold as the car sped up the slow grade from the San Diego suburb of Ramona into shadow-mottled foothills. Chinese coolies had labored, Bo remembered, beside Irish immigrants to wrest tourmaline, garnet, topaz, and gold from these hills. Hungry, she wondered how the two groups had managed to combine menus at mining camp chuckwagons. Sweet-and-sour finnan haddie? Steamed soda-bread rolls stuffed with thousand-year egg paste? In her side mirror she could see the Palomar Observatory looming whitely in the distance behind the car. Its two-hundred-inch Hale reflector telescope nightly scanned the heavens for things not visible to the naked eye. The facility's pale dome looked like a huge soup bowl inverted in the hills. Bo decided to ignore it.

"What in God's name is a fay-doe-doe and how would I

know if I liked an-dewey? Is it edible?" Hunger had become a nagging irritant.

"The best food north of Ponchatoula," LaMarche replied as he navigated a turn onto a dusty mountain road that quickly lost itself in rolling meadows. "I'm scheduled to keynote a conference in New York this weekend. Supposed to be there today, in fact, to revise the agenda or something. But I rescheduled the flight for tomorrow just so I wouldn't miss this!" At a barnlike structure beside a dilapidated general store whose rusting gas pumps still wore the round glass heads popular during the Depression, he parked the maroon Jag among at least a hundred pickup trucks. "And a *fais-do-do* is just a big get-together. Food, dancing, a little wine . . ."

Bo remembered her own admonition to spend the evening in revelry in order to forget the cherubic corpse on an operating table. She'd followed her own advice, and yet it seemed wrong.

LaMarche noticed her downcast gaze and nodded. "We'll talk about it later. Right now we'll eat, enjoy. It isn't over, you know. It won't be over until Samantha's killer is imprisoned. The others," his thin lips were ashen beneath his mustache, "will see to an appropriate punishment."

Both sets of eyes stared at nothing as physician and social worker allowed themselves the unprofessional fantasy of revenge. Even the most hardened criminals sometimes felt revulsion at the rape of a child. And lacking a restraint characteristic of the general population, they wouldn't hesitate to mete out a biblical punishment. It was likely that Samantha's killer, released to a general prison population, would relive his victim's torment a thousand times.

The satisfaction of the fantasy made Bo half sick.

"Enough," LaMarche said with finality as an accordion wheezed to life inside the building followed by the scratchy tuning of violins. "Duhon's going to cheer you up!"

Having made a conscious decision to forget Samantha Franer for at least an hour, Bo cocked an eyebrow at the dustbowl parking lot with its army of trucks and grinned. The interior of the huge shed, which had from its pervasive scent been used to store apples from nearby orchards, was lit by a series of emergency lights whose extension cords all snaked to a single generator. Long tables covered in newspaper lined the walls, and a flatbed farm wagon served as a bandstand. Over the sweet apple smell Bo noticed a pervasive odor of hot, buttery flour.

"What's that smell?" she sniffed appreciatively.

"Roux." He was steering her toward two empty folding chairs at one of the long tables.

"Roo? Kanga's baby in *Winnie the Pooh*? They're cooking baby kangaroos here? I'm calling the animal cruelty people—"

"It means . . . it's a dark, sticky sauce made of butter and flour," he answered her jibe seriously. "How about some shrimp *étouffée*?"

"Does it have roo in it?"

The answering smile was warm. Almost, Bo realized, seductive.

"No, *ma cherie*, no *roux*."

You've always been a sucker for an accent, Bradley. Remember that Portuguese environmentalist who played pan pipes and got you to donate a month's salary for the protection of freshwater clams from a dam proposal? Try not to forget that.

"Shrimp sounds fine," she agreed. "And after dinner you'll provide the promised explanations about the Franer case?"

"Dinner, a little wine, maybe a two-step. Then . . ." He was busy acknowledging greetings from some of those present who seemed to know him, but greeted him as Jacques.

"I come around sometimes when there's a Cajun band," he explained. "It reminds me of summers I'd spend down in the bayous with my uncle. His name was Pierre Auguste, but everybody just called him Oncle Gus. He could catch snakes right out of the water with his bare hands, and my aunt would make a mouth-watering jambalaya out of them . . ."

"Snake jambalaya—my all-time favorite," Bo said with a

wide-eyed smile. "And I'm really Princess Anastasia, heir to the vanquished Russian throne. *We* used to catch beluga caviar, barehanded of course, right out of the Volga. What a coincidence!"

"Mais non," came the amused reply. "I'm serious."

His gray eyes wore a pleasant, faraway look. A look not related to the unremarkable red wine they were drinking from jelly glasses. Andrew LaMarche was plainly enjoying himself.

"You come out here to get away from it all, don't you?" Bo asked. On the dance floor people from three to ninety waltzed and two-stepped energetically. "It's a different world. Away from what you see at the hospital . . . like today?"

"Yes." His look shifted to one of concern. "And what do you do, Bo Bradley? How do you get away?"

Bo jabbed a *boudin* sausage on her plate with a plastic fork. "I jog," she informed the sausage. "Mostly I paint. Usually things like this . . . things from other worlds."

"Maybe you'll paint a Cajun sausage?" he joked.

Bo looked straight ahead and sifted the remark for unpleasant innuendo. There was none. A silly comment, not a crude come-on. She wondered if she'd been out of circulation so long she was anticipating trouble that didn't exist. Or else the absence of lithium was allowing a manicky hypersexuality to surface, coloring every innocuous encounter with a brush of eroticism. Bo hoped not. The guy was just being nice in his courtly, old-fashioned way.

Several lively two-steps later, she began to wonder if her politically correct, non-animal-tested deodorant would withstand the exertion. Her hair was soaked at the neck and curling ferociously.

"Let's go outside," LaMarche suggested with flawless timing. "I do want to talk seriously about what happened today."

In the moonlit parking lot a cool breeze ruffled the taffy-colored homespun shirt Bo had hurriedly tucked into her old jeans. Lighting a cigarette, she watched its smoke dissipate beneath a towering cottonwood beside the still-raucous building. "So why did you go off half-cocked over the Franer case today?" she asked. "And why did you do that curious sculpture of the ape carrying the baby?"

LaMarche leaned thoughtfully against the cottonwood as Bo sat on a truck bumper the size of a church pew.

"I have no children," he began, looking at a point above her head. "And the ape is a sort of metaphor, I guess, for what we do. The attempt to rescue children from the *côte noir*, the dark side of human nature, or ourselves. It's always there. And we often fail. We failed today."

Bo chose to ignore the enigmatic first statement in favor of the one she deeply understood. "We didn't fail," she said. "*You* didn't fail. There was nothing you could have done. Dr. Ling's report clearly stated that Samantha's injuries were life-threatening long before she got to the hospital. Don't blame yourself for her death."

"I don't," he went on, watching the sky as if it were making gestures he couldn't decipher. "The failure doesn't lie in the child's death. That shouldn't have happened, but it did. I'm not sure anything could have prevented it. Certainly no medical intervention could have saved her. But the failure I'm talking about is something different." He lowered his gaze to Bo's face. "The failure that resulted in my behavior today is in the way we look at things. We're blind. We only see what we expect to see, even if it's not really there. I saw that in myself today. It made me angry."

"What are you talking about?"

The suddenly moody doctor was lapsing into abstraction.

"I had a child once, Bo," he muttered abruptly. "I never saw her. Her name was Sylvie. She drowned in a bathtub in New Orleans while I was still with the Corps in Vietnam. Her mother, who was not my wife, left her alone only a little while. Apparently she'd been trying to bathe her toys. She was two."

Bo listened to dust settling on cottonwood leaves and did not move. After a while she said simply, "I'm sorry, Andy."

"Whoever violated Samantha blew apart the entire world for everyone connected to her," he continued through clenched teeth. "Her whole family and everyone close to her. The murdering bastard raped and killed more than just one little girl. He raped and killed the world for those people!"

His hands, Bo noticed, were knotted into fists.

"That's how you felt when your daughter died, isn't it?"

"I don't deny that her death propelled me into pediatrics, and then into the field of child abuse. It was a way of holding the world together, of trying to make sense of the senseless. Until you . . . until recently, it's been my whole life . . ." His voice trailed off.

Bo shifted uneasily on the truck's bumper. There was no denying the intensity of his words, but there was something else. Something very personal in the narrative, and it was directed at her. An appeal? More like a declaration. So powerful in its vulnerability and candor it felt like a threat, abrading a boundary she hadn't realized was there, but now wanted to keep intact.

"You've identified with the parent in this case," she stated the obvious, creating a palpable wall between them. A wall behind which she could play social worker all night if necessary. A wall that would blunt the intimacy he offered. "I can understand that. But why does that lead you to believe this Paul Massieu isn't the perp? Why else would he run?"

The change of subject wasn't lost on LaMarche, who crossed his arms over his chest and shook his head as if reprimanding himself. After a lengthy examination of the cottonwood's higher limbs, he turned again to Bo. "In French it's called *le monde*," he began softly. "That means 'the world,' but no one's world is the same. The assumption that we share an identical world is at the root of most problems, especially the serious ones."

"What has this to do with the Franer case?" Bo asked, lost.

"Everything. Please hear me out, Bo. It's important."

The decision to listen had to be made consciously. With a brain always scanning the external environment and its own stores of imagery for constant stimulation, even in periods of relative calm such as this one, it was too easy to grasp subtlety after subtlety and nothing more. Too easy to catch merely a mood and then move on. Not easy at all to open the mind in slow silence while another spoke. Bo looked at the man who'd saved her life and that of a deaf little boy six months in the past, and decided she owed him that much, if not the deeper bond he'd reached for only minutes earlier. With a deep breath she exerted the Herculean effort necessary to mute the sweep of her mind. "All right," she said quietly.

He had been watching. "Estrella told me you've stopped taking the lithium, Bo. Do you think—"

"We're not here to talk about lithium. What was it that you wanted to say about the world and Samantha Franer?" It was difficult to arrest the lecture framing itself for delivery to Estrella Benedict first thing in the morning, but Bo managed.

"As a young man I lived in a world where men accepted no responsibility for pregnancies in women to whom they were not married. This same world included a corollary mythology that held that all female people, simply by virtue of certain bodily organs, were magically able to provide years of tedious daily care for children. Had I moved one inch outside that world, my daughter might still be alive."

"You're still blaming yourself—" Bo began.

"Let me make my point. *You're* now in another world—the world of child abuse investigation, its legality. That world makes assumptions based on previous cases. That's the way law works. In your world it's assumed that the perpetrator in a molest is the mother's live-in boyfriend because very often it is. But what if somebody from another world falls into yours?

Will you bother to try looking through his eyes before deciding what's real?"

"You seem to have forgotten that I have a rather special relationship with this issue," Bo bristled. "I have a psychiatric disorder, a passport to more worlds than most people see on a three-continent tour. In addition to that, my undergraduate degree is in art history. Sophomoric lectures on cultural perspective are scarcely necessary. I've already considered the possibility that this case isn't typical. But how do you explain the fact that Paul Massieu *ran*?"

"What about *his* world, Bo? What if he ran because something in his reality, and that of Bonnie and Samantha and Hannah, demanded that he return Hannah to it?"

Bo's ears flattened against her skull as a strand of awareness spun out ahead of her. She couldn't keep up with it, but its message was clear. "What did Bonnie Franer tell you?" she asked, watching him now as closely as he had watched her.

"The woman loves her children, Bo. She's weak, a longtime victim. That love is her only strength. She has literally nothing else. She allowed Paul Massieu into her life precisely *because* he would never hurt the girls. He offered them love and protection. She didn't care what else he did, or what he believed in—"

"How can you . . . ?" Bo interrupted. "Bonnie Franer is an extremely fragile personality, prone to depression, probably self-destructive at times. You can't have had time to interview her in any depth, anyway. How can you trust her assessment . . . ?"

LaMarche kicked an exposed root of the cottonwood. "What if Paul Massieu has simply returned Hannah to a world, the only world he knows where she'll be safe?"

The knowledge racing ahead had taken on form. Bo felt her eyes widen in the dark at what he was telling her.

"You know where Massieu is! Bonnie Franer told you, and you're withholding the information!"

There was no denial.

"Think about what I've said, Bo. Just think about it. Looking at things differently may just make it possible for you to stay in this line of work. You're good. But without a broader view the pain and disgust will break you. I don't want that to happen."

"Andy," Bo said as the senselessness of a child's death took on even more sinister ramifications, "if you're right and Paul Massieu really isn't the perp, then who is? Who destroyed that little girl? What world does he live in?"

Andrew LaMarche stretched his angular hands at his sides and turned the palms slowly skyward. "I don't know," he answered.

From the door of the sprawling shed a sonorous waltz drifted liquidly on violin strings. Bo hated the warm flush that crept up her cheeks at his earlier compliment, and the dismay that accompanied any possibility of Paul Massieu's innocence. Domestic child sexual abuse was nothing unusual; it was her turf. But the notion of a "stranger molest" opened doors on a bewildering darkness. She wondered why the idea of a child eviscerated by the sexual demands of a trusted, familiar adult seemed less horrific than the same crime perpetrated by a stranger. The answer lay in LaMarche's words. The familiar, however repugnant, constituted her world. But what if this crime had its origins in a different one?

"That's the last dance." LaMarche gestured toward the spilling light. "Would you do me the honor?"

In his arms Bo felt an odd sense of kinship, as if they were compatriots in some film noir struggle involving World War II resistance fighters. Dim lighting. Frenchmen in berets and baggy shirts. Edith Piaf singing "Non, Je Ne Regrette Rien" from a cabaret stage. The feeling was smoky, warm . . .

Snap out of it, Bradley. You're tired and your brain's turning to oatmeal. That really is Piaf. What happened to the band?

"Duhon always ends with that recording," Andrew La-

Marche said, leading her toward the door with his right arm firmly around her waist. "It's his trademark."

"Mine too," Bo nodded sleepily, aware that he was kissing the top of her head occasionally as they walked to the car, and too tired to break the mood.

On the way home Bo heard the Jaguar's motor murmuring *"le monde"* repetitively. Something about the notion, the insistent syllables of it, kept breaking and spreading in her mind like an egg. The man beside her was harboring a secret. Why? Because there were different worlds? It made little sense, but then what did? A broad view, then. Blurry, gentle. Maybe wise. Lois Bittner, Bo smiled to herself, would probably approve. Madge Aldenhoven would vaporize with rage.

"Thanks for the evening," she nodded as LaMarche saw her to her door. "I'll think about what you said."

He left with a polite nod. No future dates set. No promises to call or be called. It was good. And, Bo reminded herself, it was over. Andrew LaMarche just didn't fit into her world. Nobody did.

Inside, the answering machine on the tiled counter between her living room and lilliputian kitchen was blinking.

"Bo?" Madge Aldenhoven's voice announced, "you're going to have to fly to New York tomorrow. The police have captured the perp in the Franer case at some cult hideout in the Adirondacks. We're sending you to retrieve the sister. Your plane leaves at 6:19 A.M. for Albany. I'll meet you at the office at 5:00 with the tickets."

In the neon glare of her bathroom Bo stared at a pharmacist's brown plastic bottle half full of pinkish tablets. Lithium. A surefire way to remain uninvolved, to stop the French *"le monde"* thumping in her brain. But did it need to be stopped?

Maybe LaMarche was right. Maybe there was another way to view the broken lives that fell across her desk in orange-banded case files. Maybe more to it than disgust and helplessness. The possibility felt like new canvas, stretched and beckoning.

Bo tossed the pills in her carry-on bag for the journey, just in case. Then she fell in bed humming a French song about having no regrets, and fell asleep wondering what life would be like without them.

Chapter 9

Eva Broussard lay sleepless upon a large bent-twig bed that had belonged to one of the lodge's Prohibition-era owners. A Pittsburgh glove manufacturer with stern views on temperance, the man had given his ideas immortality in the property's deed. No alcohol could be served within the lodge walls while the government of the United States remained intact. The troubled woman turned softly, imagining a bloodless coup at that very moment in Washington, D.C. A large cognac, she thought, might muffle the incessant mating whistles of the thousand spring peeper frogs calling, bog to bog, through the Adirondack night. Hannah Franer lay asleep on a cot beside the antique bed.

In shadow the child seemed merely a younger version of the mother. The same fine blonde hair drifting across the pillowcase. The same wide-set hazel eyes, full lips, and overlarge nose that reddened at the slightest emotion. Eva wondered if the similarity between mother and daughter extended to what lay inside—that core being some might name "soul." If so, extreme caution must be exercised now. For Hannah Franer's future would lie squarely in the ways she learned to deal with the pain of the present. And even that wasn't complete. Eva was certain there would be at least one more devastating blow for the child to absorb. Grimly certain.

Soundlessly she slipped to an open casement window. Below the lodge Night Heron Lake appeared to hold floating beneath its surface scattered sparks of light identical to those in the sky above. At the water's edge a pale glacial boulder left there twelve thousand years ago by a retreating wall of ice seemed a small, abandoned moon.

"I know nothing," the rangy woman whispered in French to the stone sphere. "We don't live long enough to know anything. Our little jelly brain is just a chemical flash, like heat lightning. But you," she addressed the stone intently, "have had time to observe a great deal. And you aren't talking." On the night wind a whiff of hemlock drifted into the room. Beavers at work, damming some upper tributary of Shadow Creek. The little mammals' engineering feats seemed elegant and full of meaning compared to the chaos that lay before Eva Broussard.

The New York State Police had burst into the lodge only minutes before Paul Massieu would have made his escape across the glassy darkness of Night Heron Lake. A lightweight canoe was prepared and waiting. The anthropologist had, as was a sort of ritual among the Canadian Seekers, canoed the chain of lakes from Montreal to this wilderness outpost where he'd first seen "Them." A covert return to Canada by the same watery route seemed the safest. It would never have occurred to New York lawmen routinely checking I-87 as a courtesy to the state of California that their prey was paddling a handmade canvas canoe beneath silent miles of red spruce.

But Paul Massieu was no wizard of stealth. He'd left a paper trail as wide as the Hudson River connecting him to an organization incorporated as "Shadow Mountain Interests" with an Adirondack mailing address. When a ticket agent at San Diego International Airport told Dar Reinert, "Sure. The

French guy and the little girl? Bought tickets to Albany, New York, ETA 6:27 P.M. Albany time," it had taken only two phone calls to get an address and a New York warrant.

"You should not have run, Paul," Eva insisted through pursed lips at Albany's homey airport terminal. "It can only be interpreted as evidence of guilt."

"Bonnie begged me to get Hannah back here when she called from the hospital. That was before Sammi . . . before we knew . . ." His voice broke with emotion. "The doctor who tried to save Sammi, this doctor had already told Bonnie they'd take Hannah away, put her in a foster home. I'm not Hannah's real father; this doctor told Bonnie they'd never let me get Hannah back, even if . . . He told Bonnie the police are certain I'm the one who . . ." His eyes rolled upward as a shudder rippled across his bulky shoulders. ". . . who raped a three-year-old baby that I loved as if she were my own . . . They'd never let me have Hannah, and they won't let Bonnie have her, either, now. Bonnie's going to crack under this. I know it."

People at the airport were beginning to stare at the weeping man with a terrified little girl clinging to his hand.

"We'll talk later," Eva suggested quickly. "We need to take Hannah home now."

"They know about us," he sighed in despair. "They know we're Seekers and they think we're crazy. It's one of the reasons they think I'm crazy enough to . . ."

"Yes." The older woman nodded.

It had been something of a risk, establishing a community of people devoted to the exploration of an experience that couldn't have happened. But the rugged moors of upstate New York had cradled unconventional notions before. In a rocky field near Palmyra Joseph Smith talked to an angel named Moroni, and the Mormon Church was conceived. In Victorian Arcadia, Brockport, Ithaca, Syracuse, and Buffalo the first American mediums communed with spirits and initiated an idea that would spellbind the Western world. There was something in the land, Eva sensed, and in the ominous cloud paths forever drifting across the river valleys. Something "otherly" her own people had seen fit to honor with rituals against madness, especially at the darkest time of the year. That something had turned up again, she was sure, on the ever-receptive screen of the human mind in the form of frail but magnetically powerful beings who seemed to have come from space.

But Eva Broussard could trace social patterns in history as well as she could follow pheasant tracks in the hedgerows of her childhood. Ideas spawned in the shadow-mists of New York State never stayed there. Those that did, died. There had been no further sightings. It was time to go elsewhere, and the group had selected California for the state's renowned openness to unorthodox ideas. A desert location for privacy and an ascetic wildness that might free the group to shape whatever philosophy it would make of its joint experience. A desert location within driving distance of the Goldstone Tracking Station in Barstow, where NASA scientists watched as a computer program sifted a million radio bands of celestial static for the telltale, nonrandom blips that would prove we are not alone in the universe. Blips that could only be created by nonearthly intelligence. Eva Broussard wanted to interview those scientists, include that perspective in her research. Wanted it deeply.

Paul Massieu had been sent to purchase the land. Eva felt concern when he announced that Bonnie and the children would go with him, but they preferred to remain together. Bonnie was sure she could get a part-time secretarial job to pay for trips to Disneyland and the thousand things she wanted the girls to see. And as a lifelong resident of New York State, Bonnie Franer had hated to be cold. The prospect of a winter in sunshine was too attractive to forestall. Now her younger daughter lay dead while the other clung to the man accused of the crime. Eva Broussard had driven them away from Albany and into the Adirondack deeps, weighted with apprehension. The act that robbed Samantha Franer of her life had also slammed like a fist through Eva's fascination with a collection of strangers and their encounters with tin men in the woods. A psychological inquiry that had seemed sufficient to occupy the rest of her life paled before the anguish of the man and child now huddled in her car. Eva felt a cold, murderous resentment for the man who had shattered their lives, whoever he was. He had shattered hers as well.

Later Eva took Hannah alone to the five-sided tower and gave her, one by one, the strings of Iroquois grieving beads she'd woven for the child after the news of Samantha's death. In candlelight reflected from two hundred panes of hand-blown glass in the tower's windows, she gently recited the words in Iroquois and in English. The words Hayenwatha had given to a people who lived in cloud-shadows and sometimes perished of a terrible grieving that would only later be named depression.

"Samantha is gone and cannot return," she began the soft, chanting ritual. "Samantha has died. And you hurt so much the tears blind your eyes. With these words I wipe the tears from your eyes so you can see. These beads are my words for your eyes, Hannah."

The child took the woven rush with its irregular purple beads carved from the shells of the quahog clam. Wrapping dry, tremulous fingers about the small strip, she buried her head against Eva Broussard's ribs and sobbed. Eva sank to the floor, rocking the child against her and humming a song her own grandmother had sung in the dark. A story of the Huron prophet Deganawida in his canoe of white stone. Deganawida with a speech impediment so profound he must carry his voice with him in the person of Hayenwatha, the translator mystic. The story gave form to an Iroquois reverence for sensitive communication and human interdependence. It was also, Eva had realized years ago, an excellent therapeutic model.

After a while she said again, "Samantha is gone and cannot

return. Samantha has died. And you hurt so much there's a roaring in your ears that drowns out everything else. With these words I silence the roaring so you can hear. These beads are my words for your ears, Hannah."

When the third strip of beaded rush had been given to the child, so that her throat choked by pain might be opened for speech, Eva Broussard breathed deeply and contemplated the words she would next pronounce. They were truly necessary, she concluded. And she was prepared to undertake the responsibility.

"As the oldest woman of this tribe," she recited, stretching the definition of tribe to fit the emergency, "I adopt you and make you one with us. I adopt you. You are now a child of the longhouse people, member of the Heron Clan, great-granddaughter of Naomi Blindhawk, granddaughter of Eva Blindhawk. You belong to us now. I am your grandmother. You have a home forever."

When the New York State Police arrived to take Paul Massieu away in handcuffs, they demanded to take Hannah Franer as well.

"The child is my granddaughter, an Iroquois of the Onondaga Reservation," Eva Broussard had said, her black eyes fierce beneath a leather-banded scarf. "She cannot be taken without permission of the tribal council. And she is safe here."

A veteran of clashes with radical Mohawks near the Canadian border, the trooper was not without experience in dealing with the state's original citizens. And there were recent federal laws ensuring that the children of native peoples could not be removed from the jurisdiction of their tribes. A century-late acknowledgment that to strip a human being of his or her language, culture, and mythology is a kind of death. He glared at the blonde child snuffling in the Indian woman's skirts. She didn't look like an Indian, but then neither did a lot of the people he'd seen sitting on tribal councils. Each tribe had its own rules for determining who was one of them and who wasn't. The kid had straw grieving beads pinned to her Minnie Mouse sweatshirt. He'd seen the Iroquois beads before; it was enough. California wouldn't like it, but he wasn't about to stir up another confrontation between Indians and New York State's government.

"Okay," he rumbled, "but you're responsible for her safety. And they'll come after her from California, anyway. You'll have to turn her over then."

By 4:00 A.M. the lake and sky were merely graying patterns without identity. Nothing moved among the shaded tracings that in daylight would be trees, lake, sky. Shaking the thick stubble framing her head Eva strode purposefully back to the twig bed. The steps she had taken were meant to protect Hannah's fragile being from irreversible harm. Eva was confident that her decisions were correct, but now what? Her thinking had run down like bog water, reedy and thick with odd skitterings. No point in seining it anymore tonight. There was too much turbulence to see what might come next.

Chapter 10

Descending over the Hudson River on its approach to the Albany airport, the Boeing 767 provided a spectacular view. Sleepily Bo eyed the streams of hazy, gilded light bathing the valley below. She'd been dozing since the plane change in Chicago, and was unprepared.

"I'll be damned!" she breathed in amazement. "So *this* is what they were doing!"

Her companion in the aisle seat pulled a brimmed Red Sox cap further over an already low forehead and grimaced. The off-center set of his shoulders beneath a brown nylon jacket made clear his intent to create distance between himself and this redhead who talked to herself.

"I mean the Hudson River School," Bo explained, pulling her hair from her face with both hands. "This light! This is what they painted! You know . . . Thomas Cole, Asher Durand, Charlotte Coman . . . ?"

The man shifted his weight further into the aisle and sighed miserably. It was clear to Bo that whatever interest he might have in the renowned artists of the region was eclipsed by a deeper fascination with his own shoes.

"And even *they* never got to see the light from up here,"

she concluded, "since there were no planes in the nineteenth century."

The man appeared to be painfully at prayer.

Beyond the scratched window rivers of light, cream-colored, pinkish, sometimes deepening to pale honey or muted flax, poured through clouds and spilled on the rising ground below. The effect was stunning. Bo thought of sending Madge Aldenhoven a thank-you note quoting something from Washington Irving. The light was astonishing, and a little eerie. No wonder so many had tried to capture it in paint. Bo wondered if the shape-shifting quality of the sky had anything to do with whatever Paul Massieu's cult was up to. Aldenhoven had provided an address, but no other information about the activities of the group.

Debarking into moist spring air, Bo reminded herself to rein in some of the elation buoying her steps. The day was, in fact, a bit too wondrous. The sky entirely too awe-inspiring with its washes of golden light. Too much goodness sloshing around, and it could only be coming from one source—her own brain.

You're here to pick up an eight-year-old with a dead sister, not to rejoice in spring, Bradley.

In the airport's parking lot Bo did a series of stretches beside the beige rental car, and thought about neurochemistry. Her near-religious awe at the sky could be a trained artist's response to unusually brilliant light patterns, or it could be something else. It could be that first heady surge of euphoria that would later become a torrent of racing impressions and feeling. Mania.

"It's too bad, but the truth is, you must always be suspicious of feeling too good," Lois Bittner stated flatly years ago. "Most manic-depressives like the euphoria so much they don't want it to stop. The problem is, it won't stop, like a carousel spinning faster and faster. You must always stop and dissect your euphoria, Bo. It's the minefield between you and a battle you can never win. Sometimes it will be safe, just a little surge of glee like other people experience. And sometimes it will be your last warning. Learn to tell the difference."

Bo slid behind the wheel of the nondescript Ford and admitted that twenty years after her first skirmish with manic depression, she still couldn't tell the difference. Moreover, she was sick of worrying about it. If things got worse, she'd deal with it. In the meantime it was sheer joy to be herself again, free of the numbing medication that, however necessary, made her feel like a senile otter swimming in glue.

A map provided by the rental car agency provided easy access to a six-lane freeway unimaginatively named 90 West. Bo admired the lush greenery bordering the road and adorning its median. Southern California, more desert than its chambers of commerce would like known, could not in its dampest moment produce such fervent, undulating greens. She wondered why Massieu's group, whatever they were, had decided to relocate. And how they would respond when she took from their midst the child Massieu had broken every law to return to them.

Bo plumbed her memory for information on religious cults and utopian communities. Terms such as "wide-eyed idealists" and "vegetarian mystics" readily came to mind. Could a child-rapist arise from within such a context? Of course. Pedophiles might be anywhere. But was Paul Massieu the rapist whose violence destroyed Samantha Franer? Maybe. But if he weren't, then who was?

A shadow fell sleekly over the road, turning the emerald trees to moss. What if Andrew LaMarche were right? What if Massieu had abducted Hannah for reasons other than guilt? Then Samantha's killer was free to rape, perhaps kill, again. Might, in fact, be doing so at this very moment.

To her right Bo noticed a red barn in a field beside the road. On its side were painted three huge shamrocks, outlined in white. In spite of herself Bo reacted exactly as her grandmother would have done.

"Dia's muir dhuit," she pronounced the traditional "Mother of God be with you" salutation. "Even though ye've forgot the true sign!"

Bridget Mairead O'Reilly had told her granddaughters a hundred times that no true child of Eire would display any symbol but the harp. Still, the popular American symbol for all things Irish reminded Bo of her heritage. A heritage in which intuition had value. And her intuition was suggesting a picture in which a sexual pervert was free to select his next victim from a population of children in training pants.

The appalling notion did not diminish as Bo directed the little car to the right on Route 30, across the Mohawk River and through the town of Amsterdam. Miles later the thought had become an unprovable certainty. A sign announcing the manufacture of "Havlick Snowshoes" in a village provided the final straw. Bo had forgotten the reality of snow. Webbed contraptions for walking on it seemed, at best, apocryphal. Could there *really* be a company with employees at this very moment constructing snowshoes? Shepherd's crooks? How about butter churns? Everything was relative.

"Le monde," Andrew LaMarche's phrase rumbled pointedly in the wind from the open car window. The world. A world. One of many. This one contained snowshoes, an unknown cult, and a bereaved child who must be returned to the jurisdiction of the California court that had assumed the burden of protecting her from her sister's fate. Except that if Paul Massieu were innocent, then Hannah Franer was in no peril. And the swift action of police in two states and Bo's own hurried journey were exercises in futility. Like snowshoes in San Diego.

An informative marker placed by the state of New York informed Bo that the damming of the Sacandaga River had permanently immersed several small towns. She glanced at the steel-gray water and wondered what worlds were lost beneath it. Comparisons to the system for which she worked were inescapable. As Andrew LaMarche had pointed out, no one had bothered to ask about the world in which Samantha Franer lived. They merely obliterated it with their own. And their own was one in which the perpetrator in a molest was usually the mother's boyfriend, especially if he were odd in some way. And especially if he then kidnapped the victim's older sibling and fled across state lines. That was the world of the juvenile court, the police, the agencies of child protection. It was, Bo conceded as Shadow Mountain rose bluely in the distance, only one world.

"Ye *ken* things," her grandmother had explained. "It's in the family. Be sure to heed what ye ken."

"He's still out there," Bo thought with distaste. "I'm running all over the country, Reinert's probably on another case already, LaMarche is in a tux somewhere giving lectures over chicken-in-aspic, and this sick slimebag is going scot-free!"

An hour later she found the "cult hideout" Madge Aldenhoven had described. It was a sprawling Victorian camp with two boathouses and ten smaller cottages nestled between the looming mountain and a lake strewn with little islands. To her dismay, none of the people lounging on the wide porch of the main building seemed to speak English.

"I need to speak with the person in charge," she informed a grandmotherly woman in a hickory rocker. "I know Hannah Franer is here. I have to return her to California."

The woman's clothes were American, and she involuntarily pursed her lips at the mention of Hannah's name.

"No, no," she fumbled to hide an issue of *People* magazine she'd been reading. "No English." The second word was pronounced "Ing-glish." The Midwest, Bo guessed. Not rural.

An immense bearded man clad in a monk's robe covered by an Indian blanket rose from a small table where he was either taking apart or assembling a vegetable steamer.

"Je m'appelle Napoléon Pigeon," he announced, his French accent unmistakably native. *"Et vous?"*

"Mr. Pigeon," Bo spluttered, marveling at the name, "I'm

Bo Bradley from San Diego's Child Protective Services. I'm here to escort Hannah Franer back to San Diego where she is in the legal custody of the juvenile court. Could you take me to her?"

"Je ne parle pas Anglais," he answered, revealing tobacco-stained teeth. One upper incisor had been set with a gold quarter moon that caught and reflected the setting sun. Beneath bushy eyebrows the man's aquamarine eyes glowed with a wild, undirected kindness.

Uh-oh. Basic fanatic here, Bradley. Probably hasn't eaten meat since his pet canary died in 1953 and spends his days trying to communicate with lichen. Harmless, but you're wasting your breath.

"Thanks anyway." She smiled and moved toward a screened door festooned with millwork. Inside, groups of people read or played cards in a large L-shaped living room boasting no fewer than three stone fireplaces. The floor and ceiling bore designs of elaborate inlaid maple. The walls appeared to have been papered in canvas. Everyone smiled and nodded politely as Bo entered. Everyone who spoke, spoke in French. Flustered, Bo remembered that the lodge was only about an hour's drive from the French-speaking Canadian province of Quebec. Unfortunately there was no eight-year-old girl in sight.

"I'll be back," Bo announced irritably. She was certain that at least half the fifty people present understood her perfectly.

A scent of ginger and garlic drifted from a kitchen behind the spacious dining room. It reminded Bo that, diet or not, she was starving.

"I'll bring the police if necessary."

Nobody batted an eye. They weren't afraid of her, and merely murmured among themselves phrases she couldn't understand.

Defeated, Bo stomped back to her car and considered her options. She could involve the local police. They would have to accompany her to the lodge if she requested their help. They could kick in the door, seize the child, arrest anyone who obstructed the process. Madge Aldenhoven, in fact, would insist on it. Bo Bradley would prefer to avoid it.

Back in the village named Night Heron for the lake below, Bo rented a room in a motel called the Iroquois Inn. Then she deliberately placed a call to San Diego's Child Abuse Hotline rather than to Madge Aldenhoven's office number.

"Just tell Madge I've run into a snag, but nothing big, and I'll call her tomorrow," she reported briskly. Then she hung up before the hotline worker could ask for her phone number.

A photograph of a buck whitetailed deer in snow stared from above the motel's bed. Bo stared back and wondered what to do next. How to get inside the group without causing further trauma to the child. LaMarche had said he'd be in New York City today, addressing a conference on child abuse. By now he'd be at the speaker's table of a banquet crawling with experts on matters not normally discussed at banquets. With an abandon she chose not to dissect, Bo placed a call to LaMarche's service in San Diego and left the address and phone number of the Iroquois Inn.

"I need a French translator on the Franer case," she said. "Please ask Dr. LaMarche to phone me."

In the pine-paneled coffee shop of the inn she enjoyed an enormous hamburger and four cups of decaf while penning a postcard to Madge Aldenhoven. The postcard featured a yellow-rumped warbler eating a caterpillar.

"It's a different world here," she noted. "Love, Bo."

Chapter 11

At 7:00 social worker Rombo Perry placed his office phone neatly atop a midnight blue corduroy throw pillow stuffed in the bottom drawer of his desk. Then he placed a matching pillow over the offending instrument and kicked the drawer shut. On his desk was a steaming thermos of hazelnut coffee Martin had left for him at the admitting desk only an hour ago.

Other staff on the 3:00 to 11:00 shift at San Diego County's grimly underfunded psychiatric facility usually went out for their union-mandated half-hour dinner break. Sometimes Rombo went along, more for the sake of goodwill than desire to eat greasy burritos in somebody's car. But usually he barricaded himself in the immaculate cubicle of his office, read the paper, relaxed. He and Martin would have a light snack when he got home at 11:30. Maybe a Parmesan omelette or a small salad tossed in rice vinegar. They'd worked it out years ago. A sensible schedule for a couple in which one ran a catering business from home and the other was bound by the strictures of hospital work.

Rombo was proud of the fact that in five years he'd never missed a day of work. His clients could count on him, just as

Martin could. An ordinary, decent, hardworking man was all Rombo had ever wanted to be. And now, after years in which an addiction to alcohol made that goal impossible, Rombo had it all. For a near-sighted thirty-eight-year-old gay man who'd never top a hundred and sixty pounds no matter how much iron he pumped, it was a pretty good life. Especially, Rombo grinned to himself, for a gay man burdened with a name you'd only give to a St. Bernard. Sober for seven years now. With Martin for five. A meaningful job that he liked. Rombo Perry was content.

Unfolding the afternoon edition of San Diego's only daily, he nudged his new black wire-frame glasses upward on a boxer's crooked nose. The front page carried the story he was looking for. The story about the new patient, Bonnie Franer.

Somebody named Dr. Cynthia Ganage was quoted repeatedly as believing Bonnie Franer's three-year-old daughter had been the victim of a "sexual Satanist." Ganage insinuated that a large Satanic cult might be operating in San Diego. For that reason, she told reporters, she would immediately relocate her professional offices from Los Angeles to San Diego. She had, in fact, already leased office space in an unfinished downtown office building. Until she could move in she would continue her practice from a suite at the elegant U.S. Grant Hotel.

"As a specialist in the ritual abuse of children," Cynthia Ganage said, "I've pledged full cooperation with police and Child Protective Services."

Rombo shook his head. As a psychiatric social worker he was familiar with the interface of myth and mind. During psychosis people sometimes said they actually were popular religious figures, or had been singled out for special responsibilities or for persecution by such figures. Once stabilized, Rombo's clients were uniformly puzzled by the clarity of their experiences. "I know there aren't any devils," one had told him years ago, "but that doesn't change the fact that every third person on the bus *is* one. Don't ask me how, but I can *tell*. I know it's crazy, but it doesn't feel crazy; it feels like the most real thing I've ever known!" The human brain, Rombo acknowledged, was wired for terrors so deep and joys so exultant that names must be given to cap the sanity-threatening experiences. Devil—God. And whole cultures would react like Pavlov's dogs when one of the names was mentioned.

Disclaimers by the police department's public relations liaison did little to buffer the impact of the newspaper story. Neither did a sidebar on page four featuring the president of the San Diego Ecumenical Council warning against sensationalism in spiritual matters. The paper had handled it with kid gloves, but nothing could diminish the tabloid aura of the story. No mention was made of the fact that the mother, Bonnie Franer, was in a locked psychiatric facility under suicide watch. Rombo was sure the omission reflected nothing more than Cynthia Ganage's ignorance of the situation. Had she known, she would have used the fact to advantage, as she was using the primitive facts of human psychology. Ganage was, Rombo assessed with distaste, a real pterodactyl. A media harpy of the most repugnant stripe. The knowledge only reinforced his sense of protectiveness toward Bonnie Franer.

He'd done the intake interview himself, not that it was actually an interview. The poor creature had merely hunched on a chair in his office, rocking and clawing at herself with pale, trembling fingers. She'd said nothing. Later he'd sat with her until the sedative took effect and she collapsed on her bed in a drugged sleep.

They could only keep her for seventy-two hours. Then the law required her release. It would be Rombo Perry's job to discharge Bonnie Franer to some intermediate setting where she could receive support and care. Except there wasn't any such place. Rombo knew he'd discharge this client to the street with an antidepressant prescription in her pocket, just like all the others. There wouldn't even be money for cab fare. There wasn't really enough to keep the understaffed crisis unit open. The county had been juggling funds for years, and psychiatric services were invariably the first on everybody's cutback list.

To say that nobody cared about people with psychiatric problems, Rombo acknowledged for perhaps the ten thousandth time in his career, was to put it kindly. What people really wanted, he suspected, was for the neurobiologically ill simply to vanish. Get out of sight. Go away. Die. They were just too unpleasant. They raised too many questions, demolished too many myths.

As a young man Rombo Perry had thought the stigma attached to homosexuality was about as virulent as hate could get. He'd learned to fight because of it. Been a promising welterweight in college and later, working the Chicago boxing scene, before the booze dragged him down. But being gay, he realized later, was a picnic compared to being labeled mentally ill.

Snapping the paper shut he decided to check on Bonnie Franer and warn the psych techs to keep the *Union-Tribune* out of sight. It would only upset the tormented mother to see it.

In the lounge a few people were watching a TV movie featuring singing pirates. A man in jeans and a cowboy hat, admitted yesterday with a tentative diagnosis of obsessive-compulsive disorder, spoke animatedly on the wall phone by the water fountain. He seemed to be negotiating the sale of a tractor.

"How is Mrs. Franer doing?" Rombo asked the tech heading out of the nurses' station with a clipboard, battery-powered thermometer, and a portable blood pressure cuff.

"Fine twenty minutes ago," the woman answered. "Groggy, but calm. I'm about to go around again."

On orders from the admitting physician, Bonnie Franer

would be monitored every twenty minutes. Her vital signs and mental status would be noted, and the information filed in her chart. If she became agitated she would receive additional medication. Straitjackets hadn't been used for a quarter century.

"I'll check on her," Rombo volunteered. "You go ahead and do the others."

The door was slightly ajar and the room dimly lit by a fifteen-watt night-light that could not be turned off. Gently Rombo pushed the door open and whispered, "Mrs. Franer? It's Mr. Perry, your social worker. How are you doing?"

The rumpled bed was empty, and Rombo's first assumption was that the woman had wakened and left the room in search of a bathroom or the water fountain. But then, even though his graduate training had included thorough analysis of this possibility and he'd been to countless workshops on its prevention, he gasped and froze at the reality.

Bonnie Franer's body hung unnaturally still across the wire-webbed window, framed by a yellow sodium light on the street outside. A hospital bedsheet straining at her neck was snagged by its selvage edge to the top of one of the window bars. From the sharp angle at which her head lolled against her gaunt chest, Rombo knew her neck was broken. Instinctively he ran to gather up her weight, anyway, and ripped the sheet loose from its mooring on the vertical bar.

"Nurse!" he yelled over his shoulder. Running feet answered immediately. And pointlessly.

Bonnie Franer, sedated and stripped of belts, shoelaces, all pointed or sharp objects, confined in a space containing no breakable glass, mirrors, accessible electrical circuits, lamp cords, or weight-bearing objects more than three feet off the floor, had succeeded in taking her own life. Rombo lay the lifeless body on the bed and felt a chill spread in patches over his skin. The frail woman who'd sat rocking in his office wasn't there anymore. Whoever she was, whatever her life had been, was gone. The chill circled his right calf and then reproduced itself on both of his ears. The word "suicide" framed itself again and again in his mind, and wasn't enough. The word couldn't begin to encompass the complexity that lay before him.

As two nurses, a psych tech, and the patient in cowboy boots hovered over the bed, Rombo tried to make sense of what had happened. She'd climbed up on the seldom-used radiator, apparently, and pushed out the screen at the top of the window. Then she'd tried to tie the sheet around one of the vertical bars covering the window from the outside, but the knot hadn't held. At the lurch of her weight the knot had pulled loose, but a fold of the fabric over the top of the bar had caught and ripped through to the tightly woven selvage edge. That had been sufficient to support her hundred and two pounds. The patient in cowboy boots was beginning to wring his hands and pace in a precise diamond pattern beside the bed.

"Come on," Rombo said, wrapping an arm about the man's shoulders, "let's go get some juice and try to calm down, okay? This has nothing to do with you. Nothing at all." Shivering, the man acquiesced.

"Martin, I feel really strange," Rombo stammered into his office phone an hour later, after Bonnie Franer was pronounced dead and swiftly wheeled away on a sheet-draped gurney. "I can't seem to get it, why this woman would do that . . ."

"You work in a psychiatric hospital," the familiar voice said. "These things happen."

"I know that." Rombo felt another amoebic chill under his left arm. "But Martin, I told one of the patients this had nothing to do with him. I think I was really talking to myself, Martin, and I don't understand. I've survived being called 'fag' my whole life, my father hating me until he died, and the booze . . . I've stayed alive and it's okay now, Martin. I made it through. And this woman's daughter was murdered, but she might have made it, too. Why did I make it, and she didn't?"

There was a brief silence. "I don't know," came the final reply. "Nobody knows. But I'm going to make a shrimp bisque and chill you a bottle of that sparkling herb stuff you like. We'll talk about it when you get home."

Chapter 12

President Lincoln lilacs enjoyed an unprecedented popularity in the well-kept yards of Night Heron Village. Their heady aroma filled Bo's tiny motel room when she awoke to a knock at the door at 5:00 A.M. Never rhapsodic about morning, she managed to utter only one syllable in the general direction of the sound.

"Whaaa?" she said blearily.

"Your translator," a deep voice replied. The speaker bore telltale signs of being awake. Bo sighed.

"I don't believe this!" she yelled at the door. "It's five o'clock in the morning!"

"Got your message," Andrew LaMarche explained with grating enthusiasm. "Grabbed a red-eye out of JFK into Albany and rented a car. But not before I picked up some fresh bagels and a thermos of coffee. Thought we'd have a picnic . . ."

Bo was already pulling on the slightly rumpled navy designer slacks she'd worn the day before. They'd cost as much as a place setting of sterling, but their attractive cut made her feel thin. With the fresh cream-colored turtleneck in her carry-on bag she'd look like a Campfire Girl on her way to earning a badge in sailboat maintenance. Bo wished she had a little silk teddy or at least something more lascivious than a turtleneck in which to open the motel room door. The thought spun out lazily, even sneakily, but Bo caught it before it drifted into unconsciousness. A silk teddy? She didn't even *own* a silk teddy!

"I'll be dressed in a minute," she mentioned tersely.

"Of course." LaMarche's tone suggested that he had nothing else in mind.

In the bathroom Bo grimaced at herself through toothpaste foam. Seductiveness at 5:00 A.M. wasn't her métier. The pea green eyes looking back from an ill-lit mirror didn't seem manicky. They merely looked asleep. But who knew? An inappropriate sexuality could creep up unnoticed at any time. And the lithium would just about have worn off completely by now. A friendly Edwardian doctor might be transformed, if only briefly, into an object of epic desire.

Deftly outlining her eyes in a color identified by its manufacturer as "Persian Smoke," Bo forced herself to address the issue of why she'd called Andrew LaMarche in the first place. Pulled him away from his conference in New York with a plea for help to which she knew perfectly well he'd respond. She didn't really need his help. One call to the local authorities would bring all the backup she needed to retrieve Hannah Franer from a nest of French-speaking weirdos. Except she hadn't wanted to do it that way. She'd wanted to break through the barrier surrounding the cult, find out something about it. She'd wanted to test whether her own grasp of the situation might be useful in determining the fate of Hannah Franer, rather than subjecting the child without thought to a set of rules already in place. Madge Aldenhoven would not approve of such pointless curiosity. But Andrew LaMarche would. He was a colleague on the case, conveniently in the neighborhood. Since he spoke French it made sense to enlist his involvement. Perfect sense.

The ghost of a silk teddy, Bo decided, was just a mental

remnant. Maybe something she'd been dreaming. Quite likely some best-forgotten vignette from a past in which every manic episode involved at least one fascinating and quickly discarded new lover. It could have nothing to do with Andrew LaMarche. Bo was almost certain she wasn't getting manic again, and besides, she actually liked the man. And a cardinal rule of survival involved separating the likable ones from the merely desirable ones. A comfortable, tidy boundary.

"I'm glad you called, Bo," he said when she stepped outside. "I do have an unusual interest in this case, and the conference was really quite boring. Now, tell me what's going on."

In khakis and a thickly handknit Aran sweater over a dress shirt, Andrew LaMarche looked somewhat out of place in the chilly Adirondack dawn. A little beamish, like a city kid on a camp-out. Bo couldn't help laughing when he helped her into a Lincoln town car with plush seats and tinted glass.

"The only thing the rental agency had left," he sighed.

"I want you to see this place, this cult hideout as Madge put it," Bo began. "Everybody speaks French, or at least pretends not to speak English. It's not far, and did you mention coffee?"

She knew she'd be incoherent until molecules of caffeine joined the sluggish red soup in her veins. Conversation prior to 10:00 A.M. without that chemical boost had traditionally proven futile.

In minutes LaMarche had guided the enormous car out of town and over the dirt road to a spot at the edge of Night Heron Lake. The lodge boathouses hugged the shore ten yards from the car.

"Look," LaMarche urged, pointing.

Bo saw nothing but a red eft salamander strolling thoughtfully over a licheny log. The creature seemed almost human in an orange, lizardy sort of way. Bo had been introduced to the diaries of Samuel Pepys by an English professor with the same neckless body and pencil-thin arms.

"I'm going to lecture you on Charles the Second if you don't produce that coffee," she threatened. "Look at what?"

LaMarche pointed to a row of canoes nuzzling the shore. Bo could not remember seeing the man smile this broadly. He must, she realized with a sinking certainty of what would come next, be remembering those childhood summers with Uncle Gus in Louisiana's bayous.

"An English king not known for his love of nature? How about breakfast on the water?" He fulfilled her premonition, already out of the car. "Your Quebecers won't be up for another hour, anyway."

Bo could not bring herself to explain the extent to which the idea of coffee in a canoe at dawn sounded like hell on earth. "Sure," she muttered as the salamander vanished behind a budding silver maple. It was the least she could do, after dragging him away from New York City.

Settled backward in the canoe's forward seat, Bo breathed coffee-scented steam from the thermos top handed her by Andrew LaMarche. The coffee was excellent. She might actually live.

"I have no idea yet what this cult does, what it's about," she began as LaMarche expertly paddled the aluminum craft over glassine water. In the weak light, drifting mists turned briefly gold and then disappeared. Bo noticed that she was whispering. "But they all speak French, or pretend to," she continued. "I got nowhere."

LaMarche, making no sound as he arced the dripping paddle back and forth across the canoe, watched her with an attitude at once ambivalent and bemused. The look had nothing to do with cults. "You're cold," he observed.

Allowing the canoe to drift near the shore of a small island still shrouded in mist, he placed the paddle on the floorboards and pulled off his sweater. Leaning forward on his knees he handed the sweater to Bo, and then leaned back. The sun gilding the eastern shoreline revealed a thoughtful smile beneath his trim mustache. He appeared to have made a decision. Bo was ninety-seven percent certain she knew what that decision was.

"Thanks," she responded, holding the coffee between her feet while struggling into the sweater. Oh well, why not? Their friendship would, of course, be lost. But so what? He was quite attractive in a starchy sort of way. He was going to make a pass at her. She was going to respond as any healthy, experienced woman who hadn't had a lover in two years would respond. Bo eyed the rough floorboards of the canoe and considered logistics. From a paper bag beneath his seat Andrew LaMarche extracted a sesame bagel.

"This probably isn't an appropriate moment, Bo," he began, "but there's something I want to say."

He was, she realized, going to hand her the bagel. She remembered his kindness last year when she'd been really manic, before the lithium kicked in. He'd been there for her as no one else had ever been. It wasn't good to think about that. It would be lost, that memory, after their relationship became merely sexual. It occurred to Bo that she might want to keep that memory more than she wanted a sexual fling.

"This isn't how I imagined it would be," he said, extending the bagel to her, "but, Bo, I want to marry you."

The words were spoken softly, with a hint of self-conscious laughter visible in the gray eyes.

"You what?" Bo made a grab for the bagel as if the crusty circle of dough would explain everything. The movement threw her off center and he instinctively reached to help. In the half second as the canoe tipped irredeemably to its port side, Bo looked straight into his eyes and saw that he wasn't really joking. After that it was hard to see at all. She was swimming in ice water wearing a drenched Aran sweater that seemed to weigh three hundred pounds. Fortunately they were only about fifteen feet from the island.

"I've got the canoe," LaMarche yelled. "Just wade to shore and I'll pull it in."

Bo let her feet fall numbly through the water and discovered the lake's bottom. Her eyes and teeth flamed with cold as a dripping and slightly blue Andrew LaMarche jerked the inverted vessel onto land and turned it over.

"You're crazy," Bo panted, jumping up and down on the rocky shore to maintain what remained of her circulation, "and I don't use that term lightly."

"No, I've just found the woman I love madly and want to marry." Andrew LaMarche grinned with lavender lips. "But right now I want to avoid death from exposure." Stripping off his shirt and pants he put his wet shoes back on and did a series of jumping jacks on the rocks. Bo was amazed to see lowcut jockey shorts in revealing black silk. The garment seemed completely out of character and suggested a side to Andrew LaMarche for which the sacrifice of their friendship might fade by comparison.

"Quit staring and wring out that sweater," he laughed. "Then put it back on and keep jumping. The wool will insulate your body heat even when it's wet. As soon as I dry out we'll head back to the lodge. It's not far."

Bo wrung out his clothes and then the sweater, put it back on and kept jumping. In a few moments her torso beneath the wool actually felt warm, and she buried her aching knuckles against her stomach. An immense confusion seemed to convulse there, making her heart lurch uncomfortably.

"I did have something just short of marriage in mind," Bo said through chattering teeth as LaMarche, clothed again, paddled strenuously back to shore.

"You can see how impossible that would be in a canoe," he replied with a straight face. "Life-threatening. Comparatively, marriage is a most attractive option."

"Not an option for me. I've already done that." The words were leaden, weighted with too much history and the surprising eruption of desire. She felt as though she were suddenly in a drama for which the script had not been written. Andrew LaMarche was not playing by the rules.

"We'll see," he mused, aiming the canoe for its berth beside the others. "I intend to court you relentlessly."

Bo wondered if the term "court" had been used in this context since the Spanish-American War. "Just get me out of this damn lake before my feet have to be amputated," she suggested. The abrasive tone, she hoped, would mask the welter of confusion disturbing her composure.

In minutes the canoe scraped shore.

Napoleon Pigeon was filling a bird feeder on the lawn as they parked the car and damply got out.

"Monsieur Pigeon," Bo introduced the men, "this is Dr. LaMarche."

After what seemed to be an uproarious conversation in French, the berobed giant led them to the lodge, threw new logs on a smoldering fire, and then left them there as he hurried up the staircase. Astonishingly light on his feet, he held his homespun robe like a girl. In minutes he returned accompanied by a lean Indian woman with cropped white hair and black eyes that could, Bo thought, hypnotize snakes. Ever the gentleman, LaMarche rose to meet her, leaving a damp spot on the hearth where he'd been warming himself next to Bo. The Indian woman stifled a smile with visible effort.

After fifteen minutes of animated French conversation in which Bo heard Hannah Franer's name mentioned several times, LaMarche turned and pulled her to her feet.

"I'd like to introduce Ms. Bradley of San Diego's Child Protective Services," he intoned. "Bo, this is Dr. Eva Blindhawk Broussard, founder and director of the Shadow Mountain Seekers, a group whose members either have seen or expect to see visitors from another dimension."

Bo extended her hand to a firm, welcoming grip, and waited.

"Will you help us?" the woman asked directly, and in English. Her eyes bored into Bo's as if searching for something.

Bo knew exactly what the look meant, and returned it. A look of baseline assessment that would miss nothing. A searching out of the little twitches that hide lies, mask deception. Bo could do it naturally. Eva Broussard had learned. The two women stared, blue eyes to black, as a log tumbled in the fire and sent up a spray of sparks. Bo had expected the leader of this odd assemblage to be a marginal character, a little innocent, a little delusional. Instead she found fierce intelligence and a surprising openness.

"I don't know if I can help you; my job is to help Hannah Franer. But I'd like to know about her life, her world"—she glanced briefly at LaMarche—"before I make decisions that will affect her. Will you take me to her?"

The answer was an affirmation of their mutual assessment. "Yes," Eva Broussard replied. "Come with me."

A second unusual happening in one day, Bo mused. The woman had trusted her immediately. Now if Andrew LaMarche would just come to terms with a dawning twenty-first century . . .

"I'm going to phone my service," LaMarche said. "You go on and check on Hannah."

Following Eva Broussard up the maple stairs, Bo was not surprised at the woman's next remark.

"You thought I'd be insane, didn't you?"

"Yes," Bo answered, "but you're not."

"And you'd know, wouldn't you?"

"Yes. I have a bipolar disorder, and—"

"And so you don't miss much." Eva Broussard turned and smiled. "A remarkable quality, enviable in many ways. Unusual in a social worker. How did you fall into this job, Bo Bradley?"

"It's a long story," Bo said as they entered a large bedroom in which the little girl still slept on a cot beside a twig bed.

Eva Broussard's black eyes twinkled. "I'd love to hear it later." She laughed softly. "And here's your quarry."

Bo felt as if she'd known the woman for a lifetime, as if she'd found a friend.

For a while both of them gazed at the sleeping child whose straight blonde hair fanned across the pillow. A dusting of freckles punctuated her cheeks flushed with sleep, and her perfectly arched eyebrows were the color of dust. A huge nightgown fell off one shoulder, revealing a bony frame like the mother's. Pinned to the gown's bodice were three odd strips of woven straw with purple beads attached. Bo made a note to ask about them as Eva grabbed some dry clothes for Bo from a bureau.

"Just change in there," she gestured to a hall bathroom. "Then come downstairs and we'll fill you with hot coffee while we talk."

Minutes later Bo descended the stairs in a warm caftan and wool slipper socks, only to confront LaMarche and the Indian woman looking somberly upward, waiting for her.

"What is it?" she asked from the landing.

LaMarche held out his hand. "Bonnie Franer committed suicide last night, Bo. The bastard has killed two people now."

From above a small voice rose, panicky and shrill. "Eva! Where are you, Eva? I'm scaaared!"

"These people have come from California," Eva explained to Hannah Franer, who was huddled cross-legged on the twig bed. "This is Dr. LaMarche, who tried to help Samantha, and this is Ms. Bradley, who wants to help you."

The child's wide-set hazel eyes watched as if from a great distance. The burden of pain lay in them, and a defeated disinterest.

"Oh, Hannah," Bo sighed, joining the child on the bed, "it won't stay this way! Things will get better, they really will . . ."

Eva Broussard shot Bo a look. "This is a terrible time for you, Hannah," she began, "and I'm afraid another terrible thing has happened."

Hannah traced patterns with her knuckles on the sheet. "Where's Paul?" she asked softly. "I want Paul and mama. I want to go home." The round, pale eyes glared at Bo accusingly. "Where's Paul and my mom?"

The pleasant, old-fashioned room seemed suddenly cut off from the rest of the lodge, the rest of the world. Bo could almost smell the child's rage and despair. A musty, metallic odor warning of danger. Bo glanced at Eva Broussard for confirmation, and saw the grim nod. Hannah Franer had inherited her mother's fragility. Merely quiet and somber under normal stress loads, the child might break completely now. Bo felt a desperate sense of time running out.

"Paul is okay, but he's been taken back to California," she told the child very slowly. "The police think he's the one who hurt Samantha . . ."

"Nooo!" Hannah breathed, trembling. "Paul didn't hurt Sammi. It was Goody. Goody hurt her. She said Goody hurt her," she pointed toward her crotch beneath the baggy nightgown, "down there."

Bo felt her own pulse quickening. "Hannah, who is Goody?"

"Sammi said mama would die if she told. That Goody would kill mama." The hazel eyes were dry and widening in fear. "Where's mama? Sammi told me! He got Sammi dead because she told! Did he get mama? Is mama dead, too? Where's my mama?" The child sat upright among the bedcovers, a tense, narrow sculpture.

"Your mother is in California," Eva Broussard hedged, her bronze eyelids lowered as if she were deep in thought.

"She'd dead, isn't she?" Hannah addressed the question to Eva with a directness that made Bo wince. "She's in California, but she's dead. Goody got her and he killed her!"

"Goody didn't kill your mother," Eva said slowly and

clearly. And then, because everything that might happen later would hinge on Hannah's trust of her, Eva Broussard did not lie. "But yes, your mother, too, has died."

Bo, sitting on the bed only inches from Hannah, felt the girl's spirit turn away. Turn inward toward some flat, cool landscape where nothing moved, where there was no sound, where nothing hurt. Like a puppet slack on its strings the child curled upon herself and toppled sideways on the bed. A dark stain spread beneath her hips as she lost control of her bladder. The hazel eyes fell vacant even as Bo watched, as if the person inside simply slid down, and away.

"Mon Dieu," Andrew LaMarche uttered raggedly from the doorway. "She's gone into shock!"

"Something like that," the Indian woman replied, gathering the girl in her arms and striding toward the hall bathroom. "Bo, I'll need your help."

Deftly placing Hannah in the deep old bathtub, Eva turned on the water and adjusted its temperature to a tepid level that would cool the child's skin and gently induce a faster heart rate.

"Hold her up while I get the gown off," Broussard directed.

Bo could feel muscle tone over the small bones. Hannah was still with them.

"Bo and I are going to massage you with these washcloths," Eva Broussard explained. "It will help you get some of the hurt out. Let some of the hurt out, Hannah. The water is here to take it away."

Bo watched as Eva kneaded Hannah's pale flesh with a rough cloth, and did the same. Gradually the child's skin turned pink, but the hazel eyes remained empty.

"I am your grandmother now, Hannah," Eva went on. A note of authority rang in her voice. "And this is our way. Samantha and your mother are gone, and your hurt is terrible. You must let some of the hurt out, or you will be very sick. The water is here to take your hurt away . . . now."

Bo watched as Hannah turned her head to face the Indian woman. Slowly the small hands formed fists, extended, and curled tightly again. The child's face contorted as tears sprang up and a rasping hiss escaped her bared teeth.

"Hold her," Eva told Bo. "Don't let her hurt herself."

Hannah began to pound the water with her fists, and then to kick. In seconds she was thrashing violently, flinging gallons of water like liquid groundfire from the tub.

"Fine, that's just right," Eva encouraged until the girl relaxed in exhaustion, sobbing quietly.

Only then did Bo notice the crowd of people standing silently in the hall.

"We were afraid the chanting would disturb her," a young woman in a SUNY Albany sweatshirt addressed Eva Broussard, "so we haven't done the morning chant yet. Is she going to be all right?"

"She's much better," Eva answered, taking a stack of clean clothes from the grandmotherly woman Bo had seen on the porch yesterday afternoon. "Aren't you, Hannah?"

It was in the set of the child's shoulders. Bo saw it before the ramifications became obvious. Hannah allowed Bo to help her into clean white panties and her Minnie Mouse shirt, and pointed to the beads still pinned to the nightgown on the floor. Bo retrieved the amulet and fastened it to the sweatshirt as the child watched, but said nothing.

"Hannah?" Eva repeated.

Hannah's wide lips clamped over her teeth for a moment, and then went slack. In her eyes a deep fear struggled with her need to remain attached. Eva and Bo exchanged a glance of troubled acceptance. To push the little girl right now would be disastrous.

"It's okay if you don't want to talk." Bo smiled, hiding her dismay. "We know how scared you are. You don't have to talk until you aren't so scared."

The only person who might lead them to Samantha's killer

had just been pulled from the shock of grief only to stop talking. Hannah Franer had elected to become mute, not out of rational thinking but out of a stark terror operating in the deepest channels of her mind. Somebody named Goody had told Samantha her mama would die if she revealed what he'd done to her. But Samantha had told her big sister, Hannah. Bo could almost see the two, tucked in their Raggedy Ann sheets, one of them bleeding internally, sick, frightened. Sammi had told her big sister what the man had done, and then Sammi had died. Next Bonnie Franer had crumbled under the intolerable weight of her distorted grief and taken her own life. And that left Hannah with irrefutable proof that to talk is to die.

"We're going downstairs for a little while," Eva told her after settling her in a clean bed and assigning one of the group to read aloud from a book of poems by Robert Louis Stevenson. Hannah didn't seem to hear.

"Repetitive rhyme and meter are comforting to children," the Indian woman said as she led Bo and LaMarche to an alcove beside one of the fireplaces. "The brain of a child is not like an adult's. Somehow we've lost sight of that." Bo noticed that the woman's hands were trembling as Napoleon Pigeon laid a glazed pottery tea service on an end table, and padded away.

LaMarche noticed as well, and poured the tea with deliberate indolence. The ploy gave Eva time to regain her composure, and gave Bo an opportunity to contemplate what the term "gentleman" must have meant when it still meant anything. Her grandmother, she thought while admiring the twig chair Eva occupied, would have joined Andrew LaMarche at the altar within minutes of his proposal. Any altar. But Bridget O'Reilly's fondness for "the laddies" had been legendary. Bo monitored a similar proclivity in herself like a radioactive isotope. Dangerous when not properly contained.

"Elective mutism in children is fairly rare these days," he mentioned conversationally. "Understandable in Hannah's case, but she will need to be seen by a child psychiatrist as quickly as possible. Bo, I don't see that you have any choice but to—"

"I am a psychiatrist," Eva Broussard interjected. "I don't specialize in children, but I'm the last available adult this child knows and trusts. She must stay with me. The next days and weeks will be critical. Surely you can see that."

LaMarche smoothed his mustache with a thumb and stared into his tea. "Dr. Broussard, could you explain exactly what these people, including Paul Massieu, are doing here? And could you outline your reasons for choosing to believe that Massieu is innocent of Samantha's injuries and death?"

"Andy!" Bo slammed her cup into its saucer, creating a ripple of clove-scented air in the alcove. "You believed he was innocent from the beginning. Has the mother's suicide changed your mind? And have you forgotten that this is *my* investigation?"

Eva Broussard stood and breathed the steam from her tea. "Dr. LaMarche is asking the obvious questions. Here are the answers. In two years of close professional association with Paul Massieu, I have seen nothing to suggest that he's capable of sexual assault of any kind, particularly sexual assault on a child. His relationship with Bonnie was a healthy one, despite differences in their backgrounds and education. Paul is an unusual man, especially by American standards. More like a European. He does not feel any need to conform to some model he cannot fit. An academic, he teaches cultural anthropology at McGill, devotes his leisure time to camping and the pursuit of numerous interests that center on salvaging cultural artifacts . . ."

"What cultural artifacts?" Bo asked, recognizing that kiddie porn might just fall in that category.

Eva Broussard leaned against the fieldstone wall, one moccasinned foot propped behind her. "Adirondack guideboats, old Huguenot cookbooks in French, and eighteenth-century Roman Catholic ghost stories involving Montreal's numerous convents and monasteries. Paul collects original wine label artwork, belongs to an international organization determined to preserve the oldest known names of streets and roads, and actually lost a finger attempting to rescue a millwheel destined for extinction in Vermont. In addition to that—"

"We see your point," Andrew LaMarche admitted from deep within an overstuffed plaid love seat facing Eva. "And none of Paul's interests, insofar as you know, have involved the usual pastimes of pedophiles?"

"No. Paul has no interests that could be used to attract children. No video games, sports or soda fountain equipment, toys or pets. With the exceptions of Hannah and Samantha, I feel safe in saying that Paul has a minimal awareness of children."

Bo couldn't restrain herself. "What was he going to do with a *millwheel*?" she asked.

"I don't know," Eva answered. "It was years ago. Before he came to me for help with the experience that has created this community."

"The San Diego police say Paul's a member of a cult." Bo took the cue. "*Is* this some kind of cult?" She couldn't shake a sense that the whole interrogation was pointless. That they might as well have been whistling at each other through straws while something terrible grew worse, unchecked.

"Paul and several of the others here report having seen silvery, humanoid figures at night in these mountains. Paul and three others recall being medically examined by these figures. Those with this experience generally attribute it to contact with extraterrestrial life-forms. The experience was intense and transforming for them. They and others who believe in this experience gather here. That's all. Scarcely a cult, as the term is properly used."

"And Paul isn't delusional?" Bo croaked in disbelief.

"My question as well," echoed Andrew LaMarche.

"And Paul's," Eva continued, sitting to pour more tea. "He came to me fearing that he was going mad. You'll have to trust my assessment that he shows no evidence of any psychiatric disorder. I can't explain what happened to him. But my purpose in establishing this community is to study that experience."

The sound of padding feet alerted them to the presence of Hannah, a leggy wraith in her sweatshirt and underpants. Glaring at LaMarche, the child looked questioningly at Bo and then flung herself against Eva. The dark flesh around her eyes made her look made-up, like a classic Oriental dancer. The effect was eerie.

"I'm right here, Hannah," Eva reassured the child. "And I'm glad to see you. Why don't you get your jeans and shoes now, and then you and I will see what's in the refrigerator to drink."

As Hannah scuttled away, Eva turned to face Bo. "I will come to California," she said. "I will see to it that Hannah is in the jurisdiction of your agency. It will be better for her to see that Paul is alive, in any event. But she must stay with me."

"What are you going to do?" Andrew LaMarche asked after Eva had coaxed some orange juice into Hannah and taken her out to walk near the lake.

"There are options." Bo sighed. "California may not be the best one. Eva could take Hannah up to Canada for a while. It would take weeks, even months for the paperwork to extradite them back to California. Hannah must stay with Eva if she's to come out of this at all intact. She's like the mother . . ."

"I can see that." LaMarche nodded, buttoning the cuff of his shirt recently returned from the lodge's dryer. "She's a nervous, delicate child . . ."

Bo shook her hair, now a mat of damp tangles. "She's not delicate, for God's sake, Andy, it's more serious than that. If anything she's tough as nails to have made it this far. When will people stop embroidering these cute little terms for life-threatening situations?"

His puzzled look alerted Bo to the intensity of her own words.

"I'm on a soapbox, right? I'm overreacting. She's just a kid with a lot of losses. But Andy," Bo slapped the table where the tea service sat cooling, "it's more than that. The mother's a suicide. That doesn't happen in regular people no matter what the stress. It takes a certain . . . imbalance. Hannah's got the problem, too. I've seen it. My sister . . ."

Bo stopped herself and toyed with the hem of the caftan she was wearing.

"I'd forgotten," LaMarche said softly. "Didn't she . . . ?"

Bo looked up from the wool fabric. "Not an easy word, is it? As manic depression goes, I was lucky. I got the mania, mostly. Laurie got the depression. And yes, she commited suicide when she was twenty."

The gray eyes showed pain. "I'm sorry, Bo. No wonder you're upset."

Bo stood and walked to a window overlooking a small creek. Its splashing filled the silence. "Just trust me on this, Andy. I'm going to have to do something a little irregular."

"Irregular? What are you talking about?"

"Eva wants to take Hannah back to California, to be near Paul. She's right when she says it will improve Hannah's sense of security. The child has lost her sister and her mother within twenty-four hours. Paul Massieu has been a father to her. He's all she has left."

"But Paul's in jail."

"There'll be a bond. Surely Eva will pay it. Paul will be free until his trial, if the real perp isn't caught first."

"So what's the problem?"

Bo pushed up the sleeves of the woven caftan, and then pulled them back down. Her hands were still cold. "The problem is the system. My system. The one that sent me here to bring Hannah back."

LaMarche leaned back in his chair and crossed his arms across his chest. The body language of mistrust. Bo had expected it.

"I can certify Eva Broussard as a temporary foster parent, and she's already established a relational claim to Hannah by adopting her into her tribe as an Iroquois. That relationship will stand. It's legal. Or at least I think it is. The problem is that even though I can certify Eva, and even though she's technically Hannah's grandmother now, CPS will never allow Hannah to stay with Eva."

LaMarche shook his head. "Why not?"

"Because it's not the way the system works. In particular it's not the way my supervisor works. Madge goes by the book. Temporary foster care certifications are only used in emergency situations when a close relative or family friend steps in to save a child from going to strangers. And while I think Eva matches that profile, Madge won't. If I take Hannah back as Eva's grandchild, Hannah will have to go to an Indian foster home for weeks, maybe months, while Eva establishes residency and jumps through hoops for foster care licensing. Hannah's mental state is too fragile for that, or for any foster home. It would destroy her."

"You may be projecting, Bo. Kids are resilient. They snap back more easily than—"

Bo grabbed a copy of *Adirondack* magazine and threw it against the twig chair. "Why did I know I could count on you to remain stone deaf to what I'm saying? Hannah isn't just a kid, she's a special kid who's just lost her *world*, to quote a pediatrician I once knew. She has to remain under the care of the one person with whom she feels secure. If she's torn away and sent to strangers, we could lose her."

"You're not suggesting," his tone was distant, professional, "that Hannah may try to . . . harm herself, are you?"

"Eight-year-olds, even troubled eight-year-olds, rarely attempt suicide," Bo said through clenched teeth. "But they do learn to live in fantasy, fail to cope. If Hannah is ripped from the last person she has on earth and forced to live among strangers right now, she may very well vanish into a world of her own making. Some dim world inside her own head. That cannot be allowed to happen."

"This little girl isn't you, Bo. More to the point, she's not your sister. You've lost your objectivity." LaMarche's voice bore an impersonal sympathy. "Maybe you should rethink your decision to stop the lithium. You're getting too involved."

Bo felt the flush racing up her cheeks, her hair rising imperceptibly from her throbbing scalp. "Here is what we're going to do," she said in a deliberate monotone. "I'm going back alone today. I will say that Eva has fled to Canada with Hannah. The two of them will secretly fly out later, and rent a place. We'll secure Paul Massieu's release, and Hannah will be able to spend time with him. I'm convinced this plan is in Hannah's best interests. I ask only that you keep your mouth shut. Will you do that?"

His bushy eyebrows became one bristled rope above his eyes. "You're asking me to jeopardize my entire career by withholding information from the police and Child Protective Services, and all on the word of a . . ." He bit his lip and looked at the floor.

"Of a crazy woman? That's what you were going to say, wasn't it? Overlooking, of course, the fact that you've *already* withheld information from the police . . ." Bo stood straight and felt an astonishing calm in spite of her outrage. Why had she not expected this from him? She'd certainly expected it from everybody else. Tears swam in her eyes but she blinked them away. "Yes, I'm asking you to bend the rules on the word of a crazy woman. On the word of a woman who's been in psychiatric hospitals, in restraints, even. A woman who has to take psychiatric medication at times, and who isn't taking any at the moment. Are we abundantly clear about what I'm asking?"

Andrew LaMarche didn't return her direct gaze, but instead rose and walked to the door. "I'll keep quiet if you'll agree to let me check on Hannah at least weekly. That's the only way I can go along with this. But Bo," he turned to glance at the stairs from which a Gregorian chant drifted, "nobody's going to believe you."

"Oh, yes they will," Bo whispered as the door closed behind him.

On a low table near the plaid love seat was a phone. After dialing 619 and the information number, Bo took a deep breath. "Could I have a new San Diego listing for a psychologist named Cynthia Ganage?" she asked, and wrote the number on a matchbook advertising snowshoes.

Chapter 13

In his small office with its view of bamboo plants screening the boy's club dumpsters, John D. Litten signed a name carefully to each of a stack of documents. The quality-control response form for a supplier of volleyball nets. A work order for the June groundskeeping contract service, identical to the May work order. Copy for a classifieds ad that would notify job-seekers that the Bayview Boy's Club needed one bus driver, weekends, and a short-order cook, weekdays four to six. The name he signed was "James Brenner," a halfback who died at fifteen of an undiagnosed heart valve deformity during a high school football game in Dalton, Georgia, fourteen years ago. John Litten's signature, an efficient scrawl practiced to resemble that of a doctor, gave no clue that its writer had once been Jonny Dale Litten of Estherville, South Carolina. Jonny Dale had lived with Gramma in a trailer on "Poot Hill," right over the dump. John D. lived in a downtown loft apartment overlooking San Diego Bay. A loft apartment in a building gutted and refurbished with exposed beams and brushed-chrome doors to attract architects, photographers, designers. Half the units in the building were used as offices, empty at night. No one around to hear anything. And John D. Litten was very, very careful.

At the slightest hint of trouble he moved on, followed the wind to the next big city where he could be invisible and do exactly what he wanted. And it was time to move again. The memory of yesterday began to throb in his cock. The delicious child, pink as a rosebud as she giggled and squirmed in his lap. He'd lost control, but it was so good! Too bad the kid had died. He hadn't meant to go that far, but it was just too good to stop. And the videotape, showing a masked clown named Goody at erotic play with a naked cherub, would be worth some bucks later. Big bucks.

Beneath the Formica-topped desk John Litten felt his penis stiffen inside the gray tropical worsteds he always wore with the navy blazer. A navy blazer identical to one worn by the director of United Way. And the chief of the club's advisory council. And the Methodist minister from a wealthy suburban church who came two Wednesday nights a month to teach a Bible class. John Litten knew exactly how to blend in, to look like what people wanted to see. Except his blazer had a Pierre Cardin label and his gray tie with pinpoint navy polka dots was pure silk, from Saks. Underneath, he wasn't identical at all; he was better. Classier. And smarter.

The hallmark Litten jug ears had been surgically trimmed and contoured to lie attractively flat against his head. The baby-fine mouse-colored hair was razor-cut and given volume by an imported thickener. His crooked, rotting teeth had been capped by the United States Navy, which had also taught him how to order and distribute supplies. John Litten could get a job just about anywhere.

Stepping across the office to lock the door, he unzipped his pants and masturbated quickly into a flyer advertising tumbling mats. The flyer showed a girl in leotards, doing a cartwheel. He came almost as soon as he grabbed himself, thinking about yesterday. Then he zipped his pants, stuffed the flyer to the bottom of his wastebasket, and unlocked the door. The kid was the best he'd ever done, better than anything in his whole life. He felt like superman, like a king. He wondered if part of that was because he'd rammed himself through the very core, some barrier there, and into death. He'd never killed by mistake before. John Litten didn't make mistakes. He wondered if killing with your cock was like some kind of key to another world. Or maybe it was just killing, period.

Word was all over the papers that some psychologist was blaming devil-worshipers for what happened to the kid. A devil-worshiper who lived with the kid's mother and a sister. John Litten thought about that as he examined the shine on his black hand-sewn loafers. The psychologist wasn't stupid. People loved to hear pooky like that. People could face anything but the truth. He'd known that since he was four and Gramma saw what he did to her one-eyed old cat named Scoot. She just dug a hole in the sunflowers along the front fence, and buried Scoot with the rope still around his scrawny neck. And said, "I know it was an accident, Jonny. I know you didn't mean to hurt Scoot. You was just playin', up in that tree."

Everybody in Estherville said Jonny Dale was a liar just like his no-good whore of a mother. They said she just dropped her bastard like some little, screaming turd and took off. Jonny knew he was the bastard. And after a while he figured out that bastard meant smart.

Two years later they found Dewey Ray Clyde, the shell-shocked Korean war vet, burned up in the rusting truck cab down at the dump where he liked to drink till he passed out. They said he'd blown himself to kingdom come down there by dropping a cigarette into his jar of hundred-proof. Gramma had believed that, too, even when Jonny didn't try to hide the gasoline can. From then on Jonny Dale knew exactly how stupid people could be. How much people only wanted to see what they wanted to see. It was always easy to figure out. Usually, they'd just tell you.

"Jonny, I expect you to come to school on time, and do your lessons."

That was Mrs. Myer, who had a rubber stamp in the shape of a clown's head and ink pads in different colors. Jonny Dale liked the clown head stamped on his second-grade spelling papers when he got all the words right.

"Goody," Mrs. Myer would say, walking up and down the rows with her ink pad, "Goody for you."

Jonny didn't usually get all the words right, just most of them.

Later he heard, "Litten! Your test scores qualify you for Naval Procurement Training. Report to training at 0800 hours Monday. If you rank in the top ten percent, it's an upgrade for you."

You just did whatever they said, and then when they weren't looking you could do whatever you wanted.

But the psychologist had given him an idea. Maybe he wouldn't leave right away. San Diego was big enough to hide in for a while before moving on. It might be fun to stay around and set the stupid town on its ear before heading to Seattle or Tucson or wherever it would be. It might be fun to show them, just this once, how really, really stupid they were.

John Litten straightened his tie over the white pima cotton of his shirt and headed for the club's employee lounge. The clerk he'd been pretending to pursue for months always ate at 1:00. He'd flirt with her again today, enhancing the cultivated image of randy recently divorced young accountant, just out for a lay like all the other guys. The women who worked at the club's three-block-long facility thought he was harmless, a little cute with his pale blue eyes and Southern drawl. That was what he wanted them to think, in case anybody ever asked. He wanted them to think John Litten, known here as James Brenner, was just a short, skinny Southern boy who wouldn't hurt a fly.

"Hey, Brenner! How's it goin'?" It was Ben Skiff, a co-worker who'd invited John Litten to dinner at his home several times. Lisa, Ben's wife, was always trying to fix John up with her divorced friends.

"So-so," John grinned good-naturedly, falling in step with Skiff. "I'm gonna see an old squeeze up in Phoenix this weekend. Who knows? Maybe light an old flame."

The plan was falling easily into place. And it was going to be fun.

Chapter 14

Bo drove back toward Albany through Adirondack shadows, plagued by doubt and a metallic ache behind her nose. Finally she pulled off the narrow road into a picnic area beside the Saranac River. Wide and shallow, the river produced flutelike mutterings as it coursed over its bed of rounded stones. Miles of Boston ferns framed the water in a double band of green. In Bo's mind the ferns were associated with funerals. They'd banked Laurie's casket at Sullivan's Mortuary twelve years ago. And Grandma Bridget's casket, and then both her parents' after a faulty wall furnace claimed their lives in Mexico. Bo watched the postcard scene blur, and realized she was crying. It had been sneaking up for hours and it had nothing to do with ferns.

"I'm too old for this!" she yelled over the broad river. "Mature women do not blubber into scenery."

In the rushing water Bo heard the Bavarian accents of Lois Bittner, chortling. "Who said life was easy? Just take care of yourself, Bo. Be careful."

Bo inhaled what she was sure was almost pure oxygen, given the number of plants in the vicinity, and sighed. "I'm sick of people telling me I'm crazy when I'm not," she sniffled at the water. "The minute anybody knows about the manic depression, they feel compelled to watch me like a mutating virus and provide unsolicited opinions about medication on the hour. No matter what I do, it's suspect. I hate it!"

The river continued to mutter and chirp in a language that seemed almost comprehensible. Bo threw in excess of twenty pebbles at a midstream boulder. The last twelve hit.

Are you finished with your nauseating foray into self-pity, Bradley? Good. Now, forget Dr. Centerfold, remember that you've dealt with this for two decades, go home, and figure out who really murdered Samantha Franer.

Bo grinned at her own unspoken lecture and flung herself back into the rental car. Andrew LaMarche had already flown back to New York City and his conference. For the rest of the trip to Albany, she enjoyed a fantasy of him in his underwear in the lobby of the Ritz Carlton, struggling to remove a sesame bagel impossibly baked around his neck.

Marriage! Couldn't he see how inappropriate that concept was? How antiquated? Marriage was for people like Estrella and her husband, Henry. Younger people. Mainstream people who would buy matching lawn furniture, talk about mutual funds investment, maybe have babies. Marriage was not for free-spirited, manicky artists with jobs requiring lots of overtime. Still, he was attractive. So why couldn't he just settle for a nice, invigorating affair like every other man on the planet?

The answer nagged at Bo throughout her flight back to San Diego. Andrew LaMarche wasn't like every other man on the planet. Not at all.

Madge Aldenhoven was a pillar of bureaucratic indignation when, after crossing the continent, Bo straggled into the office at 3:15.

"How could you let this happen?" Madge seethed, pointing

to a newspaper on Bo's desk. "All you had to do was get the local police, go in there, and seize the child. Instead, you let them escape."

Bo glanced at the article's header. "Cult-Related Kidnapping in New York—Leader Evades San Diego Child Abuse Professional." It would not be necessary to read the article. She knew perfectly well what it would say. It would say that Dr. Cynthia Ganage, through a confidential source, had learned of a further development in the shocking Franer case. It would say that a mysterious dark woman, head of the cult in which accused rapist and murderer Paul Massieu held membership, had fled with the slaughtered child's sister to an unknown destination in Canada.

"I'm exhausted, Madge," Bo said, slumping into her desk chair. "There's a three-hour time difference and I haven't had much sleep . . ."

"I've placed you on probation, Bo," Aldenhoven snapped. "Your incompetence has made a laughingstock of the department and fueled an already dangerous public hysteria. If you'd bothered to read the department's directive on handling Satanic cases . . ."

Bo felt an absence of patience that demanded a voice. "There *are* no Satanic cases," she began, allowing her green eyes to widen. "I checked with the FBI's task force on cult-related crime. There has not been a single documentable case of ritualized child torture or murder anywhere in the United States. It's all media hype, Madge, nothing more. Some people rape, torture, and murder women and children. Sometimes they dress up in devil suits, clerical robes, or uniforms of the Confederate Army. Some of them get off on costumes, which conveniently serve the purpose of hindering identification by their victims. But it has nothing to do with Satanism or any other ism, and anybody who buys that crap is more interested in checkout line reading at the grocery store than in protecting children. If anybody's making a laughingstock of the Department of Social Services, it's you and whoever paid that entrepreneurial shark Ganage to peddle her pamphlets in San Diego."

Aldenhoven's face, pale under normal circumstances, had turned a greenish white that reminded Bo of kohlrabi. A throbbing vein in the woman's neck provided a dash of color. Bo wondered if her supervisor were going to hit her. She hadn't been in a real fight since bloodying Mary Margaret Fagin's nose during Mass in the third grade after Mary Margaret said dogs couldn't go to heaven. The present conflict, Bo realized, had its origins in the same muddy conceptual pool. The need to impose rational order on irrational pain. For many, a storybook Satan provided comfort when unspeakable human behavior crept out of hiding.

"You're fired," Aldenhoven said through thin, long teeth.

"You can't fire me without going through procedures, hearings, appeals," Bo countered tiredly. "I belong to the union, remember? It'll take months and you know it. By then maybe we'll have found whoever raped and killed Samantha Franer. That's all I care about."

"Your job was to protect Samantha's sister," Madge said and stormed out in a billow of Estée Lauder Youth Dew perfume and dry-cleaned polyester.

"Precisely!" Bo hissed back at her slamming office door. What would Madge Aldenhoven do, she wondered, if she ever actually saw one of the small, frightened lives CPS purported to protect? The question was moot. Madge would do whatever the procedures manual dictated, even if it dictated dropping the child off a cliff.

Sighing, Bo glanced at the newspaper article while placing a call to a rental agent in the coastal San Diego suburb of Del Mar. The agent had the perfect place—a quiet studio apartment on the beach. The summer season wouldn't begin until late June. Not too many people around. And the early-season tourists who were there—retired academics, writers, and artists—kept to themselves and wouldn't take any particular notice of an Iroquois woman and blonde, silent child. But something was wrong with the article in the paper. More there than Bo had expected.

"Police deny any connection between the victimized Franer children and last night's desecration of statuary and a grave at the city's historic Mission San Diego de Alcala," a staff writer reported. It seemed that someone had broken into the mother church of California's fabled chain of twenty-one Franciscan missions and spray-painted crude genitalia and the words "Satan rules" on floors, walls, and priceless antique statues. Since an oil-based enamel had been used, the damage was estimated at over a million dollars. The grave of Padre Luis Jayme, California's first Christian martyr, who had been killed in 1775 when local Indians burned the original mission, was also desecrated. The article concluded with a lukewarm denial by a representative of the San Diego/Imperial County Intertribal Council that local Indian activists had anything to do with the desecrations. Bo was left with a sense that he wished they had.

The article bothered her. Something new and appalling seemed to have taken form in the newsprint. Something unusual, even in her unusual line of work. What if the police were wrong and Samantha's killer really had vandalized the mission? A proud symbol of the city's history, its desecration was bound to feed the hysteria orchestrated by Cynthia Ganage. But why would the killer want further attention? Child-molesters were invariably furtive, preferring to enjoy their activities in secret. Bo had encountered many, and not one would have courted publicity, even to mislead a criminal investigation. If Samantha's killer had spray-painted penises on religious statues just for kicks, then he was a different bird entirely from the pedophiles documented in CPS case files.

"You're tired; you're getting paranoid," she told herself. But the gnawing suspicion didn't go away.

A phone call to Dar Reinert helped.

"Probably just some kids," he grumbled. "Town's full of

garage bands dreaming of heavy metal big-time. My bet is it's one of them, hoping for some spin-off publicity. They love the Satanic stuff. It frightens their parents."

His gruff assessment was reassuring.

"But what if wasn't kids, Dar, just for the sake of argument. What if it *was* the same guy that killed Samantha?"

"Then Ganage would be right, and we've got a Satanist," Reinert replied, yawning. "Except the Satanist we've got is already in jail, so he couldn't have vandalized the mission last night, so it was kids. What's bothering you, Bradley? Jet lag?"

"Dar, this ritual Satanic abuse stuff is a crock and you know it! The FBI's done a huge investigation and found absolutely nothing. How can you—"

"How long you been at CPS?" the detective interrupted. "Two, three years, right? And when you can't take it anymore you'll get a transfer over to County Employment Services, or you'll get a job with the Red Cross or a church or the human services department of some company. You're a social worker. I'm a cop."

Bo wondered what can of worms she'd opened. "So?"

There was a long silence.

"So cops can't go be cops out there in the real world. Cops can only make it down in the puddle of day-old jizz that stays alive by preying on the rest of humanity. Did you know that yesterday I just happened to bust a guy who kept his retarded sister chained in a closet while he collected her Social Security disability? Thing is, the sister died at least four years ago, but he left her chained in the closet and kept cashing those checks. Bought himself a plastic lady with real cat-fur pussy and the biggest collection of hard porn on his block. Somebody called when he started inviting the neighborhood boys in to look. I think it was the mother of the five-year-old. I only stumbled on the body by accident when one of the kids said he'd heard there was a *real* plastic lady in the closet. Do I need to tell you there was about a pound of dried semen in—"

"Dar!" Bo interrupted, tasting bile, "I was talking about the FBI's report on Satanism."

"Cops see this stuff for a lifetime, like trying to dam a river of shit that just keeps coming. A lotta cops don't mind it when evil seems to have a name. Someplace it comes from. Makes it easier to understand. Lotta people out there just like cops . . . and Satan's as good a name as any."

"So, is there anything else new on the case?" Bo asked in a fervent attempt to change the subject. In three years of professional association she'd never known Dar Reinert to talk this much.

"Only that you screwed up getting the sister back here," the detective said glumly, "and the damn ACLU's crawled in bed with Massieu, which we need like a case of jock itch."

"The American Civil Liberties Union? Why?" Bo ran her left hand through her hair and considered one of the fashionable new crew cuts. She felt weighted with unfriendly, cartoon hair.

"They're claiming he's being persecuted because of his religious beliefs, because he's in this cult. Yammering, in fact, for his immediate release based on lack of evidence. A handful of New Age types in crystals are picketing for him in front of the jail right now, opposed by a larger handful of right-wing Bible whackers with signs demanding the death penalty for Satan's disciple. I've put in for vacation time. This thing's turning into a circus."

Bo listened to her stomach growling and tried not to remember the ice-cold poultry by-product sandwich provided by the airline for lunch. It had been accompanied by one miniature chocolate mint, frozen solid. "What's this lawyer's name?" she asked.

"Gentzler. Solon Gentzler. Has a practice in L.A. but spends most of his time running up and down the state filing amicus briefs for the ACLU in religious freedom cases. He's the one that handled the Freeway Witch two years ago, remember?"

Bo grimaced. The Freeway Witch had been nothing more than a women's studies graduate student who at Christmas spelled "Mary Was Used" in twinkling lights along the chain-link fence bordering a rental property she shared with three other graduate students. The fence was visible for a mile and a half in both directions along I-805, and had so incensed members of a nearby fundamentalist group that they'd petitioned the city council for removal of the lights as a violation of community standards of decency. Gentzler had gotten miles of publicity for the concept of free speech by leaking to the press elaborate defenses that would, in fact, never be needed since the student would graduate and take a job in South America within months, the petition forgotten. A radical lawyer on the case could prove to be a threat, Bo realized. Could confuse the real issue, which was simply the preservation of Hannah Franer's sanity.

"I'll need to see Gentzler," she told the detective. "What's his number here?"

Reinert provided the number, puzzled. "What do you need to see him for?"

"Oh, just to get a sense of what he thinks of Massieu," she answered vaguely. "Technically, I'll have to hang on to this case until Hannah Franer is located. It can't be transferred or closed until then. I have to document everything I can about the suspected perp so that if Hannah is found and returned—"

"Yeah, yeah," Reinert interrupted. "Except thanks to you the poor kid's been ripped off to Canada with some loony. Great work, Bradley."

"Thanks, Dar. It's so good to know I can count on your support."

Gentzler would be sure to foul up the plan worked out with Eva Broussard. He'd operate from an agenda featuring the rights of an accused man, not the uncodified rights of a vulnerable, hurt child to heal. Bo lay her head on her desk and groaned. At this rate she might well find herself waiting tables at some desert truck stop by the end of the month, and for nothing. But maybe she could convince Solon Gentzler to back off, diminish the focus of media attention on Paul Massieu, wait for the police to wise up and find the real killer. Maybe.

"You're back!" Estrella exclaimed, lurching through the door burdened with case files, a briefcase, and a white paper bag from which rose the odor of the forbidden.

"French fries." Bo replied. "I'll pay anything. I'll wash your car with imported shampoo, train Mildred to howl 'Cielito Lindo' under your window, paint a brooding portrait of Henry for your mantel . . ."

"My car's clean, I despise 'Cielito Lindo' and so does Mildred, and Henry doesn't brood." Estrella grinned. "You've forgotten that French fries are fattening. So what happened in New York? Madge got so upset when she heard you blew it that she publicly threatened to wire your desk with plastic explosives. She mentioned fire ants, too. And something about a sheet metal box in the blazing sun."

"Madge watches too many old movies on TV." Bo nodded. "And what she's really done is to put me on probation and threaten to terminate my employment. But I'll tell you what really happened for everything in that bag."

"Deal."

As the story progressed Bo noticed Estrella's expression run the gamut from mere interest to near-Presbyterian disapproval. The latter was so incongruous Bo had to laugh.

"See?" Estrella shook a pencil at the space between her desk and Bo's. "You're laughing. This isn't funny. You're a party to evasion of a court order. You've gone too far this time, Bo, and if you're not crazy you'll meet this Broussard woman and Hannah when their plane lands tonight and take Hannah straight to the county receiving home. You filed the petition yourself. You can't just turn around and decide you don't think she should be in the system. She's already in the system and you're already in trouble! This is dangerous, Bo. You wouldn't be doing this if you were—"

"If I were what? Still taking lithium?" Bo experienced a bitterness that by now felt dusty, historical. How many times in one day would she have to defend a decision that, while unorthodox, was obviously right?

"Let's get something straight," she began, standing to lean backward against her desk, her arms crossed over a stomach already protesting the greasy food she'd just wolfed. "There's no question that even the best foster home would be damaging for Hannah right now. Madge would chew off her own right hand before bending the rules enough to let Hannah stay with Eva. The job here is, ostensibly, to protect children. And lithium or not, the only way to protect this child is to break the rules. I'm sick of hearing how I should be on medication every time I exercise what amounts to simple common sense. It's not my fault this system's a factory, and it's not your job to measure every decision I make for symptoms of madness. Either you're my friend and you trust me, or you're not and you don't. Which is it?"

"Wow!" Estrella breathed beneath raised eyebrows. "Okay, okay. We're friends. I trust you. And from what you've said, you're right about Hannah. But Bo, if this gets out you're not only out of a job, you could go to jail for contempt of court!"

Bo felt her lips curl in an impish grin. "I've got an ace in the hole. No problem."

"What ace?"

"A proposal of marriage. Fairly wealthy guy but a bit stuffy for my taste. Still, it's a backup if prison looms."

Estrella looked as if she'd swallowed a Ping-Pong ball.

"LaMarche? You're kidding!"

"Tell you about it later when I pick up Mildred from your place. Right now I have to call a lawyer, go see Massieu in jail, and meet Eva and Hannah on a 5:56 flight."

After Solon Gentzler agreed to a Saturday breakfast meeting and seven phone calls finally isolated the fact that Paul Massieu had accidentally been taken to the county jail rather than the city jail where he should have been, Bo scanned her desk for anything that couldn't wait until Monday. In the pile of pink phone memos were six more denying the existence of Jonas Lee Crowley's father, eleven that could wait, and one with no call-back number.

"Satan called," the last message told her. "Will phone again."

Probably a prank, she told herself. Maybe just a joke by somebody in the message center. Some joke. Crumpling the pink slip to a tight ball, she banked it off the wall and into the wastebasket.

"Nice shot," Estrella observed.

"I hope so," Bo answered. Outside the office window a eucalyptus tree shuddered as the afternoon began its descent toward darkness.

Chapter 15

John D. Litten left the boy's club at 5:10, near the end of the business staff's Friday afternoon exit. Most people left early on Friday. Litten made it a point to be seen keeping precisely the hours demanded in his job description. Always.

He would have liked to hang around awhile, maybe watched some kids in one of the playrooms. But he'd done that last week under the guise of inspecting a sand table for possible replacement. A little boy in nylon shorts had repeatedly brushed Litten's thigh as the child pushed a plastic alligator through the sand. Leaving, Litten had pulled off his suit jacket and carried it casually over the bouncing bulge in his pants. He'd barely made it to the men's room. Too dangerous right now to play around like that. Probably too dangerous to stay in town.

In the hospital's parking lot he waved to Ben Skiff and considered closing the whole San Diego operation. It had been easy to set up, no big deal to let go of it. In these border towns it was a joke how easy it was to find just the right woman, desperate for money and more than willing to look the other way for enough of it. Some woman as stupid and hungry as Gramma. All you had to do was set up the place, hire the woman, let her handle it, and drop in from time to time for a little noontime delight. If things got hot, you just walked. No way to trace a property rented in the name of some dead guy from another state.

He'd learned to do that in the navy, too. When John Litten discovered that close to ten thousand dollars' worth of equipment was missing and traced the paper to a career noncom named Verlen Piva, Piva made a deal. In exchange for learning how Piva was saving up a nice nest egg for his retirement from the navy at thirty-five, Litten would ignore what he'd discovered. It was, Piva told him, the simplest thing in the world to walk into any town, check the old newspaper obits for the name of some guy near your age who'd bought the farm when he was a kid. Then you could get copies of the dead guy's birth certificate. With this you could get a Social Security card, driver's license, open bank accounts in Mexico where the IRS couldn't touch you. Instant identity. Untraceable.

The rest of Piva's lesson, about fencing off military equipment to surplus stores and a hundred organizations like the Ku Klux Klan, fell on deaf ears. John Litten had a better idea and a different need entirely. As soon as he got out of the navy he tried it. And it worked.

There'd been one foul-up in Gulfport, Mississippi, when they'd nearly nailed him. But he'd put on his old uniform, murmured something at the bus terminal about trying to get home to Montgomery, Alabama, before his mama died of cancer there in the hospital, and beat it out of town. In Mobile he'd got off the bus and hitchhiked to Miami, where it had been easy to start all over. It was always easy. John Litten sometimes wondered who his father was, because his mother's family put together didn't have the brains he had in his little finger. Still, he always kept a couple of military uniforms pressed and ready. People loved to believe a man in uniform was honest. And he didn't settle in any more small towns. Only big cities where nobody knew anybody's business. Or cared.

Back in his apartment John Litten nuked a frozen dinner and knocked it back with a line of cocaine and two ice-cold cans of Yoo-Hoo. The milky drink tasted just like the stuff called Chocolate Soldier when he was a kid. Jonny Dale couldn't have Chocolate Soldier very often. Just watery powdered milk Gramma got in big boxes from the county. Now John D. could have as much as he liked. And anything else he liked.

Selecting a Scandinavian video from his collection hidden beneath a false floor in a kitchen cabinet, he watched a skinny blond boy suck off a fat man wearing nothing but a feather boa and a Viking helmet. The video was an old one. Boring. He'd only bought it for the scene where the naked children throw cake batter on one another in a kitchen. That was classic. But the fat man was a downer. Litten didn't even bother to jerk off. He had something else on his mind. Something different and more exciting than any video. And what it felt like was revenge.

Last night had been risky, breaking into that church. And then when he'd stumbled against a podium or something up there on the left side of the altar and all of a sudden that church song called the doxology was blaring, echoing in the emptiness, and he'd dropped the spray paint and run like hell out into the night, that was scary. The music had followed him out into the dark where he'd crouched inside a huge bougainvillea and watched as a guard and two nuns scuttled through the open church door and turned on the lights. The music had stopped then, but he knew it was the doxology. Gramma took him to a Baptist church in Estherville sometimes. They sang it there, too. He wondered if the music was a message from Gramma that she liked the way he was getting even with the stupidity. Except Gramma had been stupid, too. So maybe it was just nothing.

But today wasn't nothing. Today at work, when the papers came and everybody was reading them with their coffee and talking about Satanists painting the church, John Litten felt something even better than he felt with the kids. He felt control. An immense control that reached out over a whole city like an invisible hand. His hand. He had them all in his hand. All the stupid assholes who thought they knew something. The police, the newspapers, the churches. And that woman named Ganage who'd started the whole thing with her stupid crap about Satan. They wanted a Satan? He'd give them one. And squeeze their nuts until they saw themselves for what they were. Stupid. Inferior.

He'd started today. Just made a few phone calls. To the police detective named Reinert, to the stupid social worker or whatever she was who messed up getting the dead kid's sister, to the psychologist, Cynthia Ganage. They were all stupid. The messages were all the same.

Padding into the kitchen in Gold-Toe socks, John Litten replaced the videotape in its hiding place, made sure he had enough coke for a couple of lines later tonight, and shoved the two Yoo-Hoo cans and the frozen dinner tray into the trash compactor. He felt like Superman, like a king, like somebody who can tell Superman and every king in the world exactly what to do. Like somebody who can *kill* Superman and all the kings if he wants to. And he does. They're all so stupid he wants to kill them, but there are too many.

Changing to a Hawaiian shirt and Bermuda shorts to look like a tourist, Litten headed out for the strip where the youngest hookers hung out. He'd bring one back for a while maybe. Dress her up in the angel costume. But the prospect held little excitement.

What was exciting was the game he was playing with a whole city of morons. And the fact that when the time came, he was going to kill one of them just for being stupid. He wondered which one it would be.

Chapter 16

It hadn't been easy to get into San Diego County's deteriorating jail to see Paul Massieu. Bo was glad the deputies enlisted to bring him back from New York had mistakenly left him in the same jail as the other man they'd picked up on the trip, whose alleged crime had taken place outside the city limits. In the mix-up she'd been able to fast-talk her way into a technically unauthorized visit, which was also technically a felony, if anybody noticed. But nobody would.

Behind the chipped black-enameled grille in the jail's barren waiting area only one woman sat amid piles of greasy manila folders. An open bottle of nail polish remover atop an inverted romance novel revealed that Bo had interrupted meditative pursuits best enjoyed in solitude. The other staff were gone for the day. From a dusty radio Willie Nelson's voice, if not his words, was recognizable.

"Yeah, whaddaya want?" the woman said with a lack of bon vivance born, Bo was sure, of innumerable unpleasant conversations with previous visitors to the jail.

Bo unclipped the Child Protective Services ID badge from her blouse and slipped it under the grille.

"I have permission to visit a prisoner named Paul Massieu," she said.

"This isn't visiting hours."

"I know. But there are mitigating circumstances that I've already discussed with the desk sergeant. I've agreed to speak with Mr. Massieu in the regular visitors' area to save trouble. You should have an order to that effect."

"Oh, yeah. Just wait."

There was no place to sit. Bo paced the bare corridor, reading and rereading a sign explaining in both English and Spanish that to bring drugs or alcohol into the jail was a felony. The sign matched the one outside the building, which had told her unauthorized conversations with prisoners were also felonious. Felonies seemed popular. Finally the woman bawled "Bradley?" in the empty hallway as if trying to be heard over a crowd. A deputy appeared from a battered metal door and wordlessly indicated another battered metal door, which he unlocked and motioned Bo to enter.

Inside, ten stools bolted to both the cement floor and the wall faced ten small, metal-paned windows. Beneath each window on the left was a wall phone, matched by one in an identical room on the other side of the wall. Well, not quite identical, Bo noticed. The walls of the visitors' side had recently been painted. Baby blue and dirty white. The prisoners-side walls were bare concrete. As Bo stood breathing the rotting grapefruit smell of enamel paint, a door opened on the other side and a prisoner in jail blues approached one of the tiny windows, sat and picked up the phone. Bo sat opposite, and picked up hers.

"Allo?" he said softly. "Oo are you?"

The accent was like Eva Broussard's, only magnified. The voice held a tremolo of fear.

"My name is Bo Bradley. I work for San Diego County's Child Protective Services, and Hannah Franer is one of my cases," she said into the phone, watching his face through the window. "You are the sole suspect in the rape-murder of

Hannah's sister, Samantha. Serious charges, Mr. Massieu. Are you guilty of them?"

The frontal approach. Most likely to produce a telling response, if not a forthright answer. Bo watched as his right hand tightened around the plastic phone receiver held against an impressive upper jaw. The hand wore a patchwork of scar tissue and was missing its little finger. A bulky man, Paul Massieu might have looked simian except for a sort of intellectual refinement that seemed to cloak him like filtered light. He returned her interrogative stare with deep-set black eyes. Outrage, pain, confusion. But no menace. Not a hint of the disguised contempt Bo had seen in the eyes of many men who preyed upon women and children.

"When I met Bonnie," he began, struggling for precision in an uncomfortable language, "Sammi was very little. She did not know her real father. Hannah could remember him, but Sammi could not. I became like a father to Sammi." He breathed deeply and went on. "To have the trust of children is . . . is honor, *oui?*"

Bo had to nod in agreement.

"I would never break that honor. You will either believe or not . . . I could never hurt a little child. Not in any way."

Behind the riveted playhouse-sized window he exhaled. He'd answered the question. And Bo believed him.

San Diego's downtown airport was conveniently only blocks from the county jail, and Bo left Paul Massieu in plenty of time to meet Eva and Hannah's plane from Albany. Eating a bag of sourdough chips near the arrival gate she wondered why a man like Massieu—apparently healthy, intelligent, educated—would think he saw space aliens on a New York mountainside. Bo knew about delusions, about things seeming to have meaning that wasn't ordinarily there. The decaying body of an opossum on a freeway shoulder highlighted and terrible—a symbol of mindless human sprawl and its slaughter of nature. In an Italian restaurant a cheap candle flickering in a red glass had once brought Bo to tears with its message of the frailty of life, and the valor in not giving up. Emotional images. The stock-in-trade of manic depression. Always there.

But Paul Massieu had not seen just a rock or shrub that *felt* like a message from the universe; he'd actually observed something physical that shouldn't have been there. A hallucination, then. Except that Eva had said Paul didn't use drugs and had no brain injury or disorder that might produce hallucinations. So what had happened to Paul Massieu on that mountain? And for that matter why was it that unusual things always seemed to happen to people hanging around on mountains alone at night? Especially, according to Bo's grandmother, in Ireland.

Bo remembered the story of a now-dead kinsman named Paddy Danaher who threw a loaf-sized stone down a Pouleduve, or fairy-hole, on a mountain called Knockfierna late one night, only to have it thrown back in his face. Paddy Danaher's nose, Bo's grandmother had smiled, was crooked for the rest of his life. The wages of disbelief in shining creatures on mountains. Bo rubbed the bridge of her nose as the plane pulled into its gate.

"Could the silver people on the mountain just be fairies?" she greeted Eva Broussard and the tired, silent Hannah.

"You 'ave 'ad a long day, Bo. No?" Eva answered, her accent as thick as Paul's from exhaustion. "And your maiden name will be something like O'Rourke, am I right?"

"O'Reilly." Bo blushed. "And yes, it's been an interminable day. Let's get out of here before somebody recognizes us. Let's take our young lady safely to her castle on the beach where you both can get some rest. I just came from a visit with Paul," she said, leaning down to make eye contact with Hannah. "He's doing fine. And he can't wait to see you."

The child turned her freckled face abruptly from Bo's, but

a nervous smile struggled at the corners of her mouth. Bo dropped to one knee and pulled Hannah gently toward her.

"Look at me, Hannah. I know you're mad at me and that's okay. You're just eight years old and you're tired and hurt and scared. Your mother and sister are gone, you've flown across the country twice in two days, and you feel like everything's just awful. I'd be angry, too. So if you look at me and I see the mad in your eyes, it won't make me get mad back because I understand why it's there. Later maybe we can be friends. Right now it's really okay to show how you feel."

Hannah wrapped a hand tightly about the beads pinned to her denim jacket and let her lower lip protrude in a childish pout. Then she turned to glare directly at Bo, her eyes tight and narrow.

"That's all right," Bo said, nodding. "It's all right to be mad. Maybe tomorrow you could walk on the beach and throw some rocks really hard into the water. I do that sometimes, when I feel like you do. What do you think?"

A relaxation of the muscles around Hannah's eyes revealed that she was considering it.

"Good," Bo concluded, rising.

Eva Broussard removed the calf-length swirl of her lined wool coat and smiled. "You've had excellent training," she told Bo as they followed the crowd through the terminal. "Not everyone could show such sensitivity . . ."

"Not everyone's been told to stop feeling," Bo replied.

"Ah. The manic depression?"

"Yeah." Bo sighed. "It tends to give one a different view."

"Your view is a lifeline for Hannah," Eva Broussard said thoughtfully. "Without you—"

"Without me she'd be in a San Diego County foster home by now, with strangers. As it is, she's a fugitive from the legal system and in the sole care of someone I don't really know. I've trusted you intuitively, Dr. Broussard, but—"

"I know you're taking enormous risks in protecting Hannah

this way. I'll do everything I can to prove your intuitions valid." As if expecting this line of conversation, Eva Broussard reached into a black leather attaché case suspended from a matching shoulder strap and withdrew a large envelope. "Recognizing the legal difficulties you may face if things don't go as planned, I have provided for you documentation of my academic credentials, a complete professional history, and the names, addresses, and phone numbers of some thirty personal references. These include an archbishop, authorities in child psychiatry from the United States, Canada, and three European countries, as well as the current chief of the Iroquois Nation and a former U.S. president who has long admired my popular-psychology series. Each will support your decision to entrust Hannah to my care, in writing or in person if it comes to that." She smiled. "And please stop calling me Dr. Broussard. You know perfectly well that sounds like the villain in a French thriller involving unethical nuclear physicists."

Bo took the envelope, grinning. "And here we all thought the next messiah would be another *man*."

At the laughter of the two women beside her, Hannah looked up wide-eyed, and then yawned. Just like an ordinary, tired kid. Bo decided that yawn was the most beautiful thing she'd seen in years.

After settling Eva and Hannah in Del Mar, Bo made the long drive back to Estrella's house on the urban peninsula of Point Loma to pick up Mildred. At the curb she reminded herself not to say anything if the fox terrier had gained weight during her two days with the Benedicts. Estrella and Henry had been known to bake homemade dog biscuits for Mildred. Bo secretly cherished the notion that it was about time for Estrella and Henry to begin a family. An event that would eventually increase the likelihood of chocolate chip cookies as over dog biscuits.

Estrella opened the door before Bo had a chance to ring the bell.

"I was afraid you'd miss it," she said, "but you're just in time. Mildred! Mom's here. Bo, come on in the family room. You won't believe this."

Bo gathered up an elderly dog who behaved as though her mistress had just returned from years as a prisoner of war. "I won't believe *what*?" Bo asked through heartfelt canine kisses.

"KTUV's doing one of those special talk shows. And guess what the topic is."

"Pregnant teenage gang members talking about the impact of international trade on long-term budget reform? Republican nudists supporting greater restrictions on the booming snail industry? I'm too tired to watch TV, Es. I'm just going to take Mildred home and crash."

"No, you're not. Look."

As television station KTUV's logo faded over a cozy talk show set, Bo recognized one of the participants, dressed in a power-red tailored suit beside which the three other guests and the set itself seemed uniformly colorless. Cynthia Ganage. Her lipstick matched her outfit precisely. Bo sank into an overstuffed couch as Estrella placed a tray of vegetables and dip on the coffee table.

"Ganage?" Bo said, reaching for a celery stalk.

"*Sí, amiga*. And she's not there to talk about split ends."

"Our guests tonight," the host told the camera in an anchorman's bass, "are Dr. Cynthia Ganage, a psychologist specializing in Satanic child abuse, the Reverend Clyde T. Cleveland of the San Diego Whole Faith Tabernacle, Mrs. Brenda Hines-Gilroy, who has quite a story to tell us, and the Reverend Dr. Sandra Rae Harvey of San Diego's First Unitarian Church. Our topic tonight . . ." the camera moved in close, "Satan in San Diego. We'll be right back."

"Told you you weren't going anywhere," Estrella said, flinging herself beside Bo and pushing a button on the remote control. "I'm taping this for Henry. He had a meeting at the base. Wonder why they invited two preachers."

"The Unitarian's there for the rational approach, not renowned for its success in dealing with irrational issues. Watch. They'll eat her for lunch."

"A recent and rather sensational child abuse case has San Diegans thinking about an ancient symbol of evil," the host intoned after four commercials. "But does one isolated case, in which there apparently *is* a cult connection, although one involving space aliens rather than Satan, mean that America's Finest City is riddled with Satanists? Dr. Ganage?"

"It's all the same. Where there's smoke, there's fire," Cynthia Ganage said, gazing intently into the camera. "But it's bigger than that."

Bo could not think of a term to cover the muddle of non sequitur, mixed metaphor, and outright gibberish Ganage was using in lieu of coherent speech. Reverend Cleveland and Brenda whatever her name was, however, nodded as if Cynthia Ganage had actually said something.

"One of our own child abuse workers, a woman named Bo Bradley, was outwitted by these people at their hideout in upstate New York only yesterday. There can be no question that this is a conspiracy, a *nationwide* conspiracy," Ganage went on, tossing her shining hair. "And the sister of the child sacrificed here in San Diego has now been kidnapped to Canada. If this isn't a Satanic network, what is it?"

"A great way to make money?" Bo answered.

The Reverend Clyde Cleveland, sweating under the studio lights, mopped his narrow pink brow with a wadded handkerchief and spoke in a fearful whisper. The Bible, he said, told of a time when Satan would rule the earth. In his view the escalating reports of Satanic activity around the country suggested that the time was near. He didn't think it unlikely that Satanic headquarters would be in San Diego. That's why, he explained, the mission had been desecrated. Wasn't it one of the oldest churches in the country?

Ganage and the woman named Brenda nodded as if this, too, made sense.

"And what do *you* think, Reverend Harvey?" the host smiled genially. "Is there anything to all this?"

A diminutive black woman with a streak of silver hair and enormous round glasses, Sandra Harvey clasped her hands and cocked her head at the camera. "Of course there's something to this," she answered. "Take the 'd' off 'devil' and you've got evil, right?"

Everybody was nodding. Bo nodded, too. "Now make your move," she told the figure on Estrella's TV screen. "You've got their attention."

"And the highly publicized rape-murder of a little girl makes us all think about evil, where it comes from, how to stop it," Sandra Harvey continued, her words bearing the cadence of some Southern state. "Maybe it's just a little easier to think about if we give it a name like Satan, and convince ourselves that it comes from outside us, outside our social systems, our books and ideas, our collective history as a species. But to externalize—"

"People worship Satan," the woman named Brenda interrupted, her voice shrill. "They worship Satan in rituals where they make you drink blood and other . . . things. They did it to me when I was little. Then they make you forget it. You're crazy if you think there's no Satan!"

A wild, lost look in Brenda's blue eyes made Bo wince.

"We have been warned . . ." Reverend Cleveland rasped as Cynthia Ganage held a copy of her book on ritual child abuse before the camera.

"We'll be right back after these important messages," the host insisted as the scene cut to a commercial for cat litter.

"So what do you think?" Estrella asked, stretching sleepily inside a purple sweatshirt Bo had handpainted for her in gold Aztec symbols.

"I think purple's definitely your color, and I think I'm going home."

"And miss the exciting conclusion?"

"There won't be a conclusion," Bo said, struggling to lift a sleeping Mildred out of the couch. "There never is. But that clam-onion dip is fantastic, and I appreciate your taking care of Mildred. G'night, Es."

On the short drive home to her Ocean Beach apartment Bo tried to imagine a painting that would embody all the reactions spinning from Samantha Franer's death. Metallic paper dolls in murky darkness fleeing wrathful Puritan clerics in frock coats above a dusty, abandoned hell where nothing moved except the ghost of Dante Alighieri spending an eternity admiring his creation. A hanged woman on a Tarot card, the background sky raining tears. A little corpse with crystal hair. A painted quilt of a thousand random black rectangles, some glossy, some flat, some opaque, reflecting light in patterns that could make no sense. That painting would be the truth, Bo nodded to herself. A painting of evil. Inscrutable and ineradicable. It felt right.

Chapter 17

"Where can you get decent lox in this town?" Solon Gentzler bellowed through Bo's bedside phone at 6:45 A.M. With that voice, Bo thought as she struggled to hold her head off the pillow, he should have been an orator. But then as a lawyer maybe he already was. He sounded seven feet tall and deplorably alert.

"This must mean it's Saturday morning," she managed to pronounce. The words defined a sad, nearly tragic reality. She was going to have to wake up. "And there are two places for lox. One in La Jolla and one in the college area. Where are you staying?"

Lois Bittner had introduced Bo to the salty smoked salmon years ago in St. Louis. The orange fish had been folded wetly atop a bagel slathered with cream cheese. One encounter had been enough.

"Travelodge in Hotel Circle," Gentzler roared amicably. "Where I'm starving."

"I'll pick you up in an hour," Bo said into a pillowcase featuring opera-pink cabbage roses against which her hair looked like a neon wig. The linens had been purchased at a swap meet during a manic episode two years ago for their astonishingly reasonable price. Bo hated them and used them regularly, hoping they'd fade or come loose at the seams, either of which would justify donating them to a worthwhile charity. Fifty washings later they continued to look brand-new.

After replacing the phone in its cradle she removed the sheets and replaced them with a beige and cream pinstriped set. Then she folded those back into the linen closet in favor of a dramatic Southwestern design that looked like desert mountains in a hazy sunset. Sand brown, lavender, smoky purple. The message was clear.

"Do other women get these feelings as randomly as I do, or is it just women with manic depression?" she asked Mildred, still pretending to be asleep in her basket beside Bo's bed. The fox terrier raised one graying brown eyebrow.

"I mean *you* even managed an inappropriate liaison with that unwholesome miniature poodle up the street. He had *fleas*, Mil. And an insufferable attitude. What made you do it?"

The dog stretched long white legs and yawned. Then she pushed a chartreuse tennis ball from her basket onto the carpet and looked at Bo expectantly. A confusion initiated by Andrew LaMarche, whose Victorian intentions seemed at odds with his underwear, faded but did not vanish entirely.

"I'll take you out after I shower," Bo told the dog.

Fifteen minutes later, dressed in white cotton slacks and a white sweatshirt on which she'd stenciled "Aardvark Power" in teal blue acrylic, Bo let the sea breeze dry her hair as she walked Mildred. Yesterday's visit with Paul Massieu in San Diego County's crowded old jail had reinforced Eva Broussard's opinion of the man. He was innocent. Bo was sure of it, even if she couldn't say why. He just seemed so beaten and lost, sobbing in broken English across the plastic barrier between prisoner and guest, his twisted right hand with its missing finger white around the phone that enabled them to talk through the shield. A French Canadian lost in an American nightmare whose origins, Bo knew from a college research paper, lay in seventeenth-century Boston and a power-mad governor named John Winthrop.

"Why can they think I raped a child because I believe what I have seen? Because I saw those people like *papier d'argent*, like silver-paper people, on the mountain? Why does this mean that I could kill a child with sex? *C'est fou*, insane!"

"Yes," Bo agreed without argument, and then didn't know what else to say. That somebody drew a yellow face on Samantha Franer's abdomen? That five years after the landing of the *Mayflower* a woman named Anne Hutchinson was exiled to predictable Indian slaughter because she was smarter, more charismatic, a kinder leader, and another gender than the governor of the Boston Colony? That in her absence a culture deeply suspicious of yellow drawings and silver people had come into being?

"There are no silver-paper people in the Bible," Bo told Paul Massieu, "so your belief in them puts you outside the regular religious system in this country. To a lot of people that automatically makes you evil, and so it makes sense to them that you'd do evil things, like rape children. Do you understand?"

"No," Massieu had answered, wide-eyed. "I don't."

"Neither does the ACLU," Bo told him. "Don't worry, they'll help you. In the meantime," she'd lowered her voice so the supervising guard couldn't hear, "let me tell you that Eva and Hannah are here, in hiding, so that as soon as you get out of jail, Hannah can be near you. You can't mention this to anyone. She needs you desperately, Paul. You're all she has now. We're not sure she's going to make it through without permanent damage. She's stopped talking, and . . ."

He'd straightened his huge shoulders and calmed himself at the words. "She's like Bonnie. I know that. She must have gentleness and strength around her. She's like her mother . . . like her mother was. I won't fail. I'll protect Hannah."

* * *

When the aging dog tired of chasing her tennis ball Bo picked her up and carried her back to the apartment.

"You're too old for such exertion," she told the fox terrier ensconced on the freshly made bed, "and so am I. If a pediatrician with a French accent calls, tell him I've taken a vow of chastity that precludes everything, including marriage."

On the drive inland to pick up Gentzler Bo congratulated herself on Hannah's care. The child and Eva Broussard had settled quietly into the cozy little beach studio last night, and Hannah had fallen asleep to the sound of surf almost immediately. Bo and Eva had talked softly on a patio overlooking the watery curve of the planet.

"What is this place?" Eva Broussard questioned, laughing. "Where are we?"

"At the edge of a continent," Bo replied. "And in big trouble."

"You don't really mean that, do you? You don't feel overwhelmed and incapable. You know you can help this child, that you can do what makes sense."

"I run on hypomania all of the time," Bo admitted, nodding. "Even when I'm fine, I'm not like other people. Too much energy, too much arrogance. The lithium takes that away, slows me down. I'm not on it right now. And yes, I'm sure that what we're doing is the right thing for Hannah even though I'm breaking rules and could lose my job. I don't care. This makes sense. But there's something else . . ."

"Yes?" Eva Broussard questioned from a chaise lounge where she sipped cognac from a cup embossed with a conch shell design. She exuded openness, interest. "What else?"

Bo tossed back her hair, lit a cigarette and regarded the other woman. A stranger, but already a friend. It occurred to Bo that beyond Estrella, she had no friends. No husband or lover, no children, no family left alive. She'd been a loner for years, and that was okay. Mildred was good company. But it would be nice to have someone to talk to again, like Lois Bittner. Someone wise and different. Someone who could see beyond psychiatric symptoms to what lay beneath. "I'm a little slow right now," she began, "not manicky at all, so I can't put it together. But nothing about this case has felt right from the beginning. Everybody's jumped to conclusions. This woman named Cynthia Ganage is building a professional reputation as a devil-hunter, the police think anything they don't agree with must be criminal, all of a sudden somebody decides to desecrate a church, and the ACLU sees 'landmark case' written all over Paul Massieu, who's really in jail because he thinks he saw little men from outer space in upstate New York. It's a mishmash. Did he really see something up there, Eva? Did you?"

Gracefully Eva Broussard unfolded her body from the chaise, stood and stretched. "Yes, he did," she answered, "and no, I didn't. What I have seen is my own mortality reflected in the hunger of people for something to bring new ideas, to bring a way out. But their real experience eludes me. I only document it and quite possibly will never understand it. What else about the case bothers you, Bo?"

In the moonlight the woman's cropped white hair looked like a helmet. Over the Pacific Ocean Orion stood belted with stars.

"Lots," Bo went on. "Little pieces. The fact that somebody's getting away with murder and nobody cares. The parts that don't fit anywhere, like the face drawn on Samantha's stomach and—" From the screen door to the left of the patio a small, sharp intake of breath was audible beneath a canopy of coral vine.

"You may come out and join us, Hannah," Eva said quietly. "We aren't keeping secrets. We were only speaking softly because we thought you were asleep and didn't want to wake you."

The child stumbled into Eva's arms, weeping. Bo noticed

the three strands of beads pinned now to a maroon sweater with cream-colored piping. Hannah clutched at the beads with nervous fingers.

"Do you know about this yellow drawing on Samantha's stomach?" Eva asked as if the topic were not fraught with horror.

The straw-blonde head nodded. Bo exhaled smoke and forced herself to become very still.

"You saw this drawing on Samantha?" Eva Broussard's voice was like a silken rope, pulling.

A nod.

"Did Goody draw it?"

A snuffle, a shake of the head.

"Do you know who drew a yellow face on Samantha, Hannah?"

The round face turned up toward Eva, convulsing with something Bo recognized as guilt.

"Oh, Hannah," the Indian woman's eyes registered a sudden understanding, "*you* painted the mask on Samantha to make her feel better where it hurt, didn't you?"

A shuddering nod, then sobs.

Eva gathered up the shaking girl and sat on a deck chair stroking the child's hair. After a while she explained to Bo.

"It is an Iroquois tradition, rather complex. The girls have seen a midwinter celebration. I took them myself. The masks, the 'false faces,' represent things seen in dreams. At midwinter, if someone is ill with unhappiness, they search their dreams for these spirit faces, which are the things they must have in order to survive. When they know, they tell the tribe and the tribe will provide what is needed. A companion or a skill, or something like forgiveness for a wrongdoing. At all the festivals people appear in the crowd wearing these husk masks. They are for insight, for healing. Hannah was trying to heal her sister by drawing a healing mask over her pain."

Bo imagined the scene. The two little girls in their Raggedy Ann sheets, the younger one in pain and terrified that Goody would kill her mother if she told. The older one trying to manage the situation. The older one, burdened always with knowing just enough more to feel responsible.

Softly Bo had knelt beside Hannah and looked straight into the child's eyes. A clear, unveiled look in which there was no pretense. "I had a little sister, too," she said. "Her name was Laurie and she died, just like your sister Samantha did. And then my mother died, just like your mother did. And I was *so* scared and sick. But pretty soon I could start feeling better. You're going to feel better, too, Hannah. I promise."

The wide-set eyes looked back, a brittle smile spasming in the lips. Then Hannah fumbled with the safety pin holding three strips of beaded straw to her sweater. Slowly she took one of the strips off the pin and handed it to Bo.

"They're grieving beads," Eva whispered. "They represent a gift of words for one whose senses are blunted by sadness. Hannah is offering her words to help your sadness."

Beneath the bowl-shaped Pacific darkness Bo felt perfectly isolated, locked in an extended moment that embodied truths too large for her grasp. "Thank you, Hannah," she answered softly, taking the beads from a hand at once childlike and ancient. "Thank you for your words."

At the Travelodge Bo scanned the lobby for an immense attorney whose voice could be heard as far as Tijuana. Somebody who looked like a sumo wrestler, or maybe a lumberjack. No dice. The only figure obviously waiting was a short, barrel-chested guy in an alligator polo shirt that had once been white, before it was washed with something blue. Probably the same jeans he had on, which were too long and frayed where they scuffed the ground at the heel.

"Take me to your lox!" he boomed genially. "That is, if your name's Bo Bradley."

"I was expecting Demosthenes," Bo told him on the way to the restaurant.

"My folks wanted me to be a cantor," Solon Gentzler explained. "Big disappointment when I couldn't carry a tune in a washtub. There was nothing for it but to accept defeat and go to law school. Let me show you."

Throwing his head back he belted out the chorus of "Sunrise, Sunset" from *Fiddler on the Roof*. Mildred, Bo thought privately, could more accurately reproduce the tune.

"The Met's loss is the bar's gain," she agreed. "So what are you doing with Paul Massieu?"

Over a breakfast impressive for its lavish display of calories he outlined strategy.

"The guy's innocent of the charge, but that's not our point. Our thing is, the evidence for the arrest includes references to cult aspects of the case such as a symbol drawn on the victim and Massieu's admitted membership in some group that sees spaceships and metal people. Even if the guy was guilty, the arrest is no good. He's got a constitutionally protected right to exercise whatever beliefs he wants to. You can't arrest people based on their beliefs. Not in this country."

"So what will happen? When can you get him out of jail?"

Bo decided to withhold what she knew about the curious drawing on Samantha Franer's abdomen until she assessed the extent to which she might trust Solon Gentzler. So far, he seemed okay.

"They can't hold him longer than Monday. That's the law. I've signed on as co-counsel with his appointed attorney. I'll be at the preliminary hearing on Monday. We'll get him out of jail then, but of course he'll have to stay around if there's a trial. So what's your part in all this?"

Bo checked her watch and wondered why she felt so restless. Like there were forty things she should be doing instead of nursing a third cup of coffee over the ruin of an epic breakfast.

Restlessness wasn't good. It could mean trouble. She made a mental note to watch it.

"I have to document the progress of the case for juvenile court," she said casually. "The status of the alleged perp in the criminal system will be crucial to Hannah's placement, when she's located."

That last bit either sounded crisply professional or hopelessly phony. Bo wasn't sure which.

"You're bullshitting me," Gentzler said, grinning. His teeth showed evidence of successful orthodontia. "What are you really up to? Anything I need to know?"

Hopelessly phony.

"I'm not sure yet," Bo replied. "I'll know more later, I think."

"Great. You'll tell me over dinner. Seafood. I don't eat shellfish, but I love that mahi mahi. Meanwhile I'll give you a copy of everything I've got on Massieu, just to help you know more. Do you think there's any connection between this case and that church desecration?"

"Yes," Bo answered. "But not anything obvious. Do you have any kids, Solon?"

Two could play this game.

"I'm not married," he replied. "Haven't found a woman who wants what I want out of life. Somebody Jewish, traditional, smarter than I am. The usual. She's out there, though. In the meantime I'm free for dinner."

Bo wasn't going to let go of it.

"Do you care about children, about what happens to them when adults get caught in the legal system?"

Solon Gentzler gazed levelly at the parking lot outside the restaurant window. "I care about keeping this country from becoming a police state," he said. "That my life's work."

Bo grabbed her keys and stood. "That's what I thought."

Chapter 18

Bo dropped Solon Gentzler at his hotel and slipped a tape of Handel's Second Concerto for Two Choruses into the BMW's tape deck. The introduction, she mused, might make a provocative sound-back for a pantyhose promo. It would feature a lissome mother of three who just loves her job as a molecular engineer but can still toss off her lab coat in time to drink champagne with a tuxedoed husband in the spray of an Italianate fountain. The husband has chosen this moment to present her with a rope of pearls because her eyes remind him of infinity. In the final frame her reasonably priced pantyhose have not yet run. "May the king live forever!" sang two choruses as Bo miraculously located a parking space on Narragansett only doors from her apartment building. She wondered if she could find a job in advertising if Madge succeeded in getting her fired over this case. Dog food commercials might be fun. Or those ads for 900 services where you could find true love or have your palm read over the phone. Bizarre, but no more so than this case, which seemed to be tapping a vein of primitive tribalism in the community. Everybody in guarded camps of opinion, each one of which seemed to be missing something. But what?

The sudden accumulation of men in her life aside, Bo was

free of distractions and able to think clearly. No mania, not a hint of depression. Everything she'd done so far regarding Hannah Franer was, rationally speaking, perfectly sane. The child was safe in Eva Broussard's care, seeming to have begun already her journey out of grief. That Madge Aldenhoven would never acknowledge the wisdom of what Bo had done was irrelevant. So was the fact that Madge had put Bo on probation and was no doubt plotting at this very moment a future in which Bo Bradley would be merely an unpleasant memory. What wasn't irrelevant was a universal lack of insight into what was actually going on.

"So what *is* actually going on?" Bo asked the musicians of the London Symphony. In the final chords there was only music.

In her apartment Bo ignored both the blank canvas beckoning from its easel in the sunny living room and her blinking answering machine. Instead she took Mildred to a grassy park and pored over a folder of information Gentzler had given her. A clinical description of the injuries that had resulted in Samantha Franer's death, signed by Andrew J. LaMarche, M.D. Copies of warrants for the arrests of Paul Luc Massieu, thirty-six, a Canadian citizen, and Bonnie Corman Franer, twenty-nine. Bonnie Franer's warrant was stamped "Deceased." Legal documents setting forth the opinion of the American Civil Liberties Union that a San Diego County Criminal Court had screwed up royally. Cases in which the United States had opposed people named Seeger and Ballard were cited as precedents, as well as a California case in which an unspecified "People" had opposed somebody named Woody. Bo tried not to envision a woodpecker in the dock, and failed. There were also newspaper clippings.

As Mildred rolled in the grass Bo read the most recent clippings. Cynthia Ganage had suggested that Paul Massieu might be issuing orders from jail to escalate Satanic activity in San Diego as a protest against his incarceration. She suggested that San Diegans purchase her recently self-published book, *Protecting Your Children from Satanic Abuse*, available by mail order. Dar Reinert was quoted as hoping public overreaction would subside, and asked that citizens not call 911 to report Satanic graffiti in public places, which was in his opinion the work of bored teenagers seeking attention. A memorial service for Bonnie and Samantha was mentioned, to be held tomorrow afternoon at St. Theresa's Church. Father Frank Goodman would officiate.

Bo scratched the fox terrier's white chest and thought about taping the service so that Hannah could hear it later. She hoped Frank Goodman would chant something. The guy had a great voice. Like an Irish tenor, except with a name like Goodman he probably wasn't Irish.

Goodman.

The realization hit Bo at the back of her tongue. The gag reflex.

"No," she said to Mildred. It can't be. Not him. Not a priest."

But her thoughts ran on. Bonnie had taken the girls to his church. That's why he came to the hospital. Would a three-year-old call somebody named Goodman "Goody"? It wasn't unlikely.

Twenty minutes later Bo, accompanied by one exuberant fox terrier, knocked at the door of St. Theresa's rectory. "I'd like to see Father Goodman," she told the housekeeper.

He was in back, shooting baskets with an older priest wearing a cassock. In T-shirt and sweatpants, Frank Goodman looked even younger than he had at St. Mary's Hospital. "Hello." He grinned, tossing the ball expertly to the older priest and jogging toward Bo. "Aren't you the CPS investigator on the Franer case? You were at the hospital."

"Yes," Bo answered. She kept her gaze open and neutral despite the grisly suspicion that had brought her. This had to be done quickly. Mildred, sensing Bo's edginess, began to growl. "And you're Goody," Bo pronounced.

Her timing was perfect, even with a sour-tasting nausea lurking in her throat. A snake's timing. Quick and clean. He hadn't had time to prepare for the assault, and would inadvertently display some minuscule acknowledgment if he recognized the damning sobriquet. Just a second of darkness in the eyes, or a twitch in the muscle connecting jaw to skull. And Bo wouldn't miss it. She'd know. But there was nothing.

"Huh?" he said, and cocked his head at Mildred. "Dogs usually like me. What's her name?"

Bo slumped to a sitting position in the grass. "Mildred." She sighed. "And sorry, I was just running a check on your potential as an arch-deviant. You flunked."

Frank Goodman sat cross-legged beside Bo and scratched Mildred's head. From his dark curls floated the unmistakable odor of incense. Realizing that her choice of seating would inevitably produce grass stains on her white slacks, Bo decided it was divine retribution. A small price to pay.

"You thought I was the one who hurt Samantha," Frank Goodman said as though he'd solved a puzzle. "The police already checked that out. I was at a diocesan meeting the entire day she was . . . injured. Then I drove back here with Father Karolak." He nodded toward the elderly priest who continued to perform impressive slam dunks, showing off. "I read the Office in the garden in full view of two priests and the cook, ate dinner with the same two priests and a businessman from the parish who's going to pay for restuccoing the educational buildings, and watched an Agatha Christie rerun on PBS, again with Father Karolak, who is quite verbal about his preference for Dorothy Sayers. Then I went to bed. Didn't the police tell you?"

For a man who'd just been accused of one of the most

repugnant behaviors imaginable, he seemed remarkably unruffled.

"No," Bo said into her knees, "but then I didn't ask. It hadn't occurred to me yet. Not until I thought you might be an Irish tenor, except you're not Irish." Her grandmother, Bo mused miserably, would have done twenty novenas and made a pilgrimage to Muiredach's Cross, just to atone for her granddaughter's nasty mind. "Look, I'm really sorry, but—"

"Don't be," Frank Goodman said. "It happens. Priests have been known to molest children. The church is finally admitting it, and keeping these guys away from kids. So why did you call me Goody?"

"Hannah Franer, before she stopped talking altogether when she heard of her mother's death, told me and a woman named Eva Broussard that Samantha said Goody hurt her."

The priest grimaced and shook his head. "That poor kid. It makes sense that you suspected me, with the name and all. I wish I could do something for Hannah. I read in the paper that you were unsuccessful . . ."

Bo pulled Mildred into her arms and turned to Frank Goodman. "Can you keep a secret?" she asked.

"Part of the job. Want to make a confession?"

Bo considered the possibility that trusting Frank Goodman with too much information might be dangerous. "Yeah," she nodded. "But only if it's real, as in privileged communication. Do we need to go into a confessional for that?"

"Nah," he replied, "but I do need a stole to make it official. Wait right here."

In minutes he was back, with the traditional length of purple satin flapping over his T-shirt. "So?"

"I confess that I set Cynthia Ganage up with that story to keep Hannah out of the very system I got her into. To keep her out of foster care. I knew Ganage would blow it all over the papers within ten minutes and give us a cover. Hannah's here, Father Goodman. She's in very, very fragile shape, but she's with Eva, who's adopted her as an Iroquois, like a granddaughter, and since Eva's also a shrink I know she can take care of Hannah. It'll help when Paul gets out of jail and Hannah can see him. Until then, they're laying low in a beach place up in Del Mar. Waiting."

"I can go to visit Hannah at any time, if it'll help," Goodman offered. "She knows me. The mother brought the girls to church here occasionally. Hannah was the quiet one, always looked a little sad. This has got to be hell for her."

"She's like the proverbial house of cards," Bo said, throwing twigs for Mildred. "One more shock, even the smallest break in what's left of her sense of security, and we may lose her to a world inside her head. It's a tightrope right now. Dangerous. But I'll ask Eva if she thinks a visit from you would help."

Bo allowed the youthful priest to pull her to her feet. "The best thing that can happen would be the arrest of the creep who really did this." She sighed. "But there don't seem to be any good leads."

"What about the day-care center?" Goodman asked. "I told the police Samantha stayed at a center while Bonnie worked at a part-time job and Hannah was in school. Paul was gone a lot of the time, scouting for property out in the desert. Bonnie found a place for Samantha to stay. Don't you have that information in your reports?"

Her file on the Franer case, Bo realized as Mildred dropped a soggy twig on Frank Goodman's foot, had not been updated since her return from New York. But all new information would have gone through Madge Aldenhoven. And stayed there. Madge was covering her own tail, making sure Bo couldn't botch the case more than she already had. For once, Bo didn't blame her.

"Do you have an address for this day-care center?" she asked the priest.

"Sure. It's on Kramer, where it dead-ends in a cul-de-sac. But the police have already been there, I'm sure."

"Just curiosity," Bo said as she headed for her car. "I'll see you at the memorial service tomorrow. And thanks."

"Hey!" he yelled from the curb. "I forgot your penance."

Bo pretended not to hear.

A professionally lettered sign above the door identified the residence as KRAMER CHILD CARE CENTER. Gray security bars covered every window of the white-shingled house. The place looked, Bo thought, like Beaver Cleaver's suburban home converted to a jail. The house was long and rectangular and set squarely in the middle of the cul-de-sac. Behind it one of San Diego's innumerable small canyons sloped down through two hundred feet of scrub and sage to the usual seam of eucalyptus and sycamore bordering the canyon's drainage stream. Beside the driveway to the left several mature bougainvilleas created a mass of blazing magenta bracts and murderous thorns over a six-foot chain-link fence. To the right closely set white oleanders, equally mature, formed a dense, attractive wall between the day-care center and the adjoining property. An older house like thousands built in San Diego during the 1960s well maintained. And private. Very private. Bo carried Mildred, squirming, to the door and rang the bell.

"Sí?" a woman answered. In her arms a wet, naked baby boy of about a year struggled to be put down. Behind her a dark-haired girl holding an overweight orange cat stared at Bo with shy curiosity. The cat also stared, its orange tail sweeping laconically beneath the girl's arms.

"I'm Bo Bradley, from Child Protective Services," Bo began, clutching the trembling fox terrier firmly. "And although I know the police have already been here—"

But Mildred, propelled by centuries of canine honor, chose to ignore the message in Bo's grip. A series of imperious barks was accompanied by much thrashing of terrier legs and a resultant small rip in the sleeve of Bo's sweatshirt. The orange cat climbed over the girl's head, causing the child to giggle and stumble against the leg of the baby, who howled in indignation. The woman narrowed her eyes and looked at Bo as if she were there to sell something unpleasant.

"I'll just put the dog in the car and get my identification," Bo said. It occurred to her that this might be the worst interview she'd ever done. A fiasco. The woman obviously spoke Spanish, which Bo did not. And their introduction could only be described as "not conducive to confidence." Bo wondered if her own lighthearted approach might be construed as harebrained. Maybe she was getting a little silly, exuberant, overconfident. A little manic. What was she doing on a Saturday, on her own time, checking out leads with grass stains on her rump and a dog in her arms? A bad sign. Or was it?

Maybe she'd just fallen into the situation through a series of conversations and was exhibiting praiseworthy devotion to her job.

When hell freezes, Bradley. Your devotion to this job is precisely as deep as your checking account. What are you really here for?

The image of a little girl with wide-set eyes handing Bo a strip of beaded rush materialized and then vanished. Hannah had been able to reach out from the papery shell of her own threatened survival. To reach out and offer comfort to another whose pain she understood. In that act, Bo realized as she shoved Mildred into the fading BMW, the child had secured a human bond that demanded Bo's best. Nothing crazy about that. But she'd keep an eye on her thoughts, just to be sure. The minute she started feeling grandiose or dispatched by mystical forces, she'd back off. At the door the little girl hopped from one foot to the other while explaining that her mama had been giving her brother, Jesus, a bath and was now "putting pants on him."

Bo checked her own response to this news for any hint of seeping religiosity. There was none. Latin people routinely named baby boys Jesus. The girl, Bo mentally bet the BMW and a year's rent on her apartment, would be named María.

"I will be there soon," the woman's voice called from inside the house. "Luisa, take Papa Cat to the yard."

Bo cursed herself as an ethnic bigot while Papa Cat eluded Luisa by leaping atop a television and overturning a backlit representation of the Sacred Heart in a frame of starched red lace.

"What do you want?" the woman asked as she emerged from a hall to the right of the living room, still carrying the baby. Jesus, now clad in a disposable diaper and tiny white dress shirt, smiled and offered Bo the remainder of his bottle. From the scent wafting through the door, it was grape juice. Bo sighed and reminded herself that symbolism exists entirely in the mind of its observer.

"I'm from Child Protective Services," she repeated, showing her ID badge. "I'd like to talk to you about Samantha Franer."

The woman grimaced. "The police, they already be here," she said. "I tell them all the children do good here. I take care of them. And I have a helper. This bad thing did not happen to the child here." The dark eyes dropped to a point below the handle of the security door. "No man work here," she whispered, glancing at Luisa, now rolling on a flowered couch with the cat. "No man."

"But could you just tell me," Bo began, "is this your house? Are you a licensed day-care center? How are children referred—?"

"I don't want talk," the woman said, turning from the door. "I already talk to police." In the woman's back, the tense set of the wide shoulders under a thin blue sweater, Bo recognized controlled emotion. But what emotion? Grief? Fear? Whatever it was, a fierce determination held it in check. It was curious, unaccountable. And impenetrable.

Bo headed back to her car and noticed Luisa, opening the heavy security door to wave. At her open car door, Bo waved in return as something orange streaked from the house and across the yard toward the oleanders. Mildred, aroused from a nap by Bo's return, was standing on the front seat, her forelegs braced against the dash. Mildred did not fail to see the streak. With a look of delight, the dog catapulted out the open car door, around the BMW's dented rear bumper, and into the oleander. A trail of barking led downward, into the canyon.

"What next?" Bo asked a cloudless sky as she struggled past twenty yards of dense, white-flowered shrubbery. "You're too old for this," she yelled at the echoing barks. "Remember your arthritis, and you're going to get burrs." There was a predictable absence of response.

The fenced backyard of the day-care center boasted a swing set, large sand box, and several small play tables. At the back of the yard a gate in the chain-link fence opened to a narrow trail leading down into the canyon. Bo edged her way around the perimeter of the fence and began a dusty descent toward the now-stationary cacophony of barks. Mildred had, apparently, treed Papa Cat.

Except the noise had its origin off to the left of the path, halfway up the canyon's side where there were no trees. Only fragrant sage bushes, prickly pale green tumbleweeds, scrub, and rocks. Beyond the trail the canyon wall was treacherous. A terrain of loosening concretized sandstone spall, compacted under tons of seawater when San Diego had been an ocean bed. Bo slipped as a football-sized clump of dirt broke raggedly under her weight and tumbled to rest against what looked like a giant mayonnaise jar full of brown water. It *was* a giant mayonnaise jar full of brown water. Bo stared at the object as comprehension rose sluggishly in her brain. Tea. Somebody was making sun tea in a jar where there should be no people or jars, much less tea. Mildred's barks, tiring now, were only a few yards ahead. Rounding a particularly unstable out-cropping, Bo found the dog yipping upward at something on a ledge behind which a crude cave had been dug. The something was not an orange cat. It was a gargoyle, a hunkering figure Bosch might have painted if Bosch had painted urban hermits.

"Oh, my God no." Bo gasped as a sunburned face stared wildly from beneath a thatch of filthy reddish hair. The huge eyes under bleached-out lashes were more frightened than her own. But she'd seen eyes like that before. She knew what to do.

Chapter 19

At eight o'clock Bo found herself seated across from Solon Gentzler on the balcony of a La Jolla seafood restaurant whose chef, if rumors were to be believed, knew not only the secret of perfect sole blanchaille, but also the more intimate secrets of several San Diego society matrons. From the distracting flash of moonlight on diamonds about the area, Bo guessed that a few matrons were hanging around for another glimpse of his culinary style.

"I love haddock," Gentzler said with enthusiasm, shrugging off a rumpled suit jacket bearing a Beverly Hills label, "but I'm going to have the shark bisque and then just a simple poached flounder with capers. How's the wine?"

Bo gazed down the length of her own freckled arm to a crystal balloon glass in whose depths a pale golden liquid said poetic things about sun and rain in California's northern valleys. Her hair, she acknowledged, was reflecting candlelight in precisely the way her shampoo intended. And the merest dab of imported scent, strategically placed, was perhaps not the only reason Gentzler's animated gaze kept drifting to the V of a casual little green silk blouse that cost a fortune and gave her eyes a sealike depth. While she knew perfectly well where this evening would lead if she opted for that direction,

Bo chose not to analyze her presence in a candlelit restaurant with a lawyer too young to remember where he was when Kennedy was assassinated. Whatever happened, Solon Gentzler would not burden it with cumbersome considerations. Like marriage.

"The wine's lovely," she answered. "But I'm having trouble with the concept of a tuna salad that costs $27.50. Do you realize how much tuna you could buy for $27.50? People are starving, Sol, and we—"

"It's because it's fresh bluefin," he apologized for the restaurant's politically incorrect extravagance, blushing slightly. "And it's on Gentzler, Brubaker, Harris and Gentzler, the family law firm. Brubaker's my sister, incidentally. A CPA as well as an attorney. She'd tell you this dinner is a business expense."

"Who's Harris?" Bo grinned. "And I thought you worked for the ACLU."

"Harris is my dear old mother, who graduated law school four years before I did. We call her Harry. And the ACLU work is pro bono. We all do it. It's sort of a family hobby." He leaned back and stared at the darkening Pacific Ocean beyond the balcony. "My *zayde*, my paternal grandfather, made it out of the death camps. His first wife and baby son didn't. The baby's name was Solon, which explains my old-fashioned name, and why we believe so strongly in what the ACLU does . . ." he turned to smile at Bo, "among which is to make sure people like your Paul Massieu don't get hanged as rapists just because they believe in little green men."

"Silver," Bo sighed. "Little silver men. I think I'll have the broiled snapper."

The contrast was still dizzying. The afternoon's terrifying discovery with a man who called himself Zolar and lived in a canyon because a huge network of people in San Diego were trying to control his mind with radio waves. The radio waves, he said, couldn't reach him there. From Zolar to the sort of eatery weekending movie stars were known to patronize. A shift of epic proportions. Bo thought of Andrew LaMarche's *le monde* and sighed again. There were too many worlds. And Zolar had shown her the grimmest yet. She watched as Solon Gentzler reverently attacked a bowl of bisque the size of a hubcap. Could she tell him about what Zolar had shown her in the canyon? About what she was sure it meant? Would Solon Gentzler believe *anything* she said after she told him just why she was not uncomfortable chatting with madmen? Too risky. Reluctantly she conceded that she should have returned one of LaMarche's six phone calls, as Estrella advised. It was, after all, his words that had made sense of the bizarre scene Zolar showed her.

The man in the canyon behind the Kramer Child Care Center was suffering from schizophrenia, no question. Bo knew the symptoms from others met on her own psychiatric sojourns, and he'd told her as much when he named the litany of neuroleptic drugs he'd been given at a "crazy bin." Thorazine, Haldol, and Cogentin to curb the thick tongue, tremors, tics, and muscular convulsions caused by the first two. Zolar knew his way through a psychiatric pharmacy and was having no more of it. Bo wondered what his real name was. And how long it had been since he'd tried to get help for the illness. The drugs he mentioned were the old standbys, used for decades, lousy with side effects that felt worse than the symptoms they were supposed to curb. But the guy was still young and his elaborate paranoia was a good sign that he could respond well to the right medications. Bo's bet was he couldn't be much over twenty-five. He probably wouldn't have been sick longer than seven or eight years. And there were some impressively helpful new medications for schizophrenia now, if only he'd try again.

"So what is the dog here for?" Zolar had whispered from his cave after Bo defused his anxiety by sitting on the ground and performing her head-ducking act. No threatening eye contact.

No aggressive bodily movement. No invasion of his brittle and hard-won psychic sanctuary. Simple courtesy, primate-style. "They don't usually send dogs. Dogs are nicer." At six feet and well muscled, he looked like a healthy if somewhat soiled young giant, lost from myth and unaccountably stuffed into a California hillside. Bo was certain he'd played football in high school, before the pitiless chemistry in his brain made a normal life impossible.

"Dogs *are* nicer," she agreed wholeheartedly, looking at the ground. "And this is my dog, Mildred. We're not here to see you. We were at a house up there to . . . to try to help a little girl who got hurt." Bo could not have said why she chose to explain her presence in that way. It was simply the truth. A spill of dusty gravel from Zolar's ledge indicated sudden movement. Then a sharp intake of breath.

"Goody," he intoned raggedly, beginning to rock from the waist. "Goody, Goody, Goody . . ."

Bo gasped and glanced up through the scrim of her own red hair. He was crying. Incredible. How did he know that name? Either he *was* Goody, or he knew something *about* Goody. But she'd have to act fast or he'd rock and chant himself into a trance. Another world where no one could reach him. Rising slowly and away from the swaying figure, Bo grasped Mildred to her side and said, "Show us where you saw Goody. We need to know about Goody." The words, pronounced clearly and with agonizing slowness, would either have an effect or they wouldn't. He continued to rock.

But he knew something. He knew the name by which a murdered child identified her killer. How could he know? Was he that killer? The stock lunatic of countless horror stories, lurking in shadows like a half-remembered nightmare? Bo felt her abdominal muscles tighten at the thought. She didn't want it to be so. But he lived here, close to the day-care center's yard. Had Samantha somehow wandered off into the canyon and then been raped by this disoriented man?

Just because you don't want it to be so doesn't mean it isn't. Be very careful here, Bradley. Be rational.

Fat chance.

Bo summoned her wits and a vast resource of something she couldn't name, and bent them toward the ragged man. She had to know. Now. "Hear me!" she thought ferociously into the air between them. "I'll try to help you. But right now you've got to hear me." Hard to do it without eye contact. Hard to solidify any connection at all with a young man whose sole desire was to avoid a world in which people existed only to plot against him. "Show us something about Goody," she said again.

The chanting stopped as he clambered down from the ledge and stood ten feet from Bo. "Hi, Mildred," he whispered, holding out his hand toward the fox terrier. "Come on, I'll take you."

Bo felt a stab of fear. The identical fear, she realized, that others had at times felt for her. The fear of someone who does not share the same, widely agreed-upon reality as everyone else. What did he mean by "I'll take you"? What if he took Mildred? Bo hated herself for her reaction and with an inadvertent appeal to St. Francis, the protector of animals, she set the aging dog on the ground. From the side of her right eye Bo watched the man hunker, pull something from his shirt pocket. Mildred advanced, her docked tail wagging. Bo could hear the booming pulse in her own arteries as if the volume had been turned up. But it was jerky. The guy was just giving Mildred a piece of beef jerky.

As relief and a bitterly personal remorse washed over Bo, she found herself wondering where he got jerky. And tea bags for his sun tea. A glance at the little shelter revealed a sleeping bag, empty cardboard juice cartons, several bags of puffed rice cakes, a jar of chewable vitamins, and an economy-sized tub of premoistened towelettes, unopened. Not the typical clutter of the homeless mentally ill. It dawned on Bo that somebody must be providing things for him, trying to help. Another in the web of secrets lacing this innocuous urban canyon.

Seconds later he stood and struck out to the left and downhill from his cave. Bo had expected him to lead them up, to the day-care center, if anything.

"I'm Zolar," he announced as if the name were a state secret. "But they won't get me."

"No, they won't," Bo agreed calmly as she struggled to keep up. He was moving swiftly through the rough canyon, his eyes sweeping the terrain as if every shadow might hide untold danger. Bo scooped up the exhausted dog and plunged ahead, wondering if this might turn out to be the ultimate wild-goose chase.

"There!" he stopped suddenly and pointed. His grubby hand was trembling.

Bo looked where he indicated and saw nothing. Just more dusty plants, sage, countless rocks, lots of beige dirt. A basic San Diego canyon. Home to owls, rabbits, the random coyote, and people who have nowhere else to go. "Where?" she asked.

Zolar grabbed a rock and pitched it into a spreading, blue-flowered shrub. "There."

The shrub was about four feet high at its center, and about six yards beneath where they stood. Odd mounds of rubble, Bo noticed on closer inspection, peeked from beneath its spreading branches. A faint path led toward its western side from the canyon floor where a medium-sized eucalyptus dropped its bark beside the drainage stream. Bo noticed shreds of the peeling bark littering the path. How would the bark get uphill, twenty yards from its source? Unless somebody put it there, to disguise the path.

Curious, Bo had clambered down to the shrub and found a three-foot opening shored with two-by-fours, concealed behind the spreading branches. Still holding the panting dog, she'd pushed the branches aside.

"Bo? Are you on the planet?"

It was Solon Gentzler, offering a basket of sourdough rolls, piping hot. They weren't microwaved, he was sure. He could tell just by touching one.

"Sorry, I was thinking," Bo belabored the obvious. At an adjacent table a woman in enough tasteful gold jewelry to finance a small emergent nation informed her male companion that she'd had to fire her gardener because he kept sneaking off to visit his wife and children in Mexico. The woman hoped he wouldn't return and salt her lawn in revenge. Bo eyed the salt shaker on the table she shared with Gentzler and toyed with the idea of removing its lid, turning and dumping its contents into the woman's hair.

"I'm getting irritable," she told the sourdough roll on her bread plate.

"This case is getting to you." Gentzler nodded. "Have some more wine. We'll take a walk on the beach after dinner. We'll take off our shoes and talk about baseball."

"I'd like that," Bo replied as a waiter placed a pound and a half of enticing aroma before her. She didn't mention that she'd never been to a baseball game in her life. But Zolar would have. He was the type. Tailgate parties with pretty girls. A Padres baseball cap that he probably wore backward when he was younger. When he still had a life. Bo sighed and cut into the snapper with a pistol-handled knife.

What she'd seen in the canyon was appalling, and at first indecipherable. A rough cave, hand-hewn like Zolar's, but bigger. Carefully shored with boards. And pink. Somebody had spray-painted the walls and ceiling in a bright pink, and lit the dim space with at least three hundred twinkling white Christmas tree lights. Bo easily found the battery pack that powered the lights, hidden under a big pink rock with a happy face on it. When she switched it on a cheap tape recorder began to play the theme from *Sesame Street*. Candy wrappers and empty cans of a children's drink called Yoo-Hoo littered the floor beside a rolled-up futon mattress. The mattress was red with white piping, and beside it on an Astroturf mat covering the dirt floor was the cover of a magazine called *Naughty Nymphets*. Kiddie porn. For a few seconds Bo couldn't make sense of the scene. And then she remembered Andrew LaMarche's explanation of the hospital logo, Mabel Mammoth: "Bright colors make strangeness friendly."

The psychology that would help children accept the unfamiliar in a hospital could do the same in a canyon. Except a child made comfortable here would be primed not for the strangeness of surgery or medical tests, but for the grotesque strangeness of adult sex. Zolar hadn't done this, she was sure. This was the work of a mind capable of complex planning and execution. But Zolar had witnessed something, and had wept at the memory of it. Bo kicked the battery pack to pieces before ducking back through the low door, tears blurring her vision.

This, she was certain, was where somebody had raped a little girl whose hair became spun crystal under operating room lights. Somebody who called himself Goody had created this place for that reason. A place to delight children into acceptance of the intolerable. Children from the day-care center. Little ones, too young to verbalize well. Small, inarticulate people too immature to distinguish cheap paint and sparkling lights from love and safety. In her worst moments Bo had not imagined anything this diseased. She wanted to scream and tear the canyon apart, rock by rock. Above, Zolar paced and muttered.

"Oh, shit." Bo breathed against Mildred's furry side. "What will happen to him if I tell the police about this?"

The answer was a dead certainty. Paul Massieu might be off the hook, but the young man who'd led Bo to the truth would be crucified. She could see the headlines—"Canyon Crazy Arrested in Child Rape After Cult Member Goes Free." Absolutely no one would believe that Zolar hadn't built the pink hellhole, in spite of his obvious incapacity. Wasn't it similar to his own "home"? And everybody would recall that mentally ill people are universally prone to unspeakable crimes, overlooking the fact that mentally ill people are almost invariably victims, not perpetrators. Bo felt the pressure of an ethical dilemma. An Olympic headache. A desire to leave town and surface in New Zealand with a phony passport.

"You're going to love Auckland," she told Mildred. But the fantasy wouldn't take the place of the tears she'd seen in the young man's eyes when he remembered Goody. When he remembered things he must have witnessed. Zolar had wept for the horror in that canyon, a horror even worse than his own. Bo felt a kinship with the young hermit, and a need to protect him. Dar Reinert, she guessed, would produce a half-baked theory that Zolar might be Goody and not know it. That he was one of the "multiple personalities" now in vogue despite their statistical rarity. Everybody would like that theory; in a matter of days it would be regarded as hard fact. People in diverse bureaucracies would close their cases on Samantha Franer and her sister, Hannah, and an innocent man suffering from one of the most terrifying disorders in the medical annals of the human race would vanish into a prison for criminals who are also insane. There would be widespread relief. And a clever, resourceful rapist would destroy more children.

Bo gave Zolar five dollars, tried to talk to him briefly about new medications, and ascended the canyon wall. After a few yards she looked back and saw nothing. As if Zolar, the pink chamber, none of it were really there.

"And we'll leave it that way," she told Mildred. "At least until I figure out what to do."

The Kramer Child Care Center was dark when Bo left. Her banging on the security bars produced no response from inside. The nameless woman, the children, and even the orange cat were simply gone.

At home she'd phoned Dar Reinert and left a message requesting information on the owner of the Kramer Child Care Center. Then she'd phoned Estrella and begged her to go by the facility before the memorial service tomorrow. If the woman were there, Es could talk to her in Spanish. After a bubble bath shared by Mildred, she'd dressed and driven to pick up a waiting Solon Gentzler, who seemed not to notice the gray cloud nesting on the bridge of her nose as they drove toward La Jolla and its seafood.

"You're exhausted," the radical attorney mentioned much later as Bo stumbled against him on the beach. They'd gone back to her apartment after dinner so Bo could change before their walk. And he was right. She was so tired the familiar beach stretching north of her apartment seemed alien. Its piles of ropy kelp could have been somnolent, feathery eels. And a lone tourist in a Hawaiian shirt just sitting on the seawall appeared to be watching her and Gentzler as if he knew them.

"You're right. I'm so tired I don't think I can drive you back to your motel," she agreed. Something about the tourist made her think of pinball machines. A mechanical carnival of simple gravity. A steel sphere rolling down a maze. The image was cold, inexorable. And crazy.

Are you trying *to bring on another manic episode? Get some sleep!*

"I'll take a cab," Gentzler said. "Don't worry about it."

The sense of implacable cold seemed to roar, bouncing off the young lawyer's words. Bo stared at her sandy feet and listened to the roar. "Sol," she said after several seconds, "this will sound strange, but I don't feel like staying alone tonight. This isn't an invitation to carnal bliss, although I admit to toying with the idea earlier. I'm just a little shaky. I'd like it if you stayed over, if you can handle sleeping on my couch. Does that sound as crazy to you as it does to me?"

"Not crazy at all," he replied, yawning. "I'm tired, too, and the couch will be fine. Which is not to say," he grinned, "that carnal bliss holds no appeal. Rain check?"

The space on the seawall occupied by the tourist in the Hawaiian shirt was now vacant.

"Who knows?" Bo answered, although the words were really directed at herself.

After helping Gentzler make up the couch in the tan pin-striped sheets, Bo collapsed into bed and a sleep undisturbed when her answering machine on the kitchen counter clicked on several times, silently recording messages she would not, under normal circumstances, have heard until morning. But a sleep very much disturbed when something tried to beat her door down at 2:00 A.M.

"What the hell . . . ?" Solon Gentzler growled, stumbling in the darkened living room toward the door as Mildred ran between his feet, barking.

Bo pulled on a luxuriant yellow terry robe with white satin starfish appliqués on the pockets. She hated the starfish, but the robe had been a steal at a bedroom boutique sale. An unclaimed custom order. Not surprising.

Gentzler was booming, "Who is it?" in decibels usually reserved for unamplified auctioneers, and struggling with Bo's several locks.

"Dr. LaMarche," the familiar voice answered as Bo opened the door.

In the greenish exterior lights of her apartment building Andrew LaMarche's face registered dismay and then something like nausea.

"Oh, God," Bo said, turning on the interior lights and then turning them off again when she realized how she and Solon Gentzler must . . . did . . . look. "Andy . . ."

"I was terribly worried about you, Bo," he explained in a voice that struggled to remain impersonal and failed. "I've phoned several times, as has Detective Reinert and Madge Aldenhoven. You may be in danger." He noted the rumpled attorney with something like a sneer. "How reassuring to see that you're not alone." With that he turned and stalked toward the stairs, a lean figure in khakis and a wrinkled blue dress shirt with a white collar. Running after him, Bo noticed that he had on only one sock. For a second she thought she might burst into tears, but then rejected the idea. What was the point?

"Andy, what *is* it?" she called from the top of the stairs.

He stopped and turned to face her. "Cynthia Ganage, that conniving psychologist who created this whole Satanic frenzy, was murdered tonight, Bo. I didn't like her, couldn't abide what she was doing, but she didn't deserve this." He leaned against the stair railing and looked out to sea. "Reinert phoned me an hour ago, asking questions about Satanic killing as if there were such a thing. He said Ganage's body was found in the bathtub of her hotel suite, fully clothed and floating in her own blood. The killer apparently knocked her unconscious, placed her body in the tub, and then opened her left large jugular with a kitchen knife. Then he collected blood in a hotel ashtray, carried it into the sitting area of the suite, and used it to write 'Satan claims a stupid pig' on the wall. According to Reinert 'claims' was misspelled 'clams,' although it may be construed to mean 'silences.' But the reason I'm here . . ." he took a deep breath, "is that Ganage received an anonymous message earlier today saying, 'Satan called.' Reinert got an identical message and so, according to Madge Aldenhoven, did you."

"My God." Bo shuddered. "Everybody connected to the Franer case. And Andy," she remembered the man on the seawall, "there was a guy on the beach tonight watching us walk. He looked like a tourist, but there was something weird about the way he seemed to know who we were."

Andrew LaMarche's tanned face grew ashen. "Perhaps he did, Bo. Am I safe in assuming that your guest will remain with you for the rest of the night?"

"Yes," she answered. "But Andy, it's not what it looks like. He's sleeping on the *couch* . . ."

"You don't need to explain," he muttered. "As long as

you're not alone. I've already phoned Eva. She did not receive one of the Satan calls, so she and Hannah may not be at risk. I'm going there now in any event. I'll be with them if you need me."

With no further discourse Andrew LaMarche bolted down the stairs and was gone. Bo gripped a weathered support holding the roof over the walkway of her apartment building, and bumped her forehead softly against the wood.

You've done it now, Bradley. You've ruined his sugary little fantasy. There will be no more Cajun dancing.

"No big deal," Bo said aloud, and recognized a lie when she heard it. Nobody as decent as Andrew LaMarche deserved to be hurt, even if it was his own damned fault. Or if it was nobody's damned fault. Bo decided to file the entire incident for some future moment when she might redeem a personal reputation about which she had never cared one whit. But now, for some reason, did.

The news of Cynthia Ganage's grisly death only confirmed what she'd sensed all along. Paul Massieu was innocent, and Samantha Franer's unknown rapist was uncharacteristically responding to media attention by escalating his activity to church desecration and now cold-blooded murder. Not a run-of-the-mill child-molester at all. Not the ill-developed male personality she'd seen a hundred times in her work, afraid of or repulsed by adult sex, aroused by the powerless innocence of children. There had always been such men. They were noteworthy for nothing so much as their unshakable devotion to a particularly repugnant lust, no matter what therapy tried to reshape them. But beyond their clandestine sexual practices, they were usually indistinguishable from anyone else. Mail-carriers, preachers, bankers, computer repairmen. Socially adept men, often active and popular in church and community work. Not prone to criminal activity. They never regarded their torment of children as criminal, merely as their right. But this man was different. This man was playing a high-stakes game that didn't fit the profile of a common child-molester. This man, Bo conceded, was a mystery.

From the beach beyond her apartment's balcony a scent of iodine, of sea chemicals and drying kelp floated against her nose. Hannah Franer was safe. Bo inhaled sea air and congratulated herself on that much. But she was going to have to tell the police about Zolar and the pink horror in the canyon. They would have to inspect the hidden cave for fingerprints, fibers, traces of Samantha's killer. And then what would happen to Zolar? The picture made her sick.

Exactly where is your loyalty, Bradley? You're as sane as it gets, for the moment. But when the time comes to draw the line between us and them, you identify with a depressed child and a lost soul whose hospital chart would undoubtedly read "Paranoid Schizophrenia." Is this what you want?

Through a tear in the fog a patch of blue-black sky sparkled with stars. There was nothing else. No hidden meaning, no subtle, multifaceted message. No unaccountable feeling adrift anywhere. No wailing of Caillech Bera, that old Celtic barker for the sideshow called madness. Those things were not gone permanently, Bo knew. They'd be back. They were part of her. But right now they were absent, leaving a window through which stars and clear thinking were possible. Bo memorized the moment, photographed it mentally against an inevitable future when she would doubt the decision she was about to make.

"Yes," she answered her own question. "This is what I want. Being me is just fine. I knew how to protect Hannah and talk to Zolar. I didn't learn those skills being somebody else, and I'm sick of pretending to be somebody else. And there's a pederast-turned-killer out there who's going to be sorry Samantha Franer wound up on my caseload."

Back in her apartment Bo found Solon Gentzler standing gloomily before her open refrigerator. "Three pounds of carrots?" he asked. "A bag of raw broccoli, two six-packs of salt-free tomato juice, and a picture of some gorgeous broad who looks like the head of an island protectorate where art thieves vacation. Bo, why do you have no food and this picture taped to your butter bin?"

"That's Frances Lear," Bo grinned, "role-model for ladies-on-lithium who aspire to wardrobes without polyester. I'm trying to lose weight because I've been taking lithium for nine months."

The cat, out of the bag, merely sat there.

"Isn't that the stuff they make batteries out of?" Gentzler queried, still searching for edible objects.

"I haven't been eating batteries for the better part of a year, Sol. Why don't we get dressed and find an all-night diner for coffee? There's something I want to tell you. And I've got an idea I need your help with."

Chapter 20

Rombo Perry set the front elevation of the NordicTrak Pro to eight degrees and slid the videotape of Vermont scenery Martin had given him for his thirty-eighth birthday into the VCR. But no New Age Indian flutes today. Selecting his *Best of the Supremes* CD, he turned up the volume, began the hour-long acceleration of his workout, and grinned. Diana Ross had not completed the impassioned story of her decision to avoid conceiving a "Love Child" when Martin St. John, dramatically patient beneath a film of whole wheat flour, approached from the kitchen.

"I know you've been upset," Martin began, "but can this sort of adolescent regression really help?"

Martin St. John's whole wheat Parker House rolls were the flagship of St. John Catering, in demand by the thousands every weekend for the endless buffets, cocktail trays, and dinner-party fund-raisers of San Diego's upscale liberal community. Special wiring had been required for the huge vertical freezer in the spare bedroom where the partially baked delicacies were stored on wire racks. A characteristic odor of bakery yeast invariably caused passers-by in the apartment's hall to salivate, and completely defeated the hi-tech decorating scheme Rombo and Martin had chosen five years ago. Before the rolls caught on. When Martin was still carving radish roses for vegetable trays and Rombo was job hunting between twice-daily AA meetings. The cozy smell wafted from the kitchen now.

"Motown has been demonstrated to help eliminate free radicals from the bloodstream," Rombo lectured as footage of Green County, Vermont, under snow crossed the television screen. "And if I listen to one more Celtic harp and flute combo over running water, I'm going to shave my head and start wearing an orange sarong."

"The sarong has possibilities." Martin beamed, his brown eyes fudge-dark in a floury face. "But this music reminds me of the Nixon administration. Bad karma. The rolls won't rise. And you're still a wreck. The woman died two days ago, Rom. You didn't even know her, really. You've got to let go of it."

A film of sweat on his forearms reassured Rombo of his cardiovascular system's ongoing efficiency. "Let's go check on Leonor after we deliver the rolls, before the memorial service. Okay? Maybe take her a rawhide bone or something."

Leonor was the very pregnant golden retriever who would soon present Rombo and Martin with a puppy already named Watson in honor of their collection of Sherlockiana. Rombo had given Martin a traditional Holmesian deerstalker cap to celebrate the news of Leonor's successful weekend idyll with a champion retriever stud named Gothard's Brendan, brought to San Diego from Palm Springs for the occasion in a vintage Mercedes. Leonor's owner, a rotund freelance window dresser, had bartered the expected puppy for a three-year supply of whole wheat rolls. And the best part, Rombo thought, was that Watson would have a yard. A real yard, with a view.

"Sure," Martin agreed, abandoning hope of an end to the music. "Probably be good for you. Take your mind off things, huh?"

Rombo watched Martin pad, barefooted, back into the kitchen, and thought about the house as he exercised. Between his salary and Martin's burgeoning business they'd been able to save enough for a sizable down payment on a house in North Park with a canyon view. The loan had included funds for renovation of the kitchen, to be used by Martin for his money-making little rolls. There would be no more chrome furniture with black basketball-rubber upholstery. They'd even picked out a couch at Ethan Allen, incurring from friends a shower of exquisitely awful grapevine wreaths and refrigerator magnets featuring geese in bow ties pushing wheelbarrows. The house would be ready in less than a month.

Increasing the tension on the ski flywheel, Rombo breathed evenly and wondered why he wasn't dead. More than a decade of booze, poppers every night in Chicago bars, fucking around, trying to be the hot'n'hung young top everybody'd get down on their knees for. The one everybody'd want when some bartender in tit-clips and a leather jock under unbuttoned Levi's yelled "Last call, Mary!" through the smoke. It hadn't occurred to Rombo to ask himself what *he* wanted. Not until it was almost too late and he was working out of Manpower every other day, cleaning warehouses and portable toilets to pay for a room and watery shots of bar whiskey at 6:30 in the morning.

One of the derelicts in the phlegmy hotel where Rombo slept had died on the lobby's curling linoleum floor. Nobody cared. Rombo thought he'd probably stepped over the body himself that night, maybe. And then the ratlike little man in his ashtray of a cage where you paid for your room told Rombo the pile of stinking rags on the floor had once been a teacher. A high school math teacher, according to the sister whose name and phone number the cops found in the guy's room. In the acidic haze of his own breath Rombo saw the future, panicked, and did the one thing for which his father would have spit in his face. At thirty, he called his mother.

A social worker in Gary, Indiana, she drove over to Chicago, picked him up, and dumped him at the best detox program she could pay for.

"Your father's love and approval are never going to happen," she told him at the admitting desk. "You've always had mine, for what it's worth. But the important thing is to earn your own. Go for it!"

He'd slipped a couple of times after that, but picked himself up and climbed back on. When his AA sponsor in Gary offered him the chance to drive a U-HAUL truck full of furniture to San Diego for a niece in the navy, Rombo grabbed it. And loved San Diego. The airy, sunlit city seemed to promise a new life. Clean and sober. And free. Within the year Rombo had moved. Within another year he'd met Martin St. John, at whose good-natured devotion Rombo marveled. It was the life he'd always wanted. Calm. Orderly.

And an even greater miracle was that neither of them had AIDS. Tested twice in two years, they'd both been negative. Rombo hadn't been able to think about that, about how he'd been spared that and the other deaths he'd courted while dancing with his father's hatred. Now he couldn't think about anything else. The image of a frail woman hanging by the neck from a bedsheet kept asking questions he knew it was time to answer.

By 11:00 Martin had delivered the last of the rolls to a beachfront restaurant where a hundred and fifty people would gather at dusk to raise funds for a women's shelter.

"Ready to visit mama dog?" he asked Rombo. "Or ready to tell me what it is about this woman's suicide that's got you reciting Hamlet's soliloquy in the shower?"

"I didn't know you heard." Rombo cringed. "And I don't know why this thing's hit a nerve. It just rips it, you know? We have everything, the best life there is, and that pitiful, *little* woman had nothing. Absolutely nothing. Some walking pustule with his brain in his dong guts her kid, and she's gone.

They're both just gone. It's over. And that's not right, Martin. It's too unfair."

Twenty minutes later they were sitting on Maxwell Grasic's enclosed rear deck, watching a golden retriever shred the *L.A. Times* in a wooden box with six-inch-high slats over its entry. The slats and box had been sanded smooth.

"She's gonna blow tonight. I just know it," their friend announced the obvious, pacing. "I've called the vet three times today already. She told me to stop calling until something happens. I've got everything ready—towels, weak tea with sugar, sterilized scissors, a Brahms tape so they'll feel relaxed. Kevin and Barry sent flowers already—yellow roses and baby's breath in a Wedgewood dog dish. The suspense is killing me."

When the dog rested briefly from nesting, Rombo sat beside her on the gray tweed outdoor carpeting and stroked her swollen sides. Tiny movements were palpable beneath the long fur. Little kicks and nudges, and something that felt like hiccups. Leonor panted and resumed her work in the box.

"I really feel that I haven't done enough, Martin," he said when Max went inside to answer the phone. "I've spent so much time hauling myself out of the sewer that I've forgotten to live in the world. This wad of worm snot rapes little girls and all I care about is us and our house and our dog and our life. I want to *do* something. Something to help."

"Got any ideas?" Martin smiled.

"Yeah." Rombo smiled back. "I do."

Chapter 21

By 8:00 Sunday morning John D. Litten had completed the careful packing necessary for his camera equipment, TV, VCR, and sound system. Those things and his clothes would fit in the car, registered to Craig Alan Sanford, a boy who had died in a Florida water-skiing accident when he was eight. Everything else would be left behind.

Outside his ninth-story window sailboats rode the gray-blue swells of the bay beneath overcast skies as tourists queued up for cruises. The sun struggling through a weak haze both warmed him and hurt his eyes. He'd been up most of the night. And he felt strange, as though parts of him were missing. One minute the back of his head, then his left shoulder, then the muscle and connective tissue inside his right hand. His right hand was hollow. And then it was just a hand again, and his dick was gone. But when he touched it, it was there and his nasal passages seemed to evaporate in his skull. A creepy parade of empty spaces probably caused, he judged, by the two lines of coke he'd blown last night. The coke and what had happened. The way he'd felt killing that woman, even though he'd meant to do the other one. Like glass. He'd felt like a man made of frozen glass. Like a light you'd see through a telescope, blazing with cold. His dick had stayed hard all night.

Everything was different now, that was for sure. Everything changed. Like finding out a secret that's been there all along, waiting. Out of habit John Litten had prepared to leave quickly. Just leave town before there was the slightest chance of getting caught. The old, regular part of him said that was the thing to do. But something else said to wait before starting on the trip that would take him away from San Diego, away from the amazing thing he'd learned. That to become Superman, all he had to do was kill.

Dressed in jeans and a black T-shirt adorned with a printed portrait of somebody named Wittgenstein, he looked like a student at any university in the country. Nobody would remember seeing some college student walking around in downtown San Diego. And even if they did, so what? Nobody was looking for him. They didn't know what to look for. They were too stupid. Locking his apartment door carefully behind him, John D. Litten bounded down eight flights of stairs and headed into the street.

In the haze things looked strange, shimmery. Like the city, knowing who he was, had polished itself for him. Beneath his feet a brick sidewalk, its basketweave mortared lines clean and new, led toward a future John Litten could scarcely imagine. A future in which he alone knew the secret of transformation. A future in which he would play with them, all the stupid ones who knew nothing, and then kill them. He didn't know why he hadn't seen it before. It had been there, all along.

In an orange, recessed doorway something moved on the ground. Litten looked at it and for several seconds could not identify it. Something long and foul-smelling, stirring beneath damp slabs of cardboard torn from a large box. One of the slabs had the name of a San Francisco importer printed on it. And the thing under it was a man. Litten looked at the sign over the orange doorway—DICK'S LAST RESORT. It was just a darkened restaurant with a wino sleeping in its doorway. Across the street a Cost Plus dumpster revealed the source of the cardboard slab. Litten wondered why it had taken him so long to piece together the ordinary scene. And then he knew why. He'd crossed over, finally, become something completely different from the creature on the ground. So different that at first he hadn't recognized it as human. That was because he was superhuman now. A superhuman walking, almost invisibly, on the misty streets of a sleeping city. It was like something he'd read in a comic book, years ago.

On Island Avenue he crossed to an old brick hotel refurbished in a downtown development project. The Horton Grand, a plaque told him, had been built in 1886. The date meant nothing. Why would anyone care when an old building was built? It was strange. Two men in white shirts and black pants lounged against the hotel's gleaming facade. They would park cars for tips, Litten remembered.

"Pretty good breakfast," one of them mentioned. "Pricey, but good."

"Yeah?" Litten answered. Why had the man told him that? Gradually it made sense. They thought he was a tourist looking for someplace to eat breakfast. In his college-boy clothes he looked their age. The man was operating on assumptions to which John Litten would have to accommodate. He went inside, feeling like a puppet. It would be okay to eat, he guessed. Probably a good idea. But things were so strange. Why would Superman have to do what a parking attendant said?

The hotel lobby had a green tile floor and a bunch of white furniture made out of sticks. And big white birdcages lined with the edges of computer paper. John Litten had torn these edges off miles of paper in the navy. Their presence was familiar and comfortable, but he would never have thought of using them for anything. Why hadn't he thought of birdcage lining? Because there were no birds around in the navy, he decided. If there had been birds he would have thought of it. Anybody as smart as he was would have thought of it. Except nobody was as smart as he was. Not anymore.

"Breakfast, sir?" a tired-looking woman in a ruffled blouse asked. Her smile seemed to go right through his face and stick somewhere behind his head. She couldn't see what he was, couldn't really see him at all. That was good.

The hotel's restaurant was dimly lit and almost empty as he followed the woman to a wooden booth with some kind of rough, flowered pad to sit on. The same material padded the back of the booth, where your head hit. Litten looked at the fabric, the tens of thousands of little sewing stitches that made flowers and leaves, vines and birds in different colors. It looked hard to do, complicated. Why would anybody bother? Something about the fabric irritated John Litten, but he didn't know what.

A man and woman seated at a round table nearby both ordered coffee with smoked salmon and onion omelettes. Nervous, Litten gave an identical order even though he hated coffee. What was wrong with him? Why didn't he feel good, now that he'd found the secret?

Some kind of music drifted from the restaurant's speakers.

"Mozart would have enjoyed this place," the man at the table told his companion. "It's so Baroque."

"I think Salieri would have liked it better." she answered, and they both laughed.

John Litten stared into his omelette, which smelled like fish. Not spoiled fish like Gramma got sometimes from a grocery in Estherville that gave it away on Saturday nights because they were closed on Sunday. But still fish. He couldn't understand why the man and woman were laughing. What were they talking about? He felt himself frowning at them, but they didn't see. They didn't see *him*. They didn't know he was there.

John Litten wondered if he *was* there. Something wrong. Lots of things he didn't understand, couldn't name. Were the people talking about music? How could you talk about music? Why couldn't he understand what they were saying, if he was Superman? Superman would understand everything, probably even make designs with a million little sewing stitches if he wanted to. But John Litten didn't even know what to call it once it was made.

An impossible realization began to form like a half-circle cloud between his ears. An awareness of difference that had always been there, ever since he could remember. A difference nobody could see, that was now complete. He wasn't like the people at the table, not at all. He couldn't understand them and they couldn't see him. He wasn't like anybody. He'd learned how to become frozen glass, and he was alone. He would always be alone.

Leaving a twenty-dollar bill on the table he rose and swiftly left the hotel. In the vacant Cost Plus parking lot he vomited behind the dumpster. Sour, fishy coffee spewing from his throat. It felt good to get rid of it. Only stupid people drank coffee, he realized. People, period. He was no longer one of them, if he ever had been.

A somber rage, like a pillar of white granite, filled him as he straightened his torso in the shadows behind the dumpster. He hated them, that was all. And he could kill them, and become glass. A painful erection throbbed behind the button fly of his denim pants. Pulling out his cock he gasped as he ejaculated to a memory of blood, and death. It was so easy. And so good. He would never need anything else.

Chapter 22

By 10:30 Bo was toying with a cup of coffee on the patio from which Eva Broussard studied a particularly inept surfer in an overlarge wetsuit who tumbled off his board with each wave.

"I'm sure nobody was following me," Bo explained, "but I drove way inland and came down through Encinitas, just in case. Sharp turns, hiding in parking lots, backtracking. Nobody could have stayed with me. I had to talk to you."

The older woman kneaded her temples with the fingertips of both hands. "Yes," she nodded, turning from the sea after Bo explained the decision she had made. The alarming risk she would take in court tomorrow. "It's a dangerous but courageous step. If you're really ready, I'm sure it's the right one for you. And the situation has become even more complex. Do you believe there is any danger to Hannah from the man who killed Cynthia Ganage? Do you think there is really any connection at all between these two killings?"

Eva Broussard seemed distant, lost in thought. Bo couldn't read the woman's mental state at all.

"It may be that Ganage was killed by someone unconnected to this case," Bo began. "We don't know anything about Ganage. She was from L.A. The police are checking her contacts there. Maybe she had an enemy, a rejected boyfriend, somebody who wanted her dead and just used the bloody message on her wall to mislead the investigation. But . . ."

"I don't think so," Eva Broussard said, her voice barely audible, "and neither do you." Bo leaned forward in a canvas deck chair, curious. Broussard seemed anxious to complete a troubling train of thought. "There are aspects of this murder that lead me to a different conclusion. A very different conclusion. But first I must hear all that you know." The graceful Iroquois woman pulled a matching chair close to Bo's and sat. Even though the dark eyes were unfocused, Bo felt the woman's concentration like a palpable force. Eva Broussard was taking the murder of Cynthia Ganage very seriously.

"At the day-care center where Samantha stayed while Bonnie worked part-time," Bo said quietly, "I've discovered a sort of cave dug in the wall of the canyon behind the property, carefully shored with two by fours. A cave painted pink and decorated with Christmas tree lights. There's a man suffering from schizophrenia who lives in the canyon. He showed me the cave. He knew that the perp called himself Goody. I think Samantha's killer was connected to the day-care center in some way. I think he went there and took children to this place down in the canyon, and . . . did things to them. There was a battery pack in the cave—"

"A battery pack?" The raven-black eyes widened.

"Yeah. He used it to power the lights and a tape recorder. Children's music . . ."

"And perhaps a video camera as well," Eva Broussard breathed. "Have you told the police?"

Bo glanced through the picture window of the studio apartment across the patio. Hannah Franer lay on the floor playing with a huge assortment of Legos. Now and then she flipped her long hair from her face in a gesture oddly adolescent, as if an older personality were already framing itself in the childlike visage. Flute music drifted from stereo speakers through two screened windows flanking the picture window.

"Only this morning," Bo admitted. "Dar Reinert called. I'd asked him to check out the registration for the center. He told me the house is rented in the name of somebody who died in Texas eighteen years ago. A phony name, in other words. The property owner lives in Oregon, pays a management service to rent and maintain the house. The management service is actually a bankrupt realtor named Brock Mulvihill who runs his business out of his garage up in San Marcos. Mulvihill says he never saw the guy who rented the Kramer Street property; it was all done over the phone and through the mail. He says the guy's checks were good, and that he paid for a new chain-link fence around the backyard so his wife could run a playschool on the property. Mulvihill drove by the house once, three months ago on a weekend, found it well kept up, and left. No questions. The market's rotten. He was thrilled to have a responsible, solvent tenant. The center isn't licensed by the county. A Hispanic woman who ran the place has vanished, although I've got a co-worker who speaks Spanish checking this morning to see if the woman's come back. It's obvious that the perp set the whole thing up to have access to children, but there's no way to learn more until tomorrow when parents start showing up to drop off kids. I told Reinert about the cave, and about Zolar, the man who took me to it. Reinert's been out there already. Zolar's vanished, but the cave's still there. The police are checking it out now, but they don't expect to find much. Reinert, of course, now thinks Zolar is our perp. Meanwhile the media are 'cautiously exploring' the possibility of a Satanic takeover of San Diego. Ganage was their pet."

Eva Broussard sighed and remained silent for some time.

"I trust your judgment on Zolar," she said. "And even if I didn't, the elaborate preparations you describe—the construction and shoring of the cave, the paint and lights—it's all too calculated and consistent for an individual with untreated schizophrenia. No, from what you've told me, I feel safe in predicting that our killer is scarcely delusional. But more significantly, I think he's an isolate. To do what he does successfully, he can have no real contact with other people. His entire existence is a sequence of performances designed to disguise what he is inside."

"A child-molester?" Bo filled in. "That's what he is inside. I've had a lot of contact with child-molesters. This guy's not your typical—"

"No," Eva Broussard answered, "he isn't typical and that's not what he's hiding. He's hiding the fact that inside, he's nothing."

"Huh?"

"It will be almost impossible for you to comprehend, Bo," Broussard went on, the pace of her speech accelerating slightly. "You are . . . how can I say this? . . . uniquely equipped to understand the experiences of the living—joy and passion, despair and hopelessness. You *are* the masks of drama—comedy and tragedy. But this man is nowhere in that world your brain magnifies. This man is devoid of all emotional capability with the possible exceptions of anger and fear, which are in him one thing. His experience is not accessible to most people, but least of all to you. Don't even try."

Bo made a stab at digesting Eva Broussard's words, and then merely filed them for later. "If you're saying he has a mental disorder, like command voices in schizophrenia or something, that accounts for his behavior, it's like nothing I've ever seen."

"He has none of the major psychiatric disorders, least of all schizophrenia, as I've said," Broussard went on. "If anything, he'd be diagnosed with one of the personality disorders—borderline, narcissistic, one of those. But he's quite sane." She appeared to study a patch of succulent ground cover spilling over the edge of the patio. "Terms like 'personality disorder' are just categories for the inexplicable. Categories that define the ways in which some people simply cannot feel normal concern and interaction with others. But this man is plagued less by disorder than by an absence of personality altogether. He feeds on power, nothing else. His power to manipulate reality. Sexual gratification with children is an almost pure exercise of power. But now he may have found something better . . ."

Bo inhaled slowly, Eva Broussard's train of thought finding completion in her own mind. "Cold-blooded murder," she exhaled. "He's found a source of power in killing." The sun-warmed beach seemed suddenly wintry. "And just as he's certainly molested more than one child, he'll kill more than once as well."

"It's quite possible that what we have here," Broussard completed her assessment carefully, "is the birth of a serial killer."

Overhead a gull dipped and squawked, wheeling out over the sea as if to avoid the grim pronouncement hanging in the air. Bo closed her eyes and shivered.

Inside, Hannah continued to work on an elaborate enclosure made of Legos. In the space of silence as the taped music stopped and reversed, Bo heard the child's voice through the screened windows, humming tunelessly. As Hannah hummed, her lips moved. "There," she pronounced, snapping Lego to Lego. "And there."

"She's talking," Bo whispered.

"Not exactly." Broussard smiled. "She isn't aware that she's forming words as she hums. Her mind is occupied with play. But eventually she'll hear herself, and if no attention is brought to the fact that she's speaking, if it's treated as perfectly normal and unremarkable, I think she'll abandon her mutism. And then even more care must be exercised as she begins to verbalize her pain and loss. Hannah will need professional care for some time."

Bo smiled. "And love, Eva. Look what your love has done for her already."

The Indian woman's face was pensive. "Like many Americans you tend to romanticize everything, Bo. This wasn't included in my plans. After surgery for a breast cancer that may or may not have been caught in time, I determined to devote the remainder of my life to researching a particular human experience. I was content with my decision, excited about the project. Then Samantha Franer was killed, her mother a suicide, Paul in jail. These people weren't especially close to me, Bo. I'm essentially an intellectual, not what you Americans would call a people person. I would have avoided this love if there had been any way to do so, but there wasn't." She looked curiously into Bo's eyes. "I think most of us will avoid the responsibilities of love in favor of less troubling attachments, don't you?" A twinkle visible in the dark eyes was a dead giveaway.

"I understand Dr. LaMarche stayed with you and Hannah last night after Ganage's murder." Bo accepted the challenge. "Can it be that he mentioned his harebrained intentions regarding me?"

Eva Broussard's smile became a grin. "He brought Hannah the Legos but said little about you," she answered, "although his discomfiture at your not being alone last night was rather too obvious. The male ego is perhaps the most fragile construct on the planet, you know. And hopelessly transparent."

"Precisely why I don't want—"

"You owe me no explanation, Bo. That debt is to yourself, no one else. I assume you're clear on your reasons for spurning his advances?"

"The problem is, he doesn't *make* advances." Bo sighed. "He's like something out of *Godey's Ladies Book*—the perfect gentleman. Besides, I like him. I'd rather keep that. And this case is a bit distracting . . ."

"Of course," Eva Broussard agreed, rising. "So what is the next move?"

Bo stretched and checked her watch. "I'm meeting my co-worker, Estrella Benedict, at the day-care center in forty-five minutes. If the woman who runs the place has returned, Estrella can interview her in Spanish. Then we're going to the memorial service for Samantha and Bonnie. Reinert thinks there's an off chance our killer will attend, if it's not Zolar. Reinert's got cops scouring San Diego for him, too. I hate it that I involved him in this."

"Your Zolar is unmedicated and miserable," Broussard noted crisply. "If he's found and gets help, it may be his salvation."

"Spoken like a true shrink." Bo laughed. "It's clear that you've never been tied down and shot full of Haldol. But maybe you're right. And Eva . . . ?" Bo couldn't resist asking. "You seem to know quite a bit about the killer, the way his mind works. But I've checked out your credentials. All your work has involved social interaction, religious mysticism, stuff like that. Nothing published on pederasts or serial killers. How do you know so much?"

"One becomes, in a sense, what one researches," Broussard answered. "A long time ago I chose to avoid research into the dark side of human behavior. I chose to avoid it precisely because it fascinates me. Too dangerous. For one who lives by choice outside the usual interpersonal frameworks of marriage and family, intense research in psychopathology can create a distorted view of the human condition. Surely you've seen that among some of your co-workers who've come to view the world as nothing but a cesspool. Nonetheless, I keep up on others' work. Sometimes it's impossible to understand the up side without some comprehension of the depths."

"Oh," Bo replied. It was the answer she had expected. Sort of.

Forty minutes later she nosed her ratty old BMW into the curb behind Estrella Benedict's immaculate silver coupé. Estrella herself paced in the driveway of the Kramer Day Care Center, her high heels popping like BB shots. Estrella pacing was not a good sign.

"What's happened?" Bo asked, hurrying from her car to the driveway. "Was she here? Was the woman here?"

"Sí," Estrella answered, singing the monosyllable in two notes. Her cheeks twitched with something like anger. "She was here."

"So? What happened? Where is she?"

Estrella curled her lips inward over her teeth and looked at the sky. Bo could see white oleanders reflected in her friend's sunglasses. "She's gone," Estrella announced.

"Gone? You mean you talked to her and then just let her walk away? She's our only witness. She's the only person who can identify this pervert. I asked you to try talking with her, in Spanish. I didn't really think she'd be here, but—"

"She didn't think I'd be here, either," Estrella went on. "And I wish I wasn't. Bo, I hate it when you get me involved in these crazy schemes of yours. Why can't you just do your job like everybody else and then go home? You always have to go too far, know too much. You get too involved."

Estrella appeared to be on the verge of tears.

"Es, tell me what happened," Bo said, leading her co-worker to lean on the BMW. "What's going on?"

Estrella smoothed a black linen skirt obviously selected for the memorial service they were about to attend, and crossed her arms over a white silk blouse pinstriped also in black. "I told her I just got a job as a secretary to a Latino lawyer, and needed day care right away for my two little girls. I said the lawyer wanted me to start next week and wouldn't wait. I said I was desperate. And you know what she told me? You know what this illiterate peasant woman from some village in Chihuahua told me?"

"What?" Bo asked. Estrella had bowed her head, Bo realized, to avoid smearing her eye makeup with tears.

"She told me to take my babies back to wherever I came

from, to get out of the U.S. no matter how bad things were at home. She told me the devil had bought her soul here for a thousand dollars a month. That's what he paid her, Bo, to run this place and look the other way. She said he let her live here with her two kids for free, and paid her a thousand a month, cash. And sometimes he'd come by at noon and take one of the children, usually a girl but not always, for walks in the canyon. She thought it was strange, but Bo, she didn't know until Samantha's death what he was doing to the kids. She said they'd act funny, sometimes vomit later, at snack time. But no evidence of injury. He was probably . . ."

"Oh, God," Bo breathed through her nose to fight the familiar nausea, "how can something like that just walk around?"

Over Estrella's shoulder the gray house seemed to be watching from behind its white bars.

"So where is she now?" Bo went on. "Why did you let her go?"

"She told me she took her kids to Tijuana yesterday and left them overnight in an orphanage with some nuns. Then she just walked around, tried to think what to do. She's been supporting about fifteen family members back in her village with that money, Bo. Their situation is desperate. She decided to leave her children in T.J. for a week, come back and try to get more money out of the creep before taking off for home."

"My god. You mean even after she knew . . . ?"

Estrella squared her shoulders and looked at Bo over the top of her sunglasses. "Yes," she replied. "And I have to tell you that *I* advised her to leave before you got here, to get over that border and home with her kids before she wound up in jail. I told her who I really am and I told her what would happen when the police finally put this picture together. She's gone, Bo. She's safe."

"Well, well," Bo said. "The voice of doom who thinks *I'm* crazy even when I'm not has just joined the ranks. And for what it's worth, you did the right thing. The woman could have lost her kids, spent years in a California prison as an accessory to crimes she didn't know were being committed. More innocent lives ruined pointlessly. I would have done the same thing, Es."

"I know," Estrella grimaced, kicking the tire of Bo's car. "That's what's so upsetting."

Chapter 23

St. Theresa's Church, a 1950s A-frame featuring a rose window Bo suspected had been pieced from old wine bottles, given the preponderance of green, was barely visible behind four TV sound trucks lining the curb. One of the trucks bore an L.A. logo. The story was, unfortunately, gaining momentum. On the residential sidewalk across the street from the church, twenty people dressed in black held aloft hand-lettered posters. "Satan Is Loosed out of His Prison," one poster announced. "And Whosoever Is Not Found Written in the Book of Life Will Be Cast into the Lake of Fire," another picked up the refrain. From the looks on the demonstrators' faces, Bo would have bet they'd *invest* in a lake of fire if they could just throw into it everybody who didn't agree with their view of the world. She was sure she'd be among the first to be flung.

"Comforting, aren't they?" she muttered to Estrella after finding her co-worker in the milling crowd outside the church. More than half of those milling had that white-sock aura Bo associated with cops.

"Revelation," the familiar voice of Madge Aldenhoven mentioned behind them. "Written by the Apostle John while in exile on Patmos."

"There's every reason to believe the book of Revelation was

actually written by an ancestor of *mine*." Bo smiled at her supervisor. "It's so nice to see you, Madge. But what a sad occasion."

"Madre de dios." Estrella said under her breath.

"Don't forget that you're on probation, Bo," Madge murmured, narrowing her eyes. "I can tell from your attitude that you're up to something. I have to stress that I think you'd be more comfortable in another line of work. Surely you agree."

Bo saw Dar Reinert beckoning from the church steps.

"I had almost come to that conclusion on my own, but now I don't think so." Bo slid out of the conversation. "We'll know tomorrow. Right now I hope you'll excuse me while I chat with Detective Reinert."

"What did she mean by 'we'll know tomorrow'?" Madge asked Estrella.

"I have no idea," Estrella answered, shaking her head.

Dar Reinert, commandeering the church steps by sheer bulk, could not have looked more obviously official if he'd been in uniform. "You're gonna like hearing this," he grumbled into Bo's ear. "We found your nut-case Zolar last night, sleeping in a tree in Balboa Park. And here's the weird part. When we got him out of County Psychiatric and took him down to the canyon this morning, just to see if he'd say anything, this seventy-year-old retired schoolteacher who looks like she pumps iron comes crashing through the shrubbery. Says she has a house on the other side, hikes in the canyon a lot. Says she knew this psycho was there, that she gave him vitamins or something."

Bo swallowed an erupting lecture on the meaningless term "psycho" and remembered Zolar's cache of wholesome supplies. So that's where he got them. But the schoolteacher had bombed with the premoistened towelettes. They wouldn't have helped much anyway.

"Here's the part you're gonna love," Reinert went on as a small pipe organ began the Guardian Angels' Song from

Humperdinck's *Hansel and Gretel*. "This schoolteacher says your nut was in her backyard sleeping on a picnic table Tuesday afternoon from 1:30 to about 6:00. Bonnie Franer said she picked up Samantha from the day-care center at about 5:15. Your guy's got an alibi for the whole afternoon the day of the rape."

Bo couldn't tell if the news or the sentimental music were responsible for the tears in her eyes. Probably both, she decided. There had been a guardian angel for Zolar. She made a mental note to take the old schoolteacher a fifth of good Irish whiskey.

"Bradley, I didn't know you were gonna *cry* for chrissakes," Reinert spluttered. He seemed amazed when the handkerchief he pulled from the breast pocket of his jacket turned out to be a small fan of paisley stapled to a piece of cardboard. Grimacing, he wadded the object into a ball and dropped it behind one of the Hollywood junipers bending over St. Theresa's steps.

People were filing in to take seats in the little church as Bo became aware of something covered in fawn-colored cashmere, nudging her side. It was an arm, attached to the shoulder of Dr. Andrew LaMarche.

"May I?" he offered in a calm baritone.

Behind him Estrella and Madge Aldenhoven formed a smiling wall.

Bo nodded demurely, placed her left hand through the doctor's arm, and wished she were in Dixie, wherever that was. At the holy water font inside the door she dipped her fingers and touched her forehead out of childhood programming before recalling that she hadn't been attached to Roman Catholicism in any meaningful way since her first bra. The holy water ran over her left eyebrow and into her eye. Never fond of funerals, Bo measured the possibility that this might be the worst yet. In less than a minute the merely possible became hard fact.

In a quiet frenzy of courtesy LaMarche stood aside as Madge

and then Estrella entered a pew followed by Bo and finally the elegant doctor. Estrella quickly dropped to the kneeler, pulling Bo with her as if for comfort.

"Don't freak," Estrella whispered into clasped hands, "but isn't that the ACLU guy sitting in front of LaMarche?"

"Oh, God," Bo breathed. A heartfelt prayer. The unkempt mop of sandy curls in the next pew belonged to Solon Gentzler. It was going to be the funeral from hell.

"In the name of the Father and the Son and the Holy Ghost," Father Frank Goodman pronounced as everyone settled into blond and oddly Scandinavian pews. Sunlight filtering through the predominantly green rose window created an aquarium-like atmosphere. The effect was not diminished by a robed figure of Christ ascendant above the altar. In sparkling green light, the statue seemed to be drifting upward from the depths of a pale sea. Behind her Bo heard Dar Reinert's gruff whisper.

"Keep your eyes open, Bradley. See if anything looks fishy to you."

Only an invitation from Frank Goodman to join in singing "We Shall Overcome" saved Bo from an inappropriate grin tormenting the corners of her mouth. Too much watery imagery. And now the anthem of the civil rights movement? What next?

Solon Gentzler's enthusiastic and off-key rendering of the familiar song, audible above everyone else, only made matters worse. Bo was glad to cover her face with her right hand as Frank Goodman began his homily, which had to do with overcoming an evil that had destroyed a little girl and her mother. When she was certain of her composure, Bo placed her hand properly in her lap and scanned the assemblage. Lots of cops. Some of the staff from St. Mary's surgical floor. Lots of media types. A number of nuns.

Bo scanned the nuns closely for any who might not be what they seemed. If Samantha's killer were stupid enough to attend the service, an old-fashioned religious habit might make an interesting disguise. Of the twenty-seven nuns in the church, representing Benedictine, Carmelite, and Sacred Heart orders, not one could conceivably have been a man.

Frank Goodman was doing something with two roses—one creamy white, the other a tiny pink bud. He was tying the roses together with a broad silver ribbon. Estrella dabbed at running mascara with a handkerchief; LaMarche looked waxen. Bo didn't want to hear the priest's words. Didn't want to think about the lost mother and child the flowers were meant to represent.

"Humph," Dar Reinert snorted behind her.

Turning to see what had caused the detective's reaction, Bo noticed two men taking seats at the rear of the church. One was short, well muscled, and had obviously suffered a broken and badly set nose in the past. His eyes behind black wire-frame glasses were somber. His companion was taller, blond, and wore a Hollywood-style silk Armani jacket with more grace than most talk show hosts. On the jacket's lapel was a tiny gold and enamel rainbow flag.

"You know those guys?" Reinert whispered over the back of Bo's pew.

"No," she answered, turning to face the detective. "Neither one of them's from CPS. And I haven't seen them at St. Mary's, either."

"Shh," Madge admonished as everyone dropped to the kneelers while Frank Goodman led them in prayer.

Bo grabbed a program from St. Theresa's morning services out of the hymnal rack on the pew behind Solon Gentzler and carefully read announcements for a youth group car wash, a marriage encounter group for seniors, and the sung rosary group's need for an alto and a bass. As an MTV video, she mused, the sung rosary might be an unexpected hit. Anything was better than attending to Frank Goodman's words, which were about a child Bo had seen in the transitional moments just after death. Between the medical ritual and those that would follow—the closing of the eyes, the covering of the face. Rituals incongruous and horrible when performed for a tiny child.

In the pocket of her long khaki skirt Bo felt the grieving beads Hannah had given her, and allowed herself to remember her own sister. Her own hopelessness in the face of suicide. Hannah would have to face that, too, when she came to terms with her mother's death. A difficult reality to face. Pulling the strip of beads from her pocket she held them in clasped hands as Frank Goodman finished an appeal for the repose of both daughter and mother. In the front row the elderly Father Karolak succumbed to a sudden fit of coughing clearly designed to obscure Frank Goodman's words. Goodman could, Bo pondered, find himself in deep trouble for that prayer, assuming anybody heard it over Father Karolak's staged hacking. Deep trouble for including a suicide in his kindly intentions. The Roman Catholic church was not renowned for its sympathetic understanding of clinical depression's worst-case scenario. It was apparent that Father Frank Goodman didn't care.

"The man has courage," Andrew LaMarche noted quietly as they stood. "And so do you, Bo. I'm sorry that I questioned your judgment. Your decision regarding Hannah was the right one." He glanced at Madge Aldenhoven, ramrod straight in a navy linen suit beside Estrella. "I admire what you've done."

Frank Goodman, accompanied by pipe organ, was singing Gounod's Ave Maria in his fine, almost Irish, tenor. Bo fought down a resurgence of the confusion Andrew LaMarche seemed determined to promote. "Thanks, Andy," she whispered, and stuffed the grieving beads back into her pocket. When he took her hand briefly she felt ridiculous and comfortable simultaneously, but didn't pull away. Not until Solon Gentzler, in unfamiliar territory and checking the crowd for clues as to what to do next, turned to glance over his shoulder. His big smile faded to a flush of chagrin when he saw LaMarche leaning in what could only be described as a husbandly attitude against

Bo. Bo jerked her right hand from the pediatrician's left one and looked at the church's beamed ceiling. It provided, as she had known it would, no exit.

"Oh, boy . . ." Estrella pronounced through a clenched smile.

"Thank you all for coming," Frank Goodman concluded as the organist began to play an obscure but upbeat medieval gavotte. Rivulets of sweat gathered momentum and dribbled down her back as Bo stood gratefully to leave. The memorial service had possessed, she decided, all the better-known qualities of the Spanish Inquisition.

Once outside she made a dash for the shade of a well-leafed liquid amber tree at the edge of St. Theresa's property, ducked behind its trunk, and lit a cigarette. Madge Aldenhoven materialized within minutes.

"I hope you're prepared for tomorrow's hearing," the supervisor reminded her. "You will represent the department and you will say that in your professional opinion Paul Massieu is the person responsible for Samantha's death. You will recommend, on behalf of the Department of Social Services, that he be held over for prosecution. You will note in your testimony that he represents a threat not only to Samantha's kidnapped sister, but to all children. I've prepared a statement outlining the department's position on this case. All you have to do is read it."

Bo exhaled smoke at the envelope Madge was handing her, and stared at one of the tree's star-shaped leaves. "And if I don't?" she asked.

"This is a directive from the department," Aldenhoven answered as if the words were a creed. "Failure to represent an official position is grounds for immediate dismissal."

"Ah." Bo nodded, rolling the envelope into a tube and looking through it at the leaf. "I assume you have a copy of this statement against which to match my testimony."

"Yes. But of course it doesn't need to be word-for-word."

"Refreshing," Bo told the leaf. "So refreshing."

"I'll see you tomorrow, Bo." Madge smiled without authenticity, and left.

Bo stubbed out the cigarette and dropped the butt in her best purse, which would now reek of rancid filter. She never left cigarettes lying around, and also never remembered to retrieve the butts from purses and pockets. It seemed a minor problem compared to those lining up behind tomorrow's showdown. But she'd made her decision. Gentzler had it choreographed down to the last nuance. All she had to do was follow through.

"Are you Bo Bradley?" the man with the broken nose inquired, making his way across St. Theresa's robust lawn.

"Yes," Bo answered. "Why?" His attitude was businesslike, but tinged with a sort of planned determination.

"I'm Rombo Perry," he explained. "I was the social worker for Mrs. Franer. I was there when she . . . when she died."

"It was nice of you to come," Bo said, puzzled. Rombo Perry's handsome, unusual face seemed haggard. The look was inconsistent with the man's remarkable fitness. She would not have been surprised if he'd attempted to sell her a health club membership.

"I've been a little upset since it happened . . ." he explained.

"A little?" his companion in the Armani jacket interrupted, approaching from the sidewalk with obvious concern for possible damage to the grass. "It's been a dark night of the soul, let me tell you. I'm Martin St. John, by the way. We've been following the case in the papers, of course. And we're concerned about you."

Bo was relieved that St. John did not pronounce his surname "Sinjin" in the British way. The lack of affectation boded well for whatever it was they wanted to say. "Yes?" she prodded. The sky was beginning to glower in a way that whispered of early tropical storms. Bo tried to remember if one were predicted.

"I don't think Mrs. Franer's boyfriend, the one they've got in jail, hurt the little girl," Rombo Perry continued hurriedly. "It just doesn't make any sense. I think the guy that killed the child is the same guy that trashed the mission and killed that obnoxious psychologist last night."

"This Satanic nonsense is a smokescreen behind which somebody's getting away with murder," St. John added, frowning at the sky. "Is it supposed to rain?"

Bo pondered the intense interest with which people in arid regions regard precipitation, and waited for a point to be made. Any point.

"This may sound a little dramatic," Rombo Perry went on, "but have you considered the possibility that this guy may come after you next? I mean, he may have a list . . ."

It occurred to Bo that the two men standing before her were total strangers. Rombo Perry might not be a social worker at all. And what kind of name was Rombo? Jamming her hands in her skirt pockets, she strolled toward Dar Reinert, conferring with a reporter near the curb. The two followed. "I've thought of it," she admitted. "But what has it got to do with you?"

"I see you've met Mr. Perry and Mr. St. John," Reinert boomed after Bo shot him a concerned look. "I've already checked 'em out, Bo. They're who they say they are. In fact, everybody here is who they say they are. The mystery man, if there is one, didn't show."

"But he *will* show," Rombo Perry insisted. "He can't just get away with what he's done."

"We don't even know who he is," Reinert sighed, swinging his arms as if the activity would make something happen. "Massieu may have raped the little girl, and some other fruitcake may have vandalized the mission, and yet *another* nut may have taken Ganage out. This Satan crap has every loony in town sharpening knives and jumping at shadows. My take on the whole mess is, we'll never solve this case."

Bo was confident that she'd never heard so many casually inaccurate terms used at the same time. "But what if your nut/fruitcake is Samantha's killer and he isn't loony at all?" she asked. "What if he decides to kill again?"

"If he does," Rombo Perry took a deep breath, "doesn't Ms. Bradley seem the most likely victim? Of the three people whose names have been publicly linked to the Franer case—you, Detective Reinert, Cynthia Ganage, and Ms. Bradley—she is the remaining woman."

"What's being a woman got to do with it?" Reinert asked.

"He won't go after a man, a cop," St. John interjected as Bo felt a chill unrelated to the darkening sky. "He'll only go for somebody weaker than he is. If you don't have enough extra patrolmen to give Ms. Bradley a guard, at least at night, Rombo and I have decided to volunteer. Would that be all right with you?"

The question was directed to Bo.

"Uh, no, really, I'll be fine. I'm staying at a friend's tonight. But thanks," she replied. The offer was disturbing.

Martin St. John extracted a business card from his jacket and handed it to Bo. "St. John Catering" was embossed in script above a quirky pen-and-ink drawing of a place setting featuring seven forks, the last of which seemed to be falling off the side of the card.

"Just call us if you need help," Rombo added. "I'm serious."

Nodding, Bo left to find Estrella and make arrangements to spend the night in safety.

"You're finally showing some sense," Estrella agreed. "We'll expect you for dinner."

The black-clad demonstrators were gone as Bo eased her car from the curb, but something of their spirit hung over the windswept street. A sense of judgment, of irrational and relentless retribution.

Chapter 24

The streets had become a lavender web of jacaranda blossoms as the wind blew them in storms from curbside trees. Bo watched the purple carpet ripple and tear where the BMW's tires disturbed it, and then settle again when she had passed. The little flowers created a fairy-tale atmosphere in which thoughts of bloody murder seemed merely unpleasant. The leaves of a silver-dollar gum tree bristled in the wind and turned from gray-green to silver in a tremulous wave.

"Rattling silver, rattling sorrow," her grandmother's voice murmured the Irish warning out of nowhere.

"The referent there is money, not leaves, Grandma Bridget," Bo said aloud and then frowned at her own reflection in the car's side mirror.

Uh-oh. The proverbs are back. Better get some rest.

At first the residential neighborhoods she traversed en route to the freeway appeared to be making a statement about what Sunday afternoons were meant to be. Green ivy. Nice fences. A white dog and teenage boy, playing Frisbee. Then an elderly woman in a red muumuu and cat's-eye sunglasses throwing soapy water on a rose bush. Strange. Followed by two potbellied men, one black and the other white, trying to wrestle what looked like a wire sculpture of a giant amoeba off the bed of an old pickup truck with Oklahoma plates. Stranger. A cluster of children staring murderously at a utility meter . . .

Oh, right. Check it out, Bradley. Whether you like it or not, you're edging into the Twilight Zone. Quit pretending that anything's normal. Go to Estrella's and get some sleep.

Norman Rockwell had given way to David Mamet. Just as well, Bo decided. Rockwell painted a fantasy of Stockbridge, Massachusetts, as it was before Alice's Restaurant. Mamet would be more comfortable with freeze-frames of southern California collapsing on a Sunday afternoon into naked scraps of inexplicable human behavior. Weird vignettes that might be terrible and might be meaningless. Grainy snapshots lacking the narrative that would impose on them an illusion of sense. Bo turned a corner and nearly hit a longhorn chicken drifting from between two parked Nissan Pathfinders, both blue and immaculately clean. The longhorn turned out to be a wadded newspaper, caught in the wind. Or else it really was a chicken, blown in from a Depression-era newsreel, lost in time. Bo pulled the car to a stop in front of a mustard yellow bungalow with brown trim, and tried not to see the plaster elf peeking over the porch railing. An elf with pitiless, painted eyes.

This could happen sometimes, without the lithium. As if a veil of imposed coherence, of mundane ordinariness were lifted away and the raw truth made visible. The raw truth that things were stranger than they seemed to be. The first hint had been on Wednesday, when the veil began to unravel. That was to be expected, just the usual manic-depressive drift. Bo was used to it. It might happen, Lois Bittner said, when Bo was under stress. Or when she was premenstrual, or postmenstrual, or when she had the flu. It might happen with a sudden drop in atmospheric pressure, or with a poignant memory, or with indigestion. Nobody knew when it might happen, in other words. But it was happening now. Bo closed her eyes and listened to the engine's idle.

"I'm scared," she said aloud and lit a cigarette.

"So?" Lois Bittner's voice echoed in her head. "What is it that's scaring you?"

"Somebody might try to kill me, for one," Bo exhaled. "But that's not really it. It's what I'm going to do tomorrow. I'm terrified."

"This thing you're going to do tomorrow scares you more than somebody trying to kill you?" the familiar voice asked.

"A lot more," Bo answered, shivering. "Should I go through with it?"

There was no answer, only the sound of wind rustling the fronds of a palm tree in the bungalow's yard. In her mind Bo could see a picture of Lois Bittner, the wise old eyes bright and fond. The Frye boots, the long skirts, the Indian jewelry. Clothes from another era. Pastrami lunches in St. Louis restaurants that probably weren't even there anymore. The shrink's warm office in a building now leveled for a mall parking garage. The truth, unvarnished.

Bo had stayed in St. Louis for over a year after her collapse at the Holiday Inn, just to work with Lois Bittner against the shifting chemistry in her skull. They'd perused the medical literature, tried varying medications, read the famous mood-disordered writers—Keats, Poe, Virginia Woolf, Hemingway, Robert Lowell, Sylvia Plath, Anne Sexton—until Bo knew their lives and symbols, their depressions and manias, better than they had. Bittner discouraged Bo's interest in van Gogh and the other affected painters, suggesting that Bo's similar talent might forge too great an identity. In defiance Bo had freelanced an article on "Van Gogh's Use of Black" for an art journal and dyed half her wardrobe to match the artist's indigo irises. A job as volunteer coordinator for a Jewish community center of whose board Lois Bittner was a member provided a living. The position had preserved a vocational integrity useful in getting her old job back at the reservation, and then in getting this one. But a year after Bo returned to New Mexico

Lois Bittner had traveled to Germany for a conference, and died of a massive cerebral hemorrhage in a Bremen *bierstube.* Friends had arranged for her burial there. Bo was saving for the day when she would lay a pastrami sandwich on that grave.

"You're gone, aren't you?" she addressed the picture of Lois Bittner in her mind. "You're not there anymore. You're dead." The picture didn't change. But a message gleamed in the familiar eyes. "I'm not dead as long as some part of me lives in you," Bo answered for the best friend she'd ever had. "Don't blow it."

Grinning, she gunned the car to the nearest 7-Eleven and dropped a quarter in its pay phone. "This is Bo Bradley from County Social Services," she abridged her place of employment to a more serviceable label for the floor nurse at County Psychiatric. "The police have informed me that a client I know as Zolar was taken there yesterday night. Is he still there?"

The news was that Zolar, aka Patrick Darren Preble, had been taken by a family overjoyed that he was alive to a private psychiatric hospital called, like fully half of San Diego's schools, streets, and office buildings, Mesa Vista. Bo knew right where it was, only a few miles from her office. In fifteen minutes she was there.

"So Patrick," she smiled, propping her feet on the edge of the bed where he lay clean and frozen in a darkness Bo recognized as a cousin to her own so long ago, "why are you here? Ignore the voices for a minute and let me tell you about this great little Mexican restaurant up the street. Fabulous carne asada and the best chicken chimichangas north of the border. Sound good? We'll go there in a few days, and that's a promise."

A pulse of light deep in the teal blue eyes, a barely perceptible spasm near the corner of the mouth under the trimmed red beard were sufficient evidence of success. And then there was more. The blazing finale for any remaining reticence Bo might have regarding tomorrow's dive off an outgrown cliff.

"How's Mildred?" Patrick Preble inquired thickly.

Bo could only imagine the effort necessary to frame the polite and wondrously appropriate question through both the illness and the muddying medications that had given the young man back his name.

"Mildred's fine," she answered. "And she remembers the jerky you gave her."

Driving west on I-8 a half hour later, Bo turned on the radio for an explanation of the purple-gray clouds roiling above San Diego. One of them, she decided as the announcer explained that a freak tropical storm named Annabelle was swirling offshore, looked like a Kodiak bear stretching to eat a file cabinet.

It was exhaustion, she admitted. And the monumental stress of this case. There was no medication that could take away the disturbing imagery, the sense that odd and potentially horrifying realities lurked everywhere, their disguises simply gone. It was a perception Bo accepted simply as a truth few others could see. A perception to which she could give form in her paintings. Not quite delusional. Sometimes fascinating. Always unnerving.

She'd run home, pick up Mildred and a change of clothes, and get to Estrella's before the storm hit. She'd be safe at Estrella's. She could rest and calm the odd sensibility, prepare for tomorrow. It was going to be okay.

Chapter 25

Eva Broussard walked barefoot along the beach, nearly deserted as Sunday afternoon picnickers and the perennial bands of surfers fled the oncoming storm. Hannah Franer ran before her, chasing flotsam thrown on the dull golden sand by frothing waves. In the dim light the child looked magical, like one of the Jo-Ge-Oh, the Iroquois Little People said to live in the lost ravines of the Adirondack and Catskill wildernesses.

Eva watched the child and considered the reasons why all the nations of the world told stories of "little people" with magical power whose homes were hidden in natural places. Perhaps the tales were a way of honoring childhood itself, lost in each individual forever with the grim surge of reproductive chemistry at puberty. Lost, but remembered and reified in myth. The preservation of childhood, she nodded at her own thoughts, might be the telling variable in a human equation now dangerously skewed toward destruction.

The man who destroyed Samantha Franer had violated that necessity. The man who raped a three-year-old child was removed from the human community and all its future. But he wasn't the only one. Thousands of others like him, perhaps millions, walked on the earth, self-absorbed and forever alone. A terrible power lay in their ability to damage the very foundation on which human happiness must be built. A power to poison the little people, and thereby tear apart the web of life. Most of them, Eva thought as cream-colored spume bubbled and then vanished in the sand at her feet, had no awareness of the cruel distortion they threw into the future. But this one, the one who eviscerated Samantha Franer with the weapon of his own body, had somehow glimpsed it. And embraced it. He knew what he was now. And his rage at the knowledge would propel him to kill and kill until something stopped him.

Hannah seized a broken shell from the littoral and held it up for Eva to see. A penknife clam shell, purplish and similar in color to the quahog beads pinned on the child's shirt. The clams were related, their shared history documented under ancient seas. Like the two people on this Pacific beach, Eva smiled, with their shared history of stories. "Let's go sit up there," she gestured to a small amphitheater in the worn cliffs where a sandstone layer had collapsed in piles of rubble beneath a stripe of white quartz.

Hannah scrambled ahead, her golden hair streaming in the odd light. "Up there, up there," she sang into the whipping wind, ozone-scented and laden with salty chill. "Let's go sit up there."

It was a mark of the child's strong spirit, Eva conceded, that she'd been able to speak again so quickly after the horrors that locked her in silence. But her speech wasn't self-generated, not spontaneous. Not yet. Since early in the afternoon she'd repeated phrases Eva said to her in a peculiar singsong voice, as if words were audible toys to be played with, not symbols that could define Hannah Franer and her experience to the world outside her head. That experience was too terrible to define, Eva knew. But the experience also *was* Hannah Franer. If the child could not be brought to define it, that fierce, boundaried core of being called self would never wholly return.

Purple-gray clouds fringed in shifting yellow glare jostled

over the windswept water as Eva gathered her skirts and climbed into the small amphitheater beside Hannah. Cupped in the western edge of the North American continent, a dim silence seeped from the curved stone walls. Eva Broussard listened to the silence and heard the pulse of ten thousand stories, told so that people might know what they were.

Hannah sat cross-legged in jeans wet to the knee, and drew lines in the sand with her broken clam shell. The jeans, Eva noted as if from a great distance, were already snug, a little too short. The child's body was growing. Could her mind be brought in step? Far at sea filaments of lightning threaded toward an invisible horizon. In the flickering surge of light Eva saw a woman's face beneath the child's. A face like Bonnie Franer's, but also different. A firmer set to the wide jaw. A smoothness over the sandy eyebrows that in the mother had seemed a landscape of crimped cloth. The face of the woman Hannah Franer might become, if she were given tools with which to survive.

"Look how your California clam shell is purple," Eva began in the storyteller's voice she had heard in childhood, "just like your clam shell grieving beads from New York are purple. The California clam shells are *like* the New York clam shells."

"Like New York," Hannah sang in the quiet shelter, watching Eva from the sides of wide-set eyes.

"And I'm going to tell you a special story," Eva went on, almost chanting. "It is the story of Otadenon, whose name means 'The Last One Left.' "

"Last, last," Hannah sang, rocking slightly to the sound of Eva's voice.

"Otadenon was the last one left of his family," Eva continued softly. "His family had been taken away forever by something *otgont*, something very bad."

"Bad," Hannah repeated in a quavering falsetto. Her left hand reached for the grieving beads over her heart.

Eva let herself rock beside the child as she told the story, of how Otadenon, to save the life of the man who cared for him, traversed a trail guarded by two snakes, two bears, and two panthers on the way to the terrible chestnut grove where the flayed skin of a woman hung in the trees, singing a warning if anyone came near.

"Skin Woman," Hannah repeated, but did not sing. *"Ot-gont."*

"Yes," Eva replied, taking no apparent notice of the emerging conceptual connection. "And Otadenon was very, very afraid. But he tricked Skin Woman by giving her a worthless wampum belt, and got plenty of chestnuts to feed everyone, and went home. Otadenon was very afraid, but he didn't give Skin Woman his life. Otadenon was the Last One Left, and he went on being Otadenon, Hannah. He won. Can you guess who Otadenon, the Last One Left, is like?"

Hannah drew a tightening spiral in the sand with the penknife clam shell, rocking hard. "Clams like . . . New York," she pronounced, gasping. "Otadenon is like . . . me. Because I'm the Last One Left."

"Yes, Hannah," Eva whispered as the wind gusted a shower of sand up from the beach and the child's face broke in sobs. "Otadenon's story is your story, too." From deep in her heart Eva Blindhawk sent a prayer of thanks to the chain of Iroquois storytellers who had preserved through time a story that would teach Hannah Franer who she was.

After Hannah wept for a long time within the circle of Eva's arms, she looked up through matted eyelashes, her head cocked to one side. "Can there be two Last One Lefts?" she asked.

Eva was puzzled. "What do you mean, Hannah?"

"There's two Last One Lefts. Like Otadenon. I'm one, and there's another one." She smoothed her windblown hair with both hands in a businesslike gesture that made Eva smile. "I think you're not really the Last One Left when there's two. And Bo's the Last One Left, too. She said so. So me and Bo, we're the last *two* left. Kind of like sisters. See?"

In the keening of the sea wind Eva imagined she heard an ancient wooden flute, its music sent from the midwinter fire of a vanished Iroquois longhouse. Sent into the future through the mind of a child on a California beach. The gamble had succeeded; the story had given coherence to mere fragments of pain. When Hannah plumbed its depths and molded it to fit her own need, the story became a bridge to a future unimagined when the tale was first told.

"I do see, Hannah," Eva answered. "And you're very, very smart to have figured out how you and Bo are both like Otadenon, how you and Bo are both the Last One Left. You have a good mind like a *Hageota*, a storyteller. I am proud to be your grandmother."

The child's eyes glowed as a smile lit her wide, freckled face.

"I'm hungry," she mentioned, standing and stretching her arms toward the sea. "Can we get a hamburger? Can we call Bo? I want to tell her about Otadenon. Skin Woman won't get *us*!"

In a flurry of sand and pebbles Hannah scrambled from the little enclosure and dashed across the gray-lit beach, her face exultant. Eva followed, smiling. The story of Otadenon, created in a time when sickness and cold might leave anyone the sole survivor of a family, had leaped three thousand miles and probably as many years.

"Nyah-weh," Eva pronounced into the wind. "Thank you."

Chapter 26

Mildred, bored with her long day alone in the apartment, had overturned Bo's kitchen wastebasket and strewed pizza crusts, cigarette ashes, coffee grounds, and half a microwave tray of moldering macaroni-and-cheese onto the dining area carpet. The little dog's breath bore a telltale hint of Italian spices.

"I see you didn't eat the crusts again." Bo sighed. She'd forgotten to put the wastebasket on the counter, a necessary precaution when going out for extended lengths of time. "And I've got to take you out now, before the rain starts."

Mildred wagged her stubby tail in anticipation as Bo grabbed the red leather collar and leash from an easel in the dining area. Beyond her second-story deck the Pacific Ocean pounded the empty beach and gray cliffs with tons of murky saltwater. Bo could almost see the Flying Dutchman, crewed by skeletons in ragged pantaloons, floundering in the storm-driven surf. St. Elmo's fire flashing from the tattered riggings. The mainmast groaning and then breaking with a sound like blasted rock.

"Yark!" Mildred said at the door. A reminder to curb the enjoyable rush of imagination. Stay with the program. Take the dog out.

"Hurry up," Bo told the dog as they hurried toward a grassy

area abutting the seawall. Beneath the Ocean Beach pier, walls of water surged upward and split in white flumes of spray against the pier's underside. Ahead, palm trees dropped fronds on the balconies of a pink motel facing south from Newport Street. The motel seemed deserted, its sets of glass doors dark. Except there was someone on one of the balconies. A man. Short and nondescript in a black T-shirt and jeans, he appeared to be watching the storm. But Bo thought she could feel his attention shift to her and Mildred when they stopped beside a trash can on the grass. Mildred sniffed the receptacle with scholarly ardor as Bo tried not to look upward again. Had the man in the Hawaiian shirt on the beach been short? She couldn't remember. The man on the beach had been sitting on the seawall. Hard to tell if a seated figure is short. When she glanced at the balcony again, he'd gone inside. She could see the drape move slightly behind the sliding glass door, but no light. Why would he be sitting around in the dark? A lamp in the motel's street-level office indicated the presence of electricity in the building. Maybe he was watching them, unseen. Maybe he was the one who carved a hole in a canyon and painted it pink. Maybe he was the one who preserved hotel carpeting by exsanguinating people in bathtubs.

"And maybe my imagination is running at full-tilt boogie," Bo told Mildred. "Let's get to Estrella's."

Back in the apartment Bo regarded the mess on the floor and then picked up the phone.

"Es . . . Mildred's dumped the trash on the carpet. I don't want to face this when I get home tomorrow. I'll clean it up and then come right over, okay?"

Estrella mentioned several matters more pressing than tidy carpets, principally storms and blood-filled bathtubs.

"Just as soon as I can . . ." Bo promised, and hung up.

The vacuum cleaner was wedged in a broom closet among four outdated editions of *The Physicians' Desk Reference*, a striped beach umbrella, and a collapsible snow shovel Bo had kept after St. Louis for the simple elegance of its design. The storm broke just as she disentangled the vacuum's cord from a nest of dust-filmed Christmas tree lights on the closet floor. Gusting wind slammed sheets of black rain against the deck doors, making the glass wobble. In the watery design Bo imagined she saw Irish beasts from her grandmother's tales—the Dun Cow, the "slim, spry deer," a Selky seal with woeful eyes who'd once been human for a while—their mouths all wide and warning. Mildred stood growling under an easel, her ears cocked.

"It's just the storm," Bo said, suddenly edgy. Patches of orange cheese sauce had dried, flecked with coffee grounds, to the carpet's nap. Bo scrubbed the offending islands of color with a soapy sponge, rinsed and blotted the area until the carpet was spotless.

"Aye 'n' they found yer Aunt Mary Duffy," Bo's grandmother had reminded Bo's father every summer during her visits from Ireland, "dead as a stone, her rooms like a pigsty they said. 'Twas a crime 'n' a shame, such a thing." The idea had been to induce neatness in the perennially messy library of Michael O'Reilly, whose elder daughter, if now found dead, would at least not be found dead in a pigsty. Bo wondered if her father's Aunt Mary Duffy had possessed a dog with a fondness for trash. And how the negligent housekeeper had died. Outside a tree limb cracked in the wind, and fell to the street with a whoosh.

Bo abandoned the vacuum cleaner where it stood, and hurried to her bedroom closet.

"And what shall I wear to the court, tomorrow?" she sang to an Irish tune, and then finished the song. "You haven't an arm and you haven't a leg. You're an eyeless, noseless, chickenless egg. And you'll have to be put in a bowl to beg. Och, Bradley, I hardly knew ye."

The forest green bijou jacket, she decided. Matching skirt

if she could still button the waist, and cream silk blouse with a Mandarin collar. The emerald drop earrings her mother had worn onstage with the Boston Symphony. No rings. Gold watch. Don't forget the damn green shoes. New pantyhose, still in the package. It was important to look conservatively smashing for the event in which she would reveal to a hostile world just how "different" it was possible to be. As the lights flickered and then regained their normal luminosity, Bo considered how she might appear in this outfit, pushing a wire grocery cart through alleys. Pausing to glean handfuls of brown-edged lettuce from dumpsters behind restaurants. Exactly how did one hold the second glove, while grubbing through pre-used food?

But Solon Gentzler had said it couldn't happen. Not after the Disabilities Act. Madge Aldenhoven and all her demonic bureaucracy couldn't touch Bo, he'd said. And it would be a landmark step for those who would come after, like Hannah Franer. Bo remembered the child's trembling hand, the gift of grieving beads. Zolar weeping in the canyon. Her people. A lost family.

Folding the clothes neatly, Bo placed them in a waterproof duffel bag, zipped it shut, and turned off the lights. Something made a thumping noise on the deck. An overturned plant, Bo decided, clipping her car keys to the edge of her skirt pocket. Not worth dealing with in the rain. Mildred was whining near the door, her terrier eyes wolflike from fear.

"I can't believe you're losing it over a simple storm," Bo told the dog as the phone rang on the shadowy counter defining the kitchen. Bo tripped over the vacuum cleaner in a dash to answer.

"I'm leaving now, Es," she said into the phone.

"Leaving?" the voice of Rombo Perry replied. "Martin and I were thinking you might like a catered dinner and some company tonight. How about it? Breast of chicken in an orange brandy sauce over wild rice, steamed Japanese eggplant, rolls, of course, and a milk chocolate mousse. Martin's version of meals-on-wheels."

Bo leaned over to rub her ankle where it collided with the vacuum. "Sounds like heaven," she answered as she stood again, "but . . ." Something was wrong. Something moving in the dark outside. Not a potted plant. A man. "Oh shit, it's him."

Accustomed now to the dark, her eyes had been able to discern the dripping figure standing on the redwood deck. A figure in a black T-shirt with a white face on it. A bearded, old-fashioned face on a T-shirt. Distorted and ghostly on its black background. The figure wearing the T-shirt was holding something above its head in both hands. Something big. A deck chair. He was standing in the rain on her deck holding a chair over his head. As if in slow motion she saw the chair begin its descent in an arc toward the glass doors.

Bo heard the bell inside the phone jangle as it fell from the counter and hit the vacuum cleaner. Then a splintering of glass as she grabbed Mildred and ran from the apartment, leaving the door open to the wind-driven spray that blinded her as she stumbled on slick stairs, caught herself, and made it to the deserted street.

Her car was half a block away, wedged between a pickup truck and an illegally parked motorcycle with a faded surfboard chained to its gas tank. In the streetlight the hard rain made little inverted cups, brief and glasslike, as it hit the surfboard. Bo ran toward the car, imagining splashing footsteps in pursuit, the reach of a wet, pale arm. Her legs felt numb; the contraction and then expansion of large muscles necessary for running had to be thought about. The BMW seemed a receding mirage until Bo finally touched its metal surface. Grabbing her keys, she unlocked the car door and dived inside, pulling the door closed behind her and locking it. Through her rain-blurred rear window she saw the soaked figure jump the last three steps from her apartment stairs to the street, and look straight at her car. Mildred, cowering on the front seat, glanced nervously at Bo.

"We're outta here!" Bo bellowed, starting the car and pushing the motorcycle over the curb and into a streetlight pole. The surfboard cracked and split lengthwise, its two pieces making a twisted white fiberglass X over the crumpled bike. The BMW's rear wheels sent clouds of spray over the running figure whose hands grabbed and slipped on Bo's right fender as she spun out on Narragansett, away from the beach.

As he began to sprint after her, Bo thought he was going to try to catch her on foot.

"You imbecile," Bo yelled out the window, "you can't chase a car on foot!" The wind gripped her words and carried them away as the running man veered across the street and was lost between a darkened bungalow and an apartment complex whose backlit stained-glass lobby door featured dolphins rising through watery bubbles. Bo thought she felt his soul behind her like a globe of frozen ammonia. Not like dolphin bubbles. Caustic. Poisonous. She accelerated and then jammed on the brakes at Sunset Cliffs Boulevard where a fallen eucalyptus limb bisected the intersection diagonally. There was no option but to turn right, but so what? He must have gone to get his car. He'd never catch up. Bo turned onto Sunset Cliffs Boulevard where it snaked along the continent's edge. Something about his running unnerved her. An assurance, a businesslike determination that made no sense. Bo pushed down on the accelerator and within three blocks could no longer see the intersection where he'd vanished.

Six blocks later Bo took her foot off the accelerator to slow the car as the road curved left above the famous Sunset Cliffs, a sea-torn granite shelf from which the sunrise in Honshu, Japan, could easily be foreseen in North American twilight.

The car was heading into the curve too fast. Bo pressed the brake pedal gently. Nothing. Pushed it to the floor. Still nothing.

Shit, it's the brakes! He's cut the brakeline and you just pumped the last of the fluid out at the intersection. He's back there, not far, and you have no brakes!

The BMW sheared a guardrail on the right as it careened around the curve, out of control. Heavily traveled, the boulevard wore a chemical skin of oil seldom cleaned off by the pressure of a thousand rubber tires scrubbing in rainwater. San Diego's yearly rainfall could be measured with kitchen utensils. The road was an oil slick.

Bo knew the point, only one long block away, at which the sea cut a notch to within feet of the road. Another curve to the left there. A curve she could never make. The car would fishtail, flip backward into the sea. Ramming the gearshift into reverse, Bo heard the scream of warring metal as she clutched Mildred tightly to her right side and scraped the guardrail for fifty feet before plowing through it into a pile of boulders. The boulders, she remembered as the steering wheel bent under her weight, had been hauled there from the desert. Dumped there to buffer the sea where it chewed into million-dollar property. Dumped there, maybe, to stop a runaway car headed for a watery burial. As her head cleared Bo thought of the runaway truck ramps all over New England. She'd seen them as a child. Off-ramps leading to hills of gravel that could catch and stop an eighteen-wheeler with no brakes. Boulders, she smiled dizzily, were just big gravel. The BMW hissed a smell of burnt metal, but was stationary. Its front end had crumpled like a stiff blanket thrown against the rocks.

Bo tried the driver's side door. Jammed. Most of the homes fronting the sea along the boulevard were lit and gleaming yellow in the black rain. But none of the doors was open. No one coming to see what had happened. In the roar of the surf, Bo realized, the headlong crash of a car into a rockpile might not be heard. Quickly she scooted to the passenger's side, tucked Mildred under her left arm, and tried the door. It opened into a cold torrent of rain and salt spray from the tumultuous waves lashing the cliffs twenty feet from the car. The man in his car might round the first curve any moment now. But there was still time to make a dash across the boulevard to one of the houses.

As Bo struggled out of the car an enormous wave rose, serpentine from the darkness below the cliffs, and broke in a blast of spray that stung her eyes. Rivulets of seawater ran down the back of her nose, leaving a bitter taste. Mildred sneezed and lurched out of Bo's grasp, landing clumsily on the wet stone. In a second the little dog had vanished into the rocks ahead, down toward the sea.

"Mildred!" Bo yelled pointlessly. Her voice was lost in the wind. As she clambered down the rocks after the dog, Bo saw a car's lights slicing the rain in wide, misty cones.

Chapter 27

Estrella Benedict watched as Henry threaded chunks of tequila-marinated turkey on metal skewers. The turkey alternated with ripe tomatillos and ruffled black mushrooms out of a jar. After a minute Estrella noticed that she'd torn a flour tortilla into four pie-shaped wedges and arranged them in an overlapping fan design in the sink.

"Bo should have been here by now," she said, mashing the wedges into the garbage disposal. "I'm worried."

"So am I," Henry Benedict agreed. "Maybe the storm's held her up."

In a red polo shirt and baggy white cotton pants he managed to look even more like a blond Abraham Lincoln than he did in his naval officer's uniform. Estrella noted the ridge of muscle wrinkling his forehead above the brow line. The last time she'd seen the furrow that deep they'd been camping in the desert and found a nest of newborn Western rattlers writhing in a shady wash. He'd stomped them with a Tony Lama boot and then thrown up behind an ocotillo cactus. Henry Benedict, Estrella had learned in four years of marriage, didn't say much and considered the implications of everything as if those implications mattered.

"I think I'll call LaMarche and see if he's heard from her," Estrella told the front of her toaster oven.

"Already called him five minutes ago," Henry replied into a hardwood cutting board hanging from a leather loop on the wall. "He says the Indian woman called him, saying the little girl's all upset, thinks something bad's happening to Bo."

"Hannah said that? Bo said she wasn't talking, that she's been mute since they told her her mother was dead."

"Well, I guess she's talking now," Henry concluded. "LaMarche said he was going over there, to Bo's place. Nothing to do but wait."

Estrella wrapped her arms around her husband's waist and listened to his heart beating slowly, its thump echoing through his back. "Bo's special," she said into his shirt. "Things never happen for her like they do for other people. She always goes deeper or something. It's scary."

"Maybe it's just what she has to deal with," he answered. "The manic-depressive thing. Maybe she just sees deeper. But we're here for her, Strell, and she knows that."

"Yeah." Estrella sighed and stared at a bright blue wall clock with hands shaped like crayons. Bo Bradley had given them the clock for Christmas last year, with numerous hints that the godchild she was expecting as soon as they were ready would undoubtedly learn to tell time within months of birth. "But this guy that raped Hannah's sister and killed the psychologist may be smarter than we think. He's really smart, Henry. What if he's gone after Bo?"

Henry Benedict aligned the skewers evenly on a foil-covered tray and glanced at the rainy kitchen window. "What makes you think he's so smart? Do you know something about this creep I haven't read in the papers?" he asked.

And then he listened as Estrella told him about a woman from a village in Chihuahua who would probably be heading there at this moment on a fumey second-class bus strung with

Christmas tree lights, her children asleep on her lap. Somebody on the bus would have chickens in a cage, Estrella told her husband, crying. Somebody would be drunk. And somebody would be singing.

"You did the right thing, hon," he whispered as Estrella wept into his chest. "You really did."

"That's what Bo said," Estrella cried harder.

Chapter 28

Mildred, her pink skin visible under wet white fur, had wedged herself beneath a jagged rock at the edge of a drop into foaming black water that seemed alive. Bo found the white dog easily and then realized why. Her sodden blouse with its peasant sleeves and seven-button cuffs was white, too. If her pursuer were looking, he'd see her instantly.

No time left to cross the narrow road, find safety in a lighted house where people would open the door, phone the police. Nothing to do but crawl further into the rocks and hide. Nothing to do but hope the man would assume she'd made it to one of the houses, and leave. Bo pictured the house on the corner across from her ruined car. A mansion. Painted unaccountably pink. A historical landmark, in fact, with a lighted American flag in the yard. Once the home of a sporting goods magnate who'd been a lover of the mystical Theosophist Madame Tingley. Maybe the man chasing her would think Bo was in that house, safe, phoning the police. She grabbed Mildred, huddled beside a black rock, and conjured an image of the long-dead mystic. Maybe Madame Tingley's ghost would stay the hand of the killer.

As a flash of lightning tore the sky Bo looked across the vertical tube of angry water below to a flat ledge extending out to sea from behind another pile of boulders. Below the ledge was a tiny inlet, now swollen with surf.

That pink house is the Spaulding Mansion, Bradley. The cave is there, remember?

Holding Mildred in a viselike grip, Bo climbed down through ragged darkness to the surging trough of seawater she now remembered was usually a pleasant tidal estuary, full of hermit crabs and anemones. But how deep was it now? And how strong the pull as a thousand gallons of churning water receded through its channel after every wave? In the sea at the base of the five-foot-wide trough a jumble of sharp-edged rocks disappeared under the next surge of water. Barnacle-encrusted, they would shred the flesh of anything thrown against them by the outgoing torrent. Bo shifted Mildred to her right arm, waited for the thundering influx of water to peak and begin its rush back to the sea, and stepped into the trough.

The receding water, ice-cold, only came to a point two inches above her knees. On her numb feet a pair of button-sided pumps, purchased to complete a costume that suggested Katharine Hepburn in *The African Queen*, proved themselves worthy of the role and did not disintegrate. Bo made a mental note to send Nordstrom's shoe department a thank-you card, if she survived.

In the next step her left foot found a fissure, pulled back and balanced the combined weight of woman and dog on the edge of a fin-shaped rock. The next wave was rolling in, its shape like a truck-sized snake beneath the water. In a second it would arc against the rocks, higher than Bo's head, and then pull them both back down a frothing cataract to the sea. Bo pushed off, landed crookedly on her right foot, which seemed to bend, and in another step achieved the pile of rocks beyond the trough. The incoming wave plowed against her back with a force that pushed the air from her lungs and left her drenched in foam, but did not succeed in dragging her down the maelstrom of its backwash. Mildred shook her head violently against Bo's side, and struggled to be set free.

"Forget it, Mil," Bo told the dog. "You got us into this. Just ride it out."

After three more minutes of agonizing rock-crawling, Bo reached the cave. Not much as sea caves go, it looked like Atlantis to Bo. Just a hole in the continental shelf where the sea had dissolved a sandstone accretion when there was still a land bridge over the Bering Strait. Bo flung herself on the rocky floor and looked around. She'd been there before. The cave was a favorite local spot for picnics, esoteric rituals, romantic trysts. Also for the homeless, who had left mounds of trash and a stained orange blanket beside the sodden remains of a fire. Bo eyed the blanket with gratitude. It might introduce her to exotic skin diseases, but it would also forestall the effects of hypothermia. Edging toward the blanket, Bo realized there was something wrong with her right ankle. A throbbing pain. An odd limpness. Pulling off her shoe she tried to arch her toes, and watched as they responded with random, guppylike movements.

The storm was diminishing. On the fissured granite shelf that sloped downward thirty feet from the cave's mouth to a wave-lashed precipice, the rain fell now in steady, vertical strings. Bo wrung out her hair and the heavy folds of her khaki skirt. Then she dragged herself and Mildred to the fetid blanket and wrapped it around them, covering her own head so that anyone looking into the cave would see a dirty blanket thrown over a rock. Not a helpless woman with a badly sprained, possibly broken, ankle.

There was no way out of the cave except through its mouth facing the sea. Behind her left arm Bo felt the rough surface of a cement patch in the cave wall, five feet high and wider than her shoulders. Spaulding had made his fortune in more than pigskin footballs. During prohibition, Bo knew from an article she'd read in a local paper, the millionaire had dug a tunnel from a closet in the mansion and under Sunset Cliffs Boulevard to the cave. Mexican rum-runners, anchoring in the tiny cove below, would haul wooden cases of *ron negro* up the cliffs and through the tunnel to luxuriant safety. The tunnel was still there, under the street, but sealed over at both ends. Bo tried not to think of the historic crawlspace as a last, dashed hope. Mildred, snug against Bo's side under the odorous blanket, appeared to have fallen asleep. Bo hated herself for the warm tears she felt running over her cheeks.

Quit sniveling, Bradley. If it's time to die, do it so as not to disgrace your ancestors.

The words, straight from the mouth of Bridget Mairead O'Reilly, made Bo smile. Her grandmother, it seemed, never shut up. Under her breath Bo sang the Irish national anthem.

"Tonight we man the bearna baoghal," she crooned to Mildred. "In Erin's cause, come woe or weal . . ."

Beyond the cave mouth, waves crashed repeatedly over the jutting granite apron. Rain fell through winds that moaned eerily among the rocks. Mildred snored. Bo sang softly. And nothing happened. No drenched figure in black leapt to the cave's door. Nothing moved at all except the thundering surf and an occasional pebble shaken loose from the chamber's walls, probably by a car on the street above.

But if there were cars, wouldn't somebody have seen the smashed BMW and stopped to investigate? Bo glanced at the stone ceiling above her. Of course. The police would have been called by now. Might even be eight feet over her head at this very minute, asking door-to-door of the beachfront residents if anyone had seen the driver of the wrecked car. Bo focused on the churning foam beyond the cave's long, flat lip. Were there flashing red lights reflected from above? Once she thought she saw a shard of red bounce off the water, but maybe not. What if she were just sitting down here while a dozen rescuers walked above? Eventually they'd abandon their search, tow her car away, and leave. And the tide was turning.

The realization felt like a slab of ice laid over her chest. The waves beyond the cliffs loomed larger, their spray splattering closer to the ragged opening of the cave. Bo scanned the walls for a high-water line and found it two feet above her head. There was a high shelf to her left at the cave's rear. If it came to that, she could climb up there and simply wait out the storm. She probably wouldn't drown. It wasn't the threat of drowning that froze her heart. It was the Celtic belief that souls leave bodies at the turning of the tide. The time of wrenching, final transition. But whose?

In the rain-sliced dark at the cave's mouth something moved. A lump of shadow indistinguishable from a hundred others shrouded in mist became a human figure, rising from a crouch before the ragged cave opening. In his right hand an open pocketknife gleamed as raindrops slid off its four-inch blade. A short, pale man whose sodden visage was oddly reptilian, the eyes unblinking.

Bo knew he couldn't quite see her in the gloom, yet his gaze was locked to hers in a psychic connection more damning than a spotlight. He knew where she was. In that connection Bo felt the force of something alien, something savagely empty. The man was not a man, but merely a form whose hatred of what he was not seethed like invisible spume around him. Something sick and deformed from the moment of its conception. A damned soul.

"You're *nothing*." Bo thought into his eyes, her heartbeat throbbing in her fingertips.

"Don't think this Irish girl can't see straight through you. You may kill me, but it won't make you human."

As he began to advance toward her, Bo threw off the filthy blanket and stood. In her head a thousand ancestral bones clamored in brogue. On the cave floor Mildred bristled and barked.

And then another figure filled the cave opening, spun the man in the black T-shirt around by his left shoulder, and sent him sprawling on the wet rock with an uppercut to the jaw. Bo watched the knife slide sideways into a puddle of foam. The second man wore black wire-frame glasses and had a crooked nose.

"It's okay, Bo!" Rombo Perry shouted into the cave as he pulled the black-clad reptile to his feet and flattened him again with a murderous punch to the nose. "We knew he was down here, but we weren't sure you were until your dog barked."

Bo thought she could smell the blood bubbling from the face of the man scuttling away from Rombo toward the edge of the cliff. A smell like peat, swampy and burnt.

"Fight, you son of a bitch!" Rombo screamed, moving toward the cowering form. "You fucking creep, you wanna rape a few more babies? Then fight for it! Give me the chance to kill you."

Bo saw the knotted muscles beneath Rombo's wet gray dress shirt. And saw through the weakening rain what was coming.

"Don't do it, Rom!" another voice called from the rocks beside the shelf. "Let the police have him!"

Martin St. John, covered in mud, jumped down from the rubble. After him a fourth man, familiar and pale, rounded the cave entry and ran to Bo. She could only point as a huge swell, pitch black and silent, reached the southwestern edge of North America.

"Oh my God," Andrew LaMarche breathed as Martin St. John grabbed Rombo's shirt, Mildred barked, and a wave weighing more than the average two-bedroom house broke against the edge of the granite precipice. The splash knocked Martin and Rombo flat, surged up into the cave, and receded. Nothing lay at the cliff's edge now. The man in the black shirt was simply gone. Ten yards below in rocks like shrapnel something bobbed in the violent surf, and then vanished. But it wasn't a man, Bo knew. It never had been.

Chapter 29

Bo awoke wearing a U.S. Navy T-shirt in a room she recognized as Henry and Estrella Benedict's guest room. She had helped Es pick out the white-on-white striped wallpaper herself. A chaste fashion statement with the white wainscoting Henry created from strips of wood floor edging. On a bed table stood a vase containing two dozen long-stemmed American beauty roses. Beside Bo in the bed were Mildred—and Dr. Andrew LaMarche, unshaven and grinning in a matching T-shirt and Navy-issue denim bell-bottoms that obviously belonged to Henry.

"I have not compromised your virtue," he explained, shielding his eyes from the sun streaming through uncurtained windows. "You were so adamant about not remaining at the hospital that I brought you here, still sedated from the minor surgery necessary to set a few bones. Estrella didn't think you should be alone."

"My virtue is unassailable," Bo replied, "except under certain circumstances. You might just *try*, Andy."

"Very well." He flung himself to one knee beside the bed. "Will you marry me, Bo?"

"Oh God, do I have a broken leg? And I've told you—I've already been married. Can't we just be . . . something other than married? And why does my right foot smell like mouthwash?" Bo dragged herself up on her elbows and glanced at a porcelain clock beneath the roses. "It's 6:30. Plenty of time to get to court by 9:00. I would kill for a cigarette. And did all of that really happen last night, or am I delusional?"

"I take it that the issuing of banns may be premature." LaMarche shook his head, standing. "And I'd already sent my morning coat out to be pressed."

"Andy!" Bo replied with bemused irritation. "What happened after we went to the hospital? Did the police fish that guy out of the water? Who is . . . was he? Have they released Paul, now that the real perp's turned up? Did Rombo and Martin go over to my place and board up the deck doors like they said? Have you called Eva? And what about my car?"

"You have sustained rather bad displacement of the tarsal ligaments and fractures in the tibia, two metatarsals, and the great toe," Andrew LaMarche began as Bo glared at her right leg, encased in what looked like pieces of beach furniture fastened together with Velcro. "Your car has been towed to a facility that specializes in the sale of spare parts. The frame was bent. You totaled it, Bo." His face paled at the words. "You could easily have been killed."

"I think that was the idea," Bo muttered. "So who *was* that creep?"

LaMarche walked to the window and clasped his hands behind his head, stretching. "There was no identification on the body," he said. "It could be anybody. The police are trying to establish his identity through fingerprints, but there's nothing to prove that man had anything to do with the deaths of Samantha Franer or Cynthia Ganage. What it looks like," he turned to face Bo but fastened his gaze on the roses instead, "is just some guy with a personal vendetta against you. A 'fatal attraction' is the term Detective Reinert used. You live in a rather bohemian area, Bo." He looked up warily. "Without knowing it you may have engaged the warped attention of—"

"Oh, come *on*!" Bo snapped, incredulous. "Out of the blue a total stranger smashes into my home *after* cutting my brake lines, chases me through a tropical storm and comes after me with a knife in a sea cave because I live in a bohemian neighborhood? That's a plot straight out of a right-wing guide-book for women. I suppose Cynthia Ganage asked for it, too. She had the gall to make a lot of money and lease her own suite of rooms in a posh hotel. And Samantha, of course, would still be alive if only her mother had known her place and stayed at home instead of getting a part-time job. No matter what brutal, vicious thing happens, it's really some woman's fault. Is that it?"

Andrew LaMarche sat in a wicker wing-chair that squeaked under his weight. "I only said the police have hypothesized—"

"The police can't *spell* 'hypothesized,' " Bo yelled, lurching to stand and then sitting back on the bed as a sharp pain exploded in her right leg. A picture formed briefly in her brain. The stranger, his wet, wispy hair the color of chewing gum under a school desk. His eyes barely blue, almost clear. Vacant as glass. "That *thing* out there on the cliffs was Samantha's killer. Eva said he might have . . . changed, after knowing he killed Samantha."

"Changed?" LaMarche rubbed the stubble on his chin. "Changed how?"

"He might have been transforming into a . . . a serial killer. It has something to do with power. First, sexual power over little children. And then murder."

"Ganage, and then you, right? I'm not disagreeing with Dr. Broussard's train of thought, Bo. I suspect she's on to something. But there's not a shred of evidence to support such a contention. Moreover, Dr. Broussard cannot be called to advance her theory in court because the court doesn't know she's here. And even if she did, there's really nothing in her theory that exonerates Paul Massieu. The whole city's on a witchhunt, edgy over the Satanism thing. Paul is demonstrably a member of a group whose beliefs are not routinely taught from pulpits. The human race is only an eyelash away from a past framed in barbarous superstition, Bo. When they're scared they want a scapegoat. No judge is going to release Paul Massieu today. It's just not going to happen."

"Why can't they scapegoat the creep with the knife?" Bo argued. "He looked demonic to me."

"Because nobody knows about him. Massieu's visible, different, barely speaks English. Add to that the fact that he was living without benefit of marriage with a woman who committed suicide the same day her daughter's rape was made public. What would you think, Bo?"

"What I wouldn't think," Bo said while gingerly edging to her feet, "is that any set of facts, in any situation, suggests the existence of a horned mastermind on little goat feet."

"It's not the mythological details so much as a projection of otherness," LaMarche continued, wincing in sympathy as Bo stood. "It's the Other that matters. People are prone to persecute anybody who can be identified as Other. Paul has been identified. Getting him out of that isn't going to be easy."

"I intend to give it my best shot," Bo told a space just above the doctor's head. "Will you drive me to my apartment? I need to get ready for the hearing."

"Martin found a packed bag," LaMarche said, "and brought it to you, along with two dozen whole wheat rolls. Estrella and Henry are preparing breakfast. Shall we?" He stood, held his arm to her, and bowed slightly in a display of courtesy so genuine Bo felt like crying.

"Andy," she grinned, "have I told you that I'm growing fond of the way you talk?"

"I'm honored," he answered.

Downtown San Diego's steeply pitched streets gleamed in post-storm sunlight as Henry Benedict found a parking lot close to the criminal courts building. Urban jacarandas, planted in cement tubs and elegantly fenced, appeared to be lavender balloons lining the street.

"Do I look okay?" Bo asked Estrella from the back seat where her right leg sprawled and throbbed in its canvas splint.

"You look great, and the crutches are an interesting accessory," Estrella replied. "I don't understand what you're so nervous about. Everything's under control, even if Paul isn't released today. Hannah's safe and doing well with Eva. She's talking again. It may take a while longer to free Paul. Quit worrying."

As Bo hopped around the corner from the parking lot, sweating from the exertion required by the crutches, she saw them. The black-clad crew from the street in front of St. Theresa's Church, their number quadrupled. Their placards less literary.

"San Diego Says No to Satan," one declared. The woman carrying it, sixtyish in theatrical makeup and red high-top sneakers, seemed to take personal pride in her poster. Her eyes sparkled like a child's.

Bo's favorite was one that botched a traditional exorcism. "Get Thee Behind Me, Satan," it commanded, "the Lion of Judy Casts Thee Out!"

"What in hell is the Lion of Judy?" Henry Benedict whispered as they ran the gauntlet of demonstrators.

"It's supposed to be Judah." Bo grinned. The carrier of the errant sign glowered beneath a cap advertising beer brewed in Colorado. Bo was grateful for the moment. It would be a while, she thought, before she was likely to smile again.

Solon Gentzler paced inside the lobby door in a rumpled three-piece suit. He looked like a teddy bear in a mortician's costume.

"LaMarche phoned and told me what happened last night," he said, furthering the cause for canonization of the ever-proper pediatrician. "I'm glad you're all right. But right now I need to speak with you privately."

Estrella and Henry nodded and moved toward the building's smudged brass elevator doors. In the lobby of a criminal court building, Bo realized as Gentzler pulled her behind a dusty silk ficus tree bent over a row of newspaper machines, the scent of floor wax could not overcome a mustier scent of despair. In the crowd a prostitute wearing revealingly torn shorts conferred with a woman attorney in Brooks Brothers gray. A Mexican couple struggled to read the English building directory, and then bowed their heads when the man's blunt finger found the courtroom they were looking for.

"Cuatro," he pronounced sadly, "numero cuatro." The woman began to cry.

A thousand stories. All terrible.

Oh, no. Not now, Bradley. Ignore everything but the reason you're here.

"Eva Broussard also phoned me this morning," Solon Gentzler explained quickly. "She says that Hannah has begun to speak again and wanted to know if there were any way for Hannah to testify in Paul's behalf without falling into the hands of the Department of Social Services."

"No!" Bo exclaimed. "There's a petition in place. I filed it myself. She'd be seized by the bailiff and taken away the minute her identity became known."

"I told Broussard as much," Gentzler went on. "Hannah's testimony that Samantha told her somebody named Goody raped her would only be hearsay, anyway. Not admissible. Nothing can be gained by exposing Hannah to the court. I just wanted to get your feel for the idea. I *could* stall this thing, ask for a later date based on new evidence. Are you sure you want to go through with this, Bo? With public interest as high as it is, the best we can hope for is manageable bail and a quick trial date. It can't help Paul."

"I want to go through with it," Bo answered. "It's for me now. And Hannah. And a guy named Patrick who just might need a job in a few months. Let's do it!"

Criminal Court Number Seven was oak-paneled and brightly lit as Bo hobbled to the long table facing the bench. A metal sign on the broad, high desk said JUDGE ALBERT GOSSELIN.

"Who's Gosselin?" Bo asked Solon Gentzler as she sat and pushed her crutches under the table.

"Antioch Law School, graduated in '76. A Quaker, sits on the National Prison Reform Board, collects quilts as a hobby. He's a dream-come-true, but I'm afraid it won't help us today."

Bo glanced at the tiered seats behind her. Estrella and Henry, smiling. Reporters with notepads. Rombo Perry and Martin St. John in dark suits, looking like 1950s jazzmen. Andrew LaMarche, resplendent in pinstripes and vest, a gold collar pin gleaming under the most conservative tie Bo had seen west of Tulsa. Madge Aldenhoven entering through the double doors at the back of the courtroom, accompanied by a bleak man in tan gabardine whom Bo recognized from his picture in the reception area of her office building. The director of San Diego County's Department of Social Services. Bo felt a tissue-thin glacier spread beneath her skin. Madge had brought in the big dog for the kill.

Solon Gentzler grinned at a group following Madge. An older couple and a woman with masses of sandy curls identical to his own.

"My folks, my sister," he told Bo. "I told them what you were going to do; they came down to lend support. There's some pressing business to attend back in L.A. this afternoon, so I'll be leaving as soon as the hearing's over. But no matter what happens, Bo, the ACLU is behind you. Nationally, if necessary."

Paul Massieu, handcuffed and in the blue polyester uniform of the jailed, was brought in, followed by the black-robed judge.

"All rise," the bailiff roared. "The Honorable Judge Albert Gosselin presiding."

Bo smoothed her green skirt with sweaty palms as the prosecuting attorney called Dr. Andrew Jacques LaMarche, attending physician to Samantha Franer at the time of her death, to testify. From the stand LaMarche listed his credentials without looking at Bo, and then quietly described the injuries that had killed a little girl.

A representative of the San Diego Police Department outlined its case against Paul Massieu, mentioning at one point its official discomfort with the accused man's membership in a group known to hold unusual beliefs.

"Objection!" Solon Gentzler boomed. "The man's personal beliefs are not at issue . . ."

Bo was certain his voice could be heard in Denver, and equally certain that an impassioned speech had been planned for precisely this moment.

"Sustained," the judge replied briskly, dashing all hope of oratory.

Solon Gentzler took his seat, sighing.

"I call Barbara J. Bradley," the prosecuting attorney announced, and Bo summoned a picture of Lois Bittner in Frye boots, smiling. It was time to do this. Others were doing it—movie stars, novelists, publishers, and TV personalities—all throwing off secrecy and demonstrating to a misanthropic public that people with psychiatric disorders had been right there all along. That people with psychiatric disorders differed from people with diabetes only in the body part affected. Bo wanted to join them. *Would* join them, now.

"You may testify from your seat if reaching the stand presents a problem," Judge Albert Gosselin noted as Bo pulled her crutches from under the table and stood awkwardly.

"No, I'll take the stand," Bo answered. The only way. Would Bernadette Devlin do this with her back to a crowd? Never.

Madge Aldenhoven's gaze, benign and phony, followed Bo like a tracking device. The DSS director seemed to be asleep.

"It is the opinion of San Diego County's Child Protective

Services," Bo pronounced after describing herself and her credentials, "that Paul Massieu represents a danger to children."

Remember to breathe, Bradley. Here it comes.

"His release into the community at this point would constitute warrantless endangerment of our own children."

Bo had said what she was ordered to say. Madge Aldenhoven's smile was small and perfect.

"You may cross-examine," Albert Gosselin told the defense attorney.

"I defer to co-counsel of record, Solon Gentzler," the defense attorney said as Gentzler stood and strolled toward Bo. At the last-minute question in his eyes Bo merely nodded.

"Ms. Bradley," he began, "is it not true that you suffer from a psychiatric disorder known as manic-depressive illness, and that you have in fact been hospitalized for your own protection due to this illness, which can distort your perceptions of reality?"

"That is true," Bo said.

"And is it not also true that you are not currently taking any of the medications routinely prescribed for the control of symptoms connected to this illness?"

"Yes."

"Your Honor," Solon Gentzler turned toward the judge. "I have no further questions, and ask that the testimony of this witness be stricken from the record on the basis of the witness's history of mental illness."

Bo's eyelids felt metallic, her lungs flattened by the weight of her blouse. She'd wanted to do this. It was her choice. Facts that did nothing toward the restoration of normal breathing. A silence in the room collapsed upon itself like a soundless gasp, and then began to expand.

"Ms. Bradley appears perfectly competent to me," Albert Gosselin answered. "Denied. Unless there's any redirect, you may step down, Ms. Bradley."

None of the lawyers had further questions.

Bo inhaled deeply and heard the rush of air like a choir in her ears. Twenty years of shame and fear, a legacy of vicious superstition extending back to prehistory, had fallen away at her words. Out of the ancient closet, she'd joined the others, the pioneers who would make a world free of psychiatric stigma. And whatever the consequences, it felt like triumph. Her words hadn't helped Paul Massieu, given Gosselin's denial. But they had defeated a bureaucracy at its own game and released their speaker from an invisible constraint worse than any straitjacket. In the front row of seats Andrew LaMarche's eyes glowed with a fierce pride. In the back, Madge Aldenhoven pursed her lips and leaned to whisper something to her companion. Bo heard Bach's Toccata and Fugue in D in her head as she regained her seat at the table. Pipe organ. All stops out.

"If there is no further testimony . . ." the judge began as Dar Reinert appeared at the rear doors, carrying something in an evidence bag. Quickly he approached the prosecuting attorney.

"Detective Reinert has produced unexpected evidence critical to these proceedings," the prosecuting attorney noted, standing. "May we approach the bench?"

"It's a videotape of somebody in a clown suit with Samantha in the cave," Reinert whispered in Bo's ear as the attorneys flocked before the judge. "We found it in the creep's car right behind where you tossed yours. Could be Massieu, if there's anything to this Satanist conspiracy thing. You don't wanna see what's on that tape."

Five minutes later a puzzled assemblage watched as the bailiff put the tape into a VCR brought into the courtroom. On the television screen above the VCR someone in a polka-dot clown costume and smiling mask fondled a living Samantha Franer. Bo gasped at the scene. The child beneath the crystalline curls was alive, moving, smiling. The same child Bo had seen motionless and cold on an operating table. In the taped scene the little girl's unease at the man's groping hands was overcome by her delight at the sparkling lights, the candy he offered her, the balloons and trinkets. There was no sound on the tape, but Bo could almost hear the tinnily reproduced theme from *Sesame Street*. As the pale hands began to pull at Samantha Franer's blue corduroy shorts, Albert Gosselin directed the bailiff to freeze the action. Paul Massieu, his handcuffed hands held tightly against his broad chest, was sobbing.

"If the man's features are never discernible throughout this event," the judge growled at Reinert, "there is no point in subjecting ourselves to this horror. Is the face ever visible?"

"No," Reinert answered.

"But the man is obviously not Paul Massieu," Solon Gentzler began. "He's three inches shorter and—"

"A distortion caused by the camera angle," the prosecuting attorney interjected. "There's no way . . ."

Bo's head felt buoyant, her eyes full of light. The creature in the clown suit had died last night, his brain smashed to inactivity by thundering surf. The tide had turned. That leprous soul was gone. And now she would free the man who would be Hannah Franer's father, who would stand between Hannah and this nightmare.

"Your Honor," Bo grinned broadly, ignoring courtroom protocol, "did you get a look at Paul Massieu's right hand?"

Expectation filled the silent room as every eye memorized the scene before them. A pervert in a clown's costume, pulling with hungry hands at the clothing of a blonde little girl. Each hand below the costume sleeves bearing five fingers, clearly visible on the screen. Then every head turning to Paul Massieu, his black eyes still wet with tears. Slowly he spread his clenched hands for all to see the right one, scarred and bent. Missing its little finger.

Thirty minutes later Bo led Paul Massieu to a wall phone in the hall outside Criminal Court Number Seven, and gave him the number of a studio cottage in Del Mar. A cottage where he could go freely as soon as he'd gotten his clothes and effects from the jail, signed innumerable forms, and returned his blue uniform.

"Eva!" she heard him begin, *"je suis libre."*

And you're free, too, Bradley. About time.

As her friends waited in a cluster, Bo approached Madge Aldenhoven and her guest. Solon Gentzler, his parents and sister, followed.

"Well, Madge?" Bo broke the ice. "What now?"

Aldenhoven's fake smile had died. "I've known all along there was something wrong with you, Bo. Your unfortunate grandstanding here has only—"

"I scarcely see anything wrong with the courage and dedication Ms. Bradley has brought to the performance of her duties in this case," a voice boomed. "I'm Barry Gentzler, by the way." The elder Gentzler directed his remarks to the man in tan gabardine. "The Americans with Disabilities Act precludes any government agency from discharging an employee on the basis of medical disability. I feel safe in assuring you that the American Civil Liberties Union will take deep interest in any punitive action directed at Ms. Bradley as a result of her courageous disclosure here today. Our interests, as you undoubtedly know, have been known to reach the Supreme Court."

The DSS director inspected his knuckles. "There will be no punitive action." He smiled. "Ms. Bradley is one of our most valued employees."

Bo had never seen Madge Aldenhoven turn quite this unbecoming a shade of green.

"All right!" Rombo Perry whooped from the clustered group, clasping his hands over his head like the winner of the fight. "We won!"

Chapter 30

Bo lounged comfortably on a sand chair beneath a robust palo verde whose spidery limbs still boasted yellow spring blooms. In the setting Anza-Borrego Desert sun, the little flowers seemed constructed of buttery paper. She divided her time between admiration of the desert's flora and perusal of a book on the Hudson River artists. The California desert light, she decided, was simply not on a par with that of the Hudson Valley. No moisture from which those rainbow refractions might spin. Still, the desert had its own magic. Accessible only in closeup. A verity well documented by one of Bo's favorite artists, Georgia O'Keeffe. Grabbing her sketchbook and pastels, Bo concentrated fiercely on the creation of a single palo verde blossom, borne on shaded, dancing winds.

"Petals on a wet, black bough?" Andrew LaMarche quoted Ezra Pound interrogatively, flinging himself on the ground beside her after an hour of strenuous Frisbee-chasing with Paul and Hannah. Mildred lay on a blanket in the sparse shade at Bo's head, eyeing the numerous surrounding cholla cactus plants with enmity. The pediatrician had earlier extracted over thirty of the barbed cholla spines from the pads of her right front paw.

"Something like that," Bo agreed. "Pound spent thirteen

years in a psychiatric facility, you know. Privately I think of him as an uncle."

"My favorite poet," LaMarche insisted. "Are we really going to roast Hershey Bars over a campfire?"

"Of course! This camping trip is Hannah's party. No camping party is complete without S'mores. Except you roast the marshmallows. The Hershey Bars melt by themselves from the heat of the marshmallows, squashed between graham crackers. It's ambrosia; trust me."

Andrew LaMarche continued to exude skepticism as he rose to help Estrella and Martin St. John unload firewood from Henry's truck, parked beside the rented jeep that had brought the rest of them through trackless dry washes. The little canyon selected by Paul for their campsite provided shelter from the wind and a spectacular eastern exposure. Already a vanishing sun gilded the layered, rubble-strewn hills with coppery light that quickly spread to lavender, gray-brown, black. Eva Broussard, in a plaid flannel shirt, jeans, and moccasins, stood at the canyon's mouth, looking east. In the shifting light the Indian woman seemed to have sprung up from what lay beneath her feet, like one of the chollas, or catclaws, or silvery smoke trees whose eerie metallic sound in the night wind always reminded Bo of tinsel. Struggling to her feet, Bo hobbled on crutches through the sand to Eva's side.

"It's only been ten days since Samantha's death," Eva said. "And yet it seems a very long time."

"The desert does that," Bo responded, watching a particularly purple rock cloak itself in a color like ashes. "Out here things rearrange themselves somehow. It's hard to describe—like a place where the truth is free to walk in your mind. It scares some people."

"I love it!" Eva smiled and turned to face Bo. "And of course you would put it so aptly." Her gaze grew somber. "You have risked your livelihood and, finally, your life in order to help

Hannah. Why did you risk so much, Bo? What makes you do what you do?"

Bo balanced on one leg and stretched her crutches toward the color-washed hills. "Who knows?" she grinned. "I have risk built into my chemistry. Any day," she braced herself again, "may bring fears beyond anything real life can produce. It provides a somewhat larger perspective, maybe. Or it may merely be a pitiably adolescent need to defy authority."

"Merde," Eva said with conviction. "You're an exceptional person, 'with a mind that nobleness made simple as a fire.' "

Bo felt every freckle on her face resist the furious blush raging there. "Yeats," she acknowledged the compliment, "describing Maud Gonne." It occurred to her that her friends must have spent the last week holed up at a seminar on poetic imagery.

"Yes," Eva Broussard said with finality. "An Irish heroine."

As they strolled toward the ring of stones that would contain the campfire, Bo changed the subject. "I still don't get what made this John Litten the monster he was," she mentioned, making sure that Hannah was out of earshot. "When the police finally identified him through navy records using his fingerprints, his IQ scores turned out to be above average. He excelled in navy training programs. Even though he came from some impoverished South Carolina backwater, he had every chance to make something of himself. Instead he used his mind to destroy the most beautiful—"

"You've answered your question," Eva interrupted, watching Hannah as the child listened to Rombo Perry tell for the fourth time the story of a wonderful new puppy named Watson who would soon come to live with Rombo and Martin, and who would certainly play Frisbee. "It's difficult for many, especially Americans, to accept, but not every person is born with identical potential. In John Litten's case, something absolutely essential was missing. Not intelligence, but a sense of his own beauty. That inner self that is capable of seeing its own beauty reflected in other living things. Something so basic it defies description, but without it we get John Litten."

"But isn't there treatment, some training or medication . . . ?"

Eva Broussard sighed as the desert valley was lost in darkness. "It's not a psychiatric problem, Bo. It's beyond that. Maybe a century from now we'll know what it is—a mutant chromosome, or specific brain inadequacy. For now such creatures fall by default to the analysis of philosophy. They're simply evil."

The whispered word drifted and then vanished in desert darkness as Estrella helped Hannah to light the fire with a torch of dried sage. Its pungent odor filled the air like incense.

"I'm starving!" Paul Massieu bellowed happily. "Do we eat now?"

As Bo pulled her sand chair close to the fire, Paul grabbed Hannah and held her laughing over his head. From a new gray sweatshirt her grieving beads hung, gleaming in the firelight. The third of the set was pinned to Bo's jacket. As Rombo and Henry Benedict showed Andrew LaMarche how properly to load hot dogs on green oak sticks gleaned from the mountains before them, Hannah ran from Paul to Bo's side. A falling star arced faintly across the darkening sky.

"Did you see that, Bo?" Hannah asked, wide-eyed. "Do you think it's the silver people? Do you think they'll come here? What do you think they are, Bo? Paul says people have seen them here before."

"I've heard that, too," Bo answered, hugging the little girl. "And what I think they are is something like shadows we see in our mind. They're not real, but then they're not *not* real. And that's what I think, Hannah, besides thinking you're about the bravest, prettiest, smartest kid in the whole, entire desert!"

Hannah giggled and glanced at Bo's sketchbook on the ground.

"Can I see your picture, Bo?" she asked. "What is it? It looks like a flower, but it looks like a straw mask, too, all by itself in the wind. Can I have it, Bo? What is it?"

"You may have it, Hannah." Bo grinned and ruffled the golden hair. "Because it's us. It's the Last One Left."